ISBN: 978-1-326-52661-0

EQUASION

Heather Turnbull

FOR LUKE

WITH LOVE AS ALWAYS

One

It was always water. It might come in the form of a lake, a vast ocean, even a tidal wave on some occasions, but it was always water and if Addilyn had believed in some supernatural meaning of dreams then she supposed that these liquid-filled images were trying to tell her something; however, she was a realist and she knew that dreams were just the workings of the brain sorting out the input of the day during sleep, not some portent of impending doom or any such like.

Addilyn Mackenzie was thirty years old and unmarried; not by choice but largely due to the fact that no man could understand, or tolerate, her obsessive compulsive disorder – at least no man she had met to date and they hadn't been scarce until they learned of this particular quirk of hers and then they made themselves so in rather a hurry. It wasn't so much ritualistic – Addilyn didn't believe that there was anything unclean on her hands or on doorknobs or anywhere else for that matter – but her fixation about numbers was alarming.

Her problem had first manifested itself when she was a child and was put down, by all the health professionals who actually didn't know all that much about the affliction, to her needing to be fair in her love for her parents because she counted every kiss and hug she gave them, and would regularly make one of them sit and be kissed and hugged until they had caught up with the number of affections showered down on the other. Her parents tolerated this because they thought it cute, and of course they were her parents and therefore by definition bound to tolerate anything from her, but when she grew up and began to count the number of words in her school books, adding one or two if she deemed it necessary to satisfy whatever it took to placate her, they decided to seek professional counselling and that's when it all started to go wrong.

Addilyn picked up her mobile phone to see what time it was; the digits would dictate whether or not she got up – how long she had to stay in bed until such time as the digits allowed her to get up – and luckily they were displaying 08:02 and that was fine so she swung her legs sideways, pushed the duvet aside, and got wearily to her feet. She avoided looking at her mobile as she made her way to the bathroom; sometimes avoidance was necessarily or she'd get hardly anything done – and once she was washed and dressed and in the kitchen making herself a coffee, mobile still out of sight, she sighed with relief and counted the number of spoonfuls of sugar and of coffee, then poured in several amounts of milk and water until she was satisfied with the result. Then she walked through to her sitting room, switched on her television, sat down with her coffee and began to count the sips she took.

It hadn't always been that bad; indeed, Addilyn could recall when it was just a minor irritation that could easily be satiated by nothing more than reciting a short mantra that involved various mathematical formulae which in turn would develop an unwanted number into one that she could quite happily live with. No hand-washing for her, no paranoid double-checking that something was on or off, locked or unlocked; everything that caused her anxiety could be placated with a bit of mathematical juggling. That was still the case now, but the mathematical process had got a lot more complex, more complicated, as if, having mastered the basics, God now wanted to teach her some higher logic.

The coffee was delicious, and Addilyn was glad she wasn't working today. Miraculously (so her doctor opined) she was able to hold down a job as receptionist /secretary /accounts clerk /tea girl /general dogsbody to a local cabinet maker, mostly due to the fact that she had the place to herself most of the day most days, and so was able to more or less run the business on the owner's behalf and indulge her mathematical compulsions at the same time. Addilyn fancied she would have loved the job even had she not had the OCD to contend with; it was well-paid, she was near enough her own boss and the few people she did work with were pleasant, friendly and great fun. Now, though, the place was closed for the Christmas period and as today was New Year's Eve, she had another two days off before returning to work on Saturday. She found she was looking forward to it; spending Christmas alone wasn't too bad but two weeks' holiday was enough because the novelty had worn off and she was beginning to feel very bored.

So bored, in fact, that she had decided to take herself off for a brisk hillwalk for the day, planning to arrive back in town just before six when she could treat herself to a glass of wine before coming home to spend the New Year alone. She wasn't much bothered with the new year celebrations; the earth would happily revolve around the sun for far longer than the time that she had left on it, and rather than be a cause for celebration, it was a natural phenomena and no amount of counting years would ever authenticate that which it was supposed to take its basis from; the year 2014 was merely two thousand and fifteen years after the year that had come before it, and nothing to do with an event that was mythological and which had no place in the purely logical life of Addilyn Mackenzie.

Having finished her first cup of coffee, she went to prepare a second and while she waited for the kettle to boil she drew the kitchen curtains apart and was greeted with watery sunshine. It looked cold out there but at least it was dry and there wasn't too much wind, certainly not enough to cause her concern. It looked like the outing to Borger Dalr was on, and strangely Addilyn was thoroughly looking forward to it.

*

Addilyn didn't need to drive because the walk she intended to do started right outside her front door, near enough. She rented a small but luxurious flat in a listed building in the small village of Grange in Cumbria, from a landlord and his wife who lived abroad in the autumn and winter and who inhabited the ground floor of the building during the British spring and summer. They had given Addilyn their permission and blessing to use the downstairs as she saw fit, but somehow she felt as if she were trespassing if she wandered into their segment of the old house and was quite content to restrict herself to her own four rooms.

She took the precaution of wrapping up

warmly, along with carrying in her backpack a map, a canteen of water, her mobile phone (fully charged) and a few sandwiches. It was already lunchtime and she had eaten a hearty breakfast of bacon and egg rolls with orange juice and more coffee, but you never knew what might happen up there on the hills and it was always sensible to take provisions. She was a seasoned enough walker to realise that such small inclusions could well be life-savers; indeed, even though she fancied she knew the fells like the back of her hand, she still took a map just in case someone needed an ordinance survey location in order to rescue her.

Certain that she was ready, she opened her front door, climbed down the external staircase that led from the side of the building to the driveway and stopped.

"Mrs Hodgson? Is everything okay?" Addilyn dropped her bag from her shoulders and walked up to the taxi where she helped the elderly woman out of the car and took a suitcase from Mr Hodgson, also in the back of the car. "Why are you back so early?"

"Nothing's wrong, dear," Mrs Hodgson assured her. "In fact, quite the opposite! We had to come home to get ready because we've adopted a daughter!"

"Adopted? A daughter?" Addilyn was more than a little taken aback; the Hodgsons were, with all due respect, hardly the ideal candidates for guardianship over a minor – she had visions of the parentification which would be forced on the girl in a few years' time which was, she knew from experience, not the best way to garner love and respect for your parents.

"Yes," replied Mrs Hodgson, now hurrying to the front door of the lower part of the house, key already out. "No-one else would take her, she's a problem child, but when we saw her, well, we just fell in love!"

"A problem child?" mused Addilyn aloud; that was even worse; did these darling people not know how much work was involved in rearing a child with special needs?

"Yes," said Mrs Hodgson. "She has emotional problems. Apparently she hates everyone she meets, but for some reason she seemed to like us."

"That wouldn't be difficult," observed Addilyn, and she meant it: the Hodgsons were gentle people, generous, thoughtful and caring. She couldn't have wished for nicer landlords or neighbours, and that the girl picked up on this came as no surprise to her. "So, how old is she?"

Mrs Hodgson had opened the front door now and Addilyn deposited the suitcase just inside it for Mr Hodgson to take over custody of. "She's ten," she replied enthusiastically.

"Such a lovely age, don't you think?"

"Indeed," smiled Addilyn, thinking that the age was as awkward as it was lovely. Not exactly a teenager but certainly getting there, and she would be developing into a woman soon and the poor old couple would have all *that* to contend with as well. "Well, I'll help if I can," she concluded, "If you want me to, that is."

"You'd be a great influence on her!" beamed Mrs Hodgson. "Now get yourself off up your mountain. I see you're all packed and ready. Which one this time?"

"Castle Crag and Borger Dalr," said Addilyn. "Nothing too taxing, just a pleasant hike."

*

For Addilyn, walks were a perfect way to clear the mind and then think things through to their conclusion; her conscious had solved more problems during walks than her subconscious had during sleep. Or at least that's the way it seemed.

The first part of the walk was largely through forest, with the occasional view to one side or the other. It was a well-trodden path, and it was almost impossible to get lost, although anything could happen in adverse weather. Today it was cold but clear and crisp, no sign of rain with the watery sun still holding the upper hand and for a mile Addilyn walked with nothing but her thoughts and the sound of birds and other wildlife communicating with each other to keep her company. Hanging oaks bowed at her passing, while holly bushes reminded her that she was still within the boundary of Christmas, and the yew trees and ash trees for which the area was so very famous lent a contrast in both structure and colour and thus kept the visually aesthetic interest. On fells both near and far, rough-looking sheep braved the weather in their long, shaggy coats and in and around the streams and ponds mallards, moorhens and geese made noisy bathtimes.

On this particular day, Addilyn's mind was too busy considering the new addition to the house to count her footsteps; there were days when she didn't count them even if she didn't have anything else to occupy her mind, but these were few and far between. Today, though, she thought about the 10-year-old girl who would soon be living beneath her and she wondered just what kind of emotional problems she could expect to witness.

If it were associated with her upbringing, then Addilyn could empathise; she herself hadn't had a particularly good one but luckily she had been strong enough to resist the attempts to grind her into a snivelling ball of self-doubt and negative self-esteem and had ploughed through her younger years relatively successfully. If she were honest with herself, she did harbour some bitterness, but most times she just passed her parents' lack of parenting skills off to their being human and therefore not perfect. It was a mistake for them to have a child; they weren't cut out for the job of rearing offspring because they had not been willing to make sacrifices. As a younger girl, she had snubbed them from the age of sixteen when she was legally able to make her own way in the world; by the time she'd begun to understand that mothers and fathers were not the paragons of perfection but human beings with faults just like the rest of the race, it'd been too late to build bridges – a drink-driver had killed them both in an accident from which he, typically, had walked away unhurt.

She was so engrossed in her reminiscing that she didn't see the dog until she almost trod on him; luckily some kind of inner instinct warned her of his presence and she caught herself just in time and side-stepped him. At least she thought it was a 'him'; his hair was too long to be sure but he *looked* like a male dog, and when she greeted him with an enthusiastic "hello, beautiful boy!" and wasn't corrected by his human, she assumed that a male was indeed what he was.

“You're a dog lover,” the middle-aged woman pointed out as dog-walkers tend to do when they meet someone who readily fusses their charge. “I can always tell.”

“Yes, I like dogs,” confirmed Addilyn. “I used to always have dogs, but I'm out working every day now so it wouldn't be fair to have one.”

“Some dogs don't mind being alone during the day,” opined the woman.

“No dogs don't mind being alone during the day,” corrected Addilyn. “But they tolerate it to please their humans!”

The woman smiled but said nothing. There was going to be an awkward silence now, Addilyn realised, and it was her fault; while what she said was certainly true about dogs not liking being left alone, she supposed that she could have been a little more judicious because now it was evident that the woman did just that. She was about to apologise for her tactlessness when the dog began to growl quietly in the back of his throat, the hair on his haunches standing up on end, his eyes steadfastly watching a nearby tree.

“Hello? Is there anyone there?” Addilyn called. She walked towards the tree, curious to see if anyone was hiding behind it, even more curious to know why.

Just as she was within a few feet of it, a child – a boy, judging from his attire – ran suddenly into view and just as suddenly into the distance, around a bend in the pathway and out of sight. Addilyn hadn't time to have a good look at his face, but she would never forget the look in his eyes for that few seconds that they locked with hers; expressing mostly fear, she was sure than just for a moment they glowed with an incandescence that could only come from within.

She turned towards the woman who was crouching next to her dog, trying to comfort him. For his part, the dog was trembling violently as if palsied.

"What was it?" whispered the woman, briefly glancing up at Addilyn before turning her attention back to the dog.

"Just a little boy," replied Addilyn lightly, although she suspected he was a bit more than that.

*

Her walk didn't last more than a couple of hundred yards before Addilyn realised that she was no longer enjoying it and that she would be better off going home and conserving her energy for a time when her mind wasn't reeling over what she knew to be impossible; and as if God agreed, there was a sudden flash of lightning which Addilyn took to herald the onset of rain.

It heralded the start of a scream instead.

Addilyn turned towards where the sound had come from and started towards it without even stopping to consider whether or not that was a good idea. Retracing steps that she had already taken, she hurried as quickly as she could back the way she had come until the dog she had just met came bounding towards her with his tail low, ears flat back and a low whimpering in his throat that communicated fear and panic. He wouldn't even accompany her as Addilyn closed in on the body that she now noticed lay prone between two large trees, and she didn't need to get right up to it to know that the woman was dead.

In the darkness of more, thicker, darker foliage there came a rustling sound, and Addilyn looked up just in time to see a pair of bright, glowing eyes before the boy disappeared deeper into the woodland with a cry that sounded more anguished than triumphant.

Two

That night, numbers invaded her sleep with a vengeance and Addilyn didn't think it was because of any kind of anxiety, even though the day had been an anxious one.

After her initial shock, Addilyn spurred into action. She had called the police from her mobile and she had told them when they arrived about meeting the woman for the first time with the dog, about the boy in the trees, about hearing the scream and finally about coming back to find her lying motionless on the ground. When they asked about the boy, she told them that she had seen him a second time but that she didn't think he was responsible; she didn't know why she held that opinion but she did think it was the correct one. She didn't mention his glowing eyes.

She went along with them to the station as requested and went through the rigmarole of being re-questioned and being told not to go anywhere without notifying them. She asked if she would be fingerprinted, but they said that there was no reason to do that just yet, but that she should keep herself available for further questioning should the need arise. She agreed and she also offered to take the dog home when the police mentioned that they were going to take him to a home; they weren't bad places, at least not up here in Cumbria where one hundred percent of the indigenous population adored dogs – and animals in general – but she still didn't like the thought of the dog being alone after losing his human without anyone to comfort him and so she'd taken the lead from the police after they'd done what they wanted with it, and led the dog back to her flat where he made himself comfortable in front of her real coal fire. As far as she knew, he'd stayed there all night.

She hadn't told the Hodgsons about what had happened because she didn't think they needed to know. They were happy at the prospect of becoming adoptive parents – still somewhat bizarre in Addilyn's opinion, but hey, whatever – and she didn't want to spoil their mood by telling them something that they could do nothing whatsoever about anyway. So she had returned to her flat, built the fire up, and spent the rest of the day sipping hot sweet tea and staring into the caverns of yellow and orange which reminded her of the boy's eyes; when it got to ten o'clock at night she went to bed and began to count.

Counting at night wasn't new to her and it didn't involve sheep either, but the way in which her compulsion was conducting her brain's energy was slightly disturbing because it was a method that she was not familiar with. She tossed and turned until she was both frustrated and angry, and then suddenly she fell asleep with not a number in her mind's sight.

*

New Year's Day was nothing special in the Mackenzie flathold, but the busy sounds downstairs indicated that it was going to be extra-special for the Hodgsons, and when she got up Addilyn found a note posted through her letterbox informing her that the young girl was arriving today and that she was invited to a welcome tea party at five o'clock. She shook her head and smiled; tea parties weren't her scene but of course she would attend this one because not only was she curious to meet the emotionally-disturbed child but also because she wouldn't dream of letting the Hodgsons down or hurting them in any way.

She had named the dog Shadow because he had a big black splodge on his otherwise white back that looked a bit like a man's shadow, with a head splodge and two small splodges to the sides that could be seen as arms if you were drunk or had a vivid imagination. Although he had a collar on, there was no name tag, no identification or telephone number, so Addilyn had no way of knowing what the woman had called him. Shadow, however, happily answered to that name so he obviously didn't mind it and all was well with him.

Rather than take him out for a walk. Addilyn merely took him into the back garden she shared with the Hodgsons and let him do what he had to do there. The events of yesterday were beginning to dawn on her now, as if her shock were biding its time before it let itself loose on her emotions. Perhaps that was why she didn't sleep well – but, no, it wasn't that, surprise though that might be; it was the numbers and the way in which they tumbled relentlessly around her brain, like the punishment the powers-that-be insisted they were.

She had been a few times to see the powers-that-be which were more commonly known as therapists, but she stopped attending when she realised that they really didn't have a clue as to what she was going through. Their training had equipped them to deal with the standard human with standard problems and there was no such thing as a standard human and certainly not a standard problem. It was obvious that the characteristics of the mental disorder would differ from person to person because they were based on that very person's psyche; what one person feared, another would laugh at, and they did have it right when they said it was a punishment. Somewhere deep down inside her, or somewhere way back in her past beyond her conscious memory, something had happened for which she had to suffer and that was true of everyone that had to put up with the total inconvenience of compulsive behaviour; the fact that it reared its ugly head at the most inopportune times stood testament to that.

Now she was sitting on the sofa with a cup of coffee on the table in front of her and Shadow leaning on her knees, head down but still alert. When she absently fussed his ears, his tail wagged as if one were a switch to start the other one off.

Suddenly there was a commotion downstairs and Addilyn knew that the little girl had arrived. There was much greeting and, Addilyn could image, shaking of hands and grinning. Then, after five minutes, the commotion stopped and after a brief gap in which there was silence, there came a soft knock at her door at which Shadow half-yapped but didn't bother with a full-blown bark; it was as if he knew that the caller was a friend – either that or he didn't have the confidence yet to bark in case it wasn't the right thing to do.

Addilyn answered the door and saw Mrs Hodgson standing there all flustered and not as happy as Addilyn expected her to be.

"Is everything all right?" she asked the older lady.

"Oh, Addilyn, dear, I don't know what I've done!" fretted Mrs Hodgson, wringing a handkerchief in her hand which Addilyn suspected she had been crying into. "I mean, Marcia is a lovely girl but I think I may have bitten off more than I can chew!"

Addilyn didn't have the heart to agree, even though this conversation was inevitable, she had suspected. "Now, I'm sure that's not right," she soothed instead. "You are quite easily the most able woman I have ever known and it'll no doubt take a little while to get used to motherhood."

Mrs Hodgson nodded but didn't look sure. She seated herself on the sofa without being invited and Addilyn offered to make a tea.

"Thank you, dear, that would be lovely," Mrs Hodgson answered, then, while Addilyn went into the kitchen to brew a pot, she continued more loudly: "I always wanted children, but Larry couldn't have them. So when this opportunity arose I jumped at it without thinking it through properly."

"So how exactly *did* the opportunity arise?" called Addilyn as she dropped a couple of tea bags into the pot.

"A phone call just before Christmas," replied Mrs Hodgson. "A gentleman who said he had it on good advice that my husband and I would make excellent foster parents. Said he′d been talking to an old friend of ours."

"That′s an unconventional way of doing things," observed Addilyn. "Usually there are forms to fill in, searches to be implemented, references to obtain..."

"Yes, but apparently this little girl was so hard to find a home for that he was willing to forego all the red tape."

"She must be a monster, then!"

"Oh no, she′s quite sweet. But..." Mrs Hodgson hesitated and waited till she had taken the mug of tea from Addilyn before continuing. "Oh, dear, but she′s rather strange and she keeps doing things with numbers! She counts things, things like her steps, she even counted the number of sips of milk she took from the beaker I gave her! Larry thinks she might be – you know – sort of retarded and that scares me."

"Sounds more like OCD to me," said Addilyn, her heart having quickened at the mention of such familiar symptoms. "That′s not retarded in any way."

She almost added that she ought to know, but then thought better of it; people still viewed any problems with the mind symptoms of mental abnormality, and Addilyn didn′t want her landlady thinking she was anything but totally in corpus mentis.

That was another problem of OCD, she'd discovered: sufferers were loathe to share their experiences with anyone except their therapists and so tended to face the fears their illness produced totally alone, and she fancied she might be a help to the little girl in that regard if in no other way.

"Well, would you let me know what you think when you come to tea later?" asked Mrs Hodgson. "I don't want her getting too comfortable if she can't stay, that wouldn't be at all fair on her. I just wish they'd warned me and maybe then I wouldn't have been so shocked."

"They probably assumed that you would turn her down just like the rest seem to have done," remarked Addilyn. "Maybe that's the very reason it wasn't mentioned."

"Oh, the poor little thing!"Mrs Hodgson sipped a drop more tea and then set the mug down on the floor, "I'd better get back. I'll be giving the girl a complex if I keep ignoring her just when she's arrived."

"All right," said Addilyn. "You go and maybe have a chat with her, learn more about her, and I'll be there in about an hour."

"Oh, thank you, dear, I knew I could rely on you!"

Addilyn smiled and showed her landlady out of the door. When she closed it she couldn't help but think that there was something rather strange about this adopting/fostering business, or at least in this particular case.

*

Shock is a strange thing; generally it materialises long after the event which caused it and this was certainly true for Addilyn who had still not properly expressed the emotions she must have felt upon finding a dead body, especially a dead body that she had been talking to not long before. Even as she shuffled about her flat finding something to wear to an informal tea party that was neither too casual nor too flamboyant, her mind was more on her landlady as the weird circumstances that had led up to the recent discussion than on what she had experienced yesterday. It was as if her brain had shoved the incident to the murky depths of her memory to be accessed at a later time when its recollection would be less painful.

In a way she was looking forward to meeting Marcia; she and the little girl had something in common at least and a shared characteristic was a good stepping stone to a pleasant relationship. She also was aware that wanting to befriend the little girl didn't completely lie with a desire to help her with her compulsions; Addilyn was lonely and always had been – her parents put paid to any chance of her giving her trust completely and as well as her compulsions, her constant suspicions also frightened away prospective partners and she had given up on love and marriage. She wasn't all that bothered, however; she only had to look at how it'd turned out for her mother and father and she deemed herself lucky to have avoided it.

She sighed and took out a pair of black trousers from her wardrobe; she'd gone and depressed herself now with thoughts of the past and that wasn't the mood she wanted to be in when she went downstairs. She crossed to her chest of drawers and selected a coral-coloured jumper; not too smart, but not too scruffy. She dressed and checked herself in the mirror, quickly tidied her fine, unruly mousy brown hair – her hairdresser had called it 'dark ash blonde' but Addilyn was under no misconception that it was anything other than plain old mousy brown – and went to meet the new addition to her landlord's and landlady's family.

Mrs Hodgson had apparently forgotten all about her misgivings of earlier on. She bustled Addilyn into the sitting room where a table had been laden with enough sandwiches and cakes for twenty, let alone four, and then she introduced her to the little girl who sat quietly on the settee colouring in a book and who hadn't even looked up when Addilyn had entered the room. Then she left them to get acquainted while she busied herself in the kitchen making tea.

Except, Marcia wasn't just colouring, Addilyn realised; Marcia was mouthing words and Addilyn instinctively knew she was counting. And she wasn't block-colouring, she was jotting, as if she were filling in the blank areas of the picture with dots. Addilyn crossed over to the settee and sat next to her. Marcia didn't look up, but neither did she move; she carried on with her work and now Addilyn could hear the numbers as Marcia whispered them to herself.

"That's pretty," she remarked, careful not to emphasise the way in which the girl was executing her crayons; you never brought attention to OCD lest it make the sufferer embarrassed or upset.

"I wish I could colour like other children do," replied Marcia, still not looking up from her work.

"Can't you?" asked Addilyn, carefully

"No." Marcia put down her yellow crayon, picked up her red one and proceeded to dot the next blank area on her picture. "I have to count the dots, work it out."

"Work what out? You're doing colouring, not sums!"

"I'm always doing sums. Not simple ones

either. Sometimes they quite frustrate me."

Addilyn smiled at the mature vocabulary. "Well, you're not doing sums now, you're colouring in a bird and a very beautiful bird it's going to be!"

"It's called a 'mouflon'. Silly name for a bird but I didn't choose it. It's not quite that bright either but it is quite colourful."

"I've never heard of a 'mouflon'," Addilyn remarked.

"No, well, you wouldn't. You don't see them around here. Nobody does."

"Well, I'd like to see one if they're that pretty. Where can you see them?"

"Where I used to live. There were loads of them. But not here."

"And where did you used to live?"

Suddenly the front door opened and Marcia jumped up from the settee and ran to greet Larry Hodgson who had been out to the local inn for his Sunday afternoon drink and discussion on farming, the weather and all things Borrowdale.

"Larrilee!" she whooped delightedly as he scooped her up in his arms.

Addilyn stood up. "Good evening, Larry," she said. "You're just in time for the party!"

"I know," said Larry. "I got my orders to be back on time. Couldn't afford to be late, she gets so grouchy."

"Lawrence Hodgson, I am *never*

grouchy!" Mrs Hodgson appeared at the door connecting the sitting room to the kitchen, carrying a tray of tea. The smile on her face showed that she was not in the slightest bit offended by her husband's comment.

The tea was hot and sweet and always tasted better than hers, Addilyn fancied. The sandwiches were packed, some with cold meat, some with cheese, some with chopped boiled egg. The cake, Mrs Hodgson declared, was home-made and quite the best she had ever made. There were also bowls of crisps and bread sticks and peanuts and a bowl of strawberry jelly. The spread reminded Addilyn of the Christmas parties at school when she was younger than Marcia; they used to sit at a long table that extended the length of the school hall on the afternoon they broke up for the Christmas holidays and they'd wear gaily-coloured hats and eat off paper plates and out of paper bowls that were ruffled at the edges. She had loved those parties and they constituted one of the very few happy memories of her childhood that she possessed.

Marcia meanwhile was more interested in 'Larrilee' than the food. She was making a big fuss of the big man, and he was making an even bigger fuss back; Addilyn could see that he, at least, was more than happy with their new family member.

"Larrilee?" she whispered with a grin.

"When Marcia was first introduced to Larry," Mrs Hodgson explained, pouring tea into china cups which rested on matching saucers. "She was nervous and tripped over her words. 'Larry' came out as 'Larrilee' and it stuck."

"It's cute!" Addilyn accepted the tea Mrs Hodgson was handing her. "Thank you. So what about you? What does Marcia call you?"

"Oh, just Josie, the same as everyone else. We weren't about to insist on 'mum' and 'dad'; we're not her parents."

"That's as maybe, but you don't have to be related to be a mum and dad and I reckon you'll manage it in no time. She's settled in so remarkably well."

"Yes, that quite surprised us too. She's hardly been any trouble at all. In fact, if it weren't for the counting and the numbers fixation, I'd say she was no trouble whatsoever." She paused, then continued: "You said it was OCD earlier. Do you know about it?"

Addilyn hesitated because she hated to lie to these lovely people. "I've had some experience," she said carefully.

"So will it pass, do you think?"

"It might, but even if it doesn't it can be handled. I'd say give her a few months to get used to her new environment and it might even disappear. If it's brought on by stress, it likely will."

"Yes, good idea." Mrs Hodgson put her cup down, stood and fetched a plate of sandwiches. "Here, this is the best ham, honey roasted with spices." She offered the plate to Addilyn and Addilyn took two. "I have to get her into school," Mrs Hodgson continued as she offered Larry and Marcia a sandwich and they both took two as well. "I'm wondering which is the best."

"I'll check the catchment area for you," said Addilyn. "Let you know tomorrow."

"I think maybe she'll be better when she has more to do and meets kids her own age. After all, we old fossils can't be much fun twenty-four hours a day!"

"You're not old fossils!" said Addilyn with a chuckle. "And Marcia seems perfectly happy in your company. Aren't you, Marcia?"

Addilyn turned to the girl and the girl looked up from examining her sandwich and looked her straight in the eyes, a smile on her face.

Addilyn started, inhaled suddenly and almost choked on some ham.

"Oh, my, are you all right?" Mrs Hodgson was beside her in a second and patting her back quite sharply.

For a second, Addilyn did nothing but stare at the girl. The eyes weren't glowing any longer but Addilyn knew that she hadn't been mistaken. Just like the little boy she had seen yesterday, this little girl had eyes that had radiated a bright gold light then returned to normal a few seconds later. She turned her attention away from Marcia and back to Mrs Hodgson.

"I'm sorry, Mrs Hodgson," she said. "I just remembered something that I simply *have* to get done for work tomorrow! Thank you so much for inviting me, and I wish I could have stayed longer. But..."

Addilyn was on her feet and walking towards the front door even as she spoke.

"There's still so much left!" said Mrs Hodgson.

"Josie, she wants to go home," said Larry, quietly. He looked up at Addilyn with such an expression of sympathy that she would have sworn he knew what she had seen because he'd seen it too. Addilyn nodded an acknowledgement to him then let herself out of the house.

"Thank you for visiting," she heard Marcia shout as she closed the door behind her, but Addilyn refused to look back. Instead she shuddered and hurried round to the side of the building where the outside steps led to the sanctuary of her own flat.

*

That night she dreamed of the tidal wave again. It was, as usual, huge and threatening, visible in the distance and getting nearer by the second. Addilyn knew that there was no running away from it; wherever she was, however fast she ran, she wouldn't be able to distance herself from it sufficiently for its effect to be anything but totally destructive.

Yet she couldn't – wouldn't – look away. It was an awesome sight, powerful and dangerous, but also beautiful and majestic, nature at her best, God reminding His people that He had the last say, not them. Her heart beat not just with fear but also with excitement and awe.

Then she noticed the bright little speck atop the giant wave and as the wave glided soundlessly towards her, she saw that it was Marcia, somehow surfing the top of the wave and riding it effortlessly without any board.

Marcia saw her too and waved happily.

Three

It may have been the dream or it may not, but the next morning Addilyn awoke in a flood of tears. Shadow, who slept on the bed, now approached her and snuggled in as if he understood what she was feeling, which he probably did.

Well, it was about time, she reasoned. She was beginning to worry because she had not vented her feelings about what she had witnessed on New Year's Eve, not only because she was aware that suppressed emotions could lead to much stress and bad health in general, but also because she was beginning to wonder what kind of hard-hearted person she had become not to cry about someone losing their life, probably by murder. She had always been tough, that was true, but that was because she'd had to be; yet by the same token she only had to see a tear-jerking film and she was tear-jerking with the best of them. Sometimes she wondered from where she got such a compassionate heart – certainly not her parents, that was for sure.

She knew she should take some time off, maybe see someone about coping with what she had witnessed and was now beginning to digest and react to, but then she remembered Marcia downstairs with the glow in the eyes that she had seen in the boy on the day of the woman's murder and the shudder that coursed through her body convinced her that she would be better off at work away from here. She needed room to think, to come to turns with the sudden development of totally bizarre events that had come into her life with a vengeance, and she longed for the boring old days when the most exciting thing to happen was a phone call from her employer asking her to do an extra shift overtime. Besides, it was always quite busy at this time of year because although sales weren't great after the festive season, there was a lot of cleaning, polishing and resurfacing to do on items of furniture that had been marked or scratched during the celebrations. She didn't want to let Donald Gittins either, what with him being good enough to employ her and tolerate her 'problem' – indeed, he was the only one around here other than the medical team looking after her who knew anything about it – and besides, she wanted to hear what was going around about the death of the woman.

She was pleased that at last she had been able to cry, although she knew she could not afford the luxury of completely breaking down until tonight, when she would have the evening and the whole of Sunday to come to terms with, and make sense of, all that had happened. So she straightened herself up, checked her appearance (she had applied some concealer around her red eyes to hide the fact that she had been crying) and judged herself passable. A quick saunter to her car which was parked at the side of the building and she was on her way. She prayed that she would hold up for the duration.

*

Considering that January was supposed to be a quite depressing time of year, post-Christmas, bad weather, credit cards maxed out and the like, everyone Addilyn knew was chirpy and cheerful. She had been greeted with a wish for a happy new year by Donald Gittins and she could hear him now as he hummed away over some project he was working on and obviously enjoying. Addilyn smiled to herself and realised that she should regard herself as lucky, and under any other circumstances she would have. However, the cloud of despondency seemed determined to rain on her today and she pushed up an umbrella of defensive resistance, focussing her attention on writing out the New Year cards that Don had purchased for her to send to his customers. They were the very same ones that he had sent Christmas cards to, but Don always made sure his Christmas cards carried only Christmas greetings, which meant that anyone whom he wished a happy new year would have to receive a separate communiqu□ saying as much.

Just then the door to the reception opened and, along with a gust of cold wind, a young boy entered. He would be maybe twelve, probably not more than that, although Addilyn had to admit she was pretty useless at guessing ages. Kids grew up so quickly these days; girls she estimated were old enough to order a drink at a bar were actually only fourteen or fifteen, and although she would've loved to ask the lad how old he was, she knew that wasn't very professional and instead she just smiled at him and greeted him a good morning.

"Hello," he said, a little shy but not overly so. "I want a coat of arms on a wooden coaster. Can you do that?"

"I should think so," smiled Addilyn. "Do you have the coaster?"

"No, I'd want a coaster and then the coat or arms painted on, or maybe chiselled in."

Addilyn smiled at the description the boy gave the intricate artwork that her boss so lovingly produced. "It may be a little expensive," she warned.

"That's okay. It's a birthday present for my stepdad. I just want him to know I love him."

"That is really sweet of you." Addilyn's smile grew wider. "So what coat of arms is it?

His surname?"

"Yes. It's 'Greenwood'. I haven't brought a photograph because I wanted to see whether you could do it first."

"That's okay." Addilyn keyed in a few commands on her computer, then: "There we go. 'Greenwood': knight's head above a shield with three Xs on – "

"That's it!" The boy was so excited that Addilyn was reluctant to tell him how much it would cost. The reluctance turned to dread when he added: "Could it be painted too?"

"Could what be painted?" Don Gittins came into the reception area from the glass door behind Addilyn's desk and had caught the back-end of what the lad had said.

"This young man would like a wooden coaster made, with his – er – with a coat of arms on it, and painted if possible," Addilyn explained. "And I haven't quoted him for it yet..."

"It's going to be a lot, isn't it." The boy sounded so dejected that Addilyn felt for him.

"Usually," Don Gittins said, "But luckily you've come on the first day of the New Year sale. How long have we got to make this coaster?"

"A month." The lad was looking at Donald Gittins as if he dared to hope that he might be able to afford it after all. "His birthday is 31st of January."

"I see," said Don, and he pretended to think hard. "Soooo," he said at length, "With the sale discount and because we don't have to start on it straight away... I'm afraid it's going to be twenty pounds, young man."

"Twenty pounds?" repeated the boy. "Oh, wow, I can afford that! But..."

"Four weekly instalments of five pounds will be fine. Now, you give Miss Mackenzie here all the details and I'll even add a spray for free."

"Wow, thanks!"

"You're welcome." He turned to leave the office, then backed up. "A cuppa would be great when you have a minute," he said to Addilyn, and she realised then that she hadn't asked him as she usually did.

"Of course," she replied, and before she could apologise for not asking sooner, he had left her to sort the boy out. She turned her attention back to him. "So, would you like to bring your own design in or shall I look for one online?"

"I'll bring it in with my first two-fifty," said the boy. He hesitated, then: "What's the free spray?" he asked.

"We spray it with polyurethane so that if anything gets spilled on it, it won't warp," explained Addilyn. "It's just a preventative measure."

"Cool."

The boy swivelled on his heel and started towards the door. He opened it, then turned to Addilyn. "Thanks," he said. "I'll be in next Saturday afternoon if that's okay?"

"That's absolutely fine."

"Only I work Saturday mornings, and I need my wages to pay the instalment."

"No problem."

"See you then, then."

"You will. Bye bye."

"Bye."

*

The kettle, cups and various beverages – black tea, lemon tea, coffee, hot chocolate and Ovaltine – were kept on a small table in the corner of the office so that Addilyn could make tea without having to lose sight of the front door and anybody who might come in. There was no bell to alert staff to the entrance of a potential customer, so when Addilyn handed her boss his mug of tea, she held the door open with her foot so that she could see the door as well as Donald Gittins.

"That was nice of you," Addilyn remarked as she handed the mug to him. "I was going to quote him around sixty."

"Oh, I know his granddad – or step-granddad if you want to be precise – and have done for years. They live in out your way, in

Rosthwaite. His son is married to some vague cousin of your Mrs Hodgson's. They never had children because they intended to leave this backwater for the pavements of gold in London but five years down there persuaded him that it was only fool's gold. So he came back, she stayed there to look for a sugar-daddy, and he remarried. Lena's a lovely girl, very quiet, same goes for her son Josh, whom you just met. Quite frankly I think they're good for Dathan because he needs someone to keep him in check and to curb his extravagant ideas."

"It was still sweet of you! And I'm sorry about the tea, it just went clean out of my head for some reason."

"I did wonder. You are okay, aren't you...?"

"I'm fine, I just..." Addilyn suddenly recognised an opening to fish for information and seized it gratefully. "I'm just a bit upset about that lady who was found dead. Right on my doorstep too."

"Oh, God, yes; I read about that this morning!" said Don. "Terrible business! She was only in her forties. Not a local, mind, but still..."

"Did they find out what killed her?" Addilyn asked as she sipped her own drink, hoping she sounded nonchalant.

"They said it was a stroke or a heart

attack." Don paused, then: "It was out past the Flock Inn tea rooms, just before you get to the river. Don't you walk there sometimes?"

"Yes. Yes, I do. In fact, I was on my way there when I saw a commotion and turned back because I wasn't in the mood. New Year's Day and all that! Must've been the vultures feasting on an eyeful of misery."

"People will be people, Addilyn, and people are morbid by nature." He paused to finish his tea. "Now, when you've rinsed the mugs, could you post the cards and pick me some A4 paper while you're at it, please?"

"No problem," smiled Addilyn as she took the mug from Don and stepped back into the reception room. She was pleased to be able to get out for a walk.

*

They'd publicised a stroke; after all the questions she'd answered and the insistence by the police officer who had interviewed her at length on the cause of death being murder, they had now told the public that it was a stroke – and Addilyn wasn't anywhere near as annoyed as she was curious.

For a start, there was the matter of the police covering up a murder; unless they had discovered evidence to the contrary, of course, but then she would have expected them to inform her. They hadn't accused her, not at all, but still it would be a matter of courtesy, especially in view of her having found the body, as far as they were concerned.

Besides, if they *were* going to cover up such a huge thing, they wouldn't be leaving her to walk and talk freely. They'd have done something to make sure that she couldn't contradict them and for a moment her heart fluttered as she imagined some pre-constructed accident waiting to happen to her back home before she shook her head at the stupidity of the idea.

The police had changed their minds and for one reason or another they had failed to notify her of their findings. Or maybe they had tried to when she was visiting with the Hodgsons and, finding her not at home, decided that leaving a note wasn't very appropriate. They might even get in touch still, now that the media had got a hold of the story.

Addilyn clutched the cards extra-securely as her hands shook so violently that she feared she would drop and soil their envelopes. When she had posted them and sauntered up Station Road for the paper, she walked back to work slowly with the intention of asking for the rest of the day off.

As it turned out, she didn't need to.

*

The car had careened off the road and must have been travelling some because the front window to the right of the entrance door was completely smashed and the car bonnet was only inches away from Addilyn's desk. Glass littered the floor around it and there were a few scattered shards outside the window as well. Don Gittins was standing on the pavement outside, regarding the damage with horror.

"Don, what the hell?" Addilyn ran the last few steps as soon as she saw that something had happened. "Are you okay?"

"Pissed, but that's the extent of it." Don regarded her for a moment, then took her hand. "Thank God you were out of the office, eh? Never complain about my New Year cards again!"

"Did you see it?" she asked him, looking at what was left of the shop front and the blue car that even from here she could see was badly smashed at the front.

"No, I was out back, looking for some spare wood for Master Josh's coaster, as it happens. I heard a terrific bang, and ran out here to see that – " Don pointed at the car " – parked in my shop."

"Thank God no-one was hurt!" breathed Addilyn. She knew she'd had a lucky escape, but she also wondered if maybe it had been meant for her.

"Yes, indeed. It's always the same, though, isn't it. These drunks get up and walk away from the crash scene while innocent victims suffer."

"The driver was drunk?" Addilyn was almost relieved to hear it because it meant the crash was an accident and not a purposeful attempt at keeping her quiet.

"Must've been, although he legged it before the police got here." Don was still angry; desolation at the ruination of his property was yet to occur to him. "Raving about some glowy-eyed creatures, the bloody idiot. The police are looking for him now."

"Glowy-eyed creatures?" Addilyn back-tracked.

"Yeah, said they were coming for him." Don wore an expression of pure disgust. "Wish they would," he growled. "We don't need the likes of him on the streets!"

"Glowy-eyed creatures..." mused Addilyn.

Don snorted. "Yeah, stupid, isn't it."

"Absolutely," said Addilyn.

Not, she added in thought.

*

Don had sent her home then; pointless her staying and nowhere for her to sit anyway, he'd shrugged, and Addilyn was glad for the excuse to leave. She had plenty to think about, and she fancied that Don was about to lose his cool and she didn't want to be around for that – more for his sake than hers; she didn't care if he lost his temper or if he broke down because she would have understood either reaction or both, but she knew him well enough to appreciate that he wouldn't have wanted her to witness either or both.

It was hard concentrating on driving, there were so many things running haphazardly through her mind, but one car accident was quite enough for one day, Addilyn told herself. She watched the road more cautiously than she needed to, but she got home in one piece and once there she sat in her car for a few minutes and tried to calm down.

A tapping on her window brought her out of her reverie and she turned to see Marcia outside, waving and smiling. Her eyes, Addilyn noted with relief, were perfectly normal. She got out of the car and smiled back uncertainly.

"Hello, Marcia," he said.

"Hello, Addilyn. I'm sorry if I scared you the other day." The little girl was looking engagingly cute today with her long hair in bunches and sporting a big heavy sweater with a woolly sheep embroidered on top of the knitting.

"It's all right."

"But what did I do?" asked Marcia. "I wanted to come and ask but Josie said best not."

"I think you know what you did," remarked Addilyn, not wanting to play this game of Marcia's.

"I don't!" protested Marcia. "I was with Larilee and you were talking to Josie and then you looked at me and suddenly you jumped up and left. I even shouted goodbye but you didn't shout back."

"Marcia, enough already." Addilyn began to walk to her external stairway. "I know you're different so it's pointless pretending."

Marcia looked downwards, as if she were studying the front of her sturdy black patent shoes, and for a moment Addilyn thought she might be crying and felt guilty even though she considered her annoyance totally justified.

"It's okay to be different," she added hastily. "But your eyes frightened me."

"My eyes?" said Marcia, looking up at Addilyn again.

"Yes," confirmed Addilyn.

"They lit up again." It was more a statement than a question, and Addilyn could see Marcia's bottom lip begin to quiver. "Didn't they."

"Yes," Addilyn said again.

"They told me it'd go away." Marcia's eyes

were watering now and for some reason, Addilyn wanted nothing more than to hold the girl and reassure her; if that's maternal instinct, she thought, it's a long time emerging...

"So you *do* know about it." Addilyn let her go and held her at arm's length, regarding her seriously, searching her little face for any signs of deceit, and finding none.

"That isn't me, that's Daji," said Marcia, and her tone was one of petulant indignity. "Sometimes he comes into my body and I can't get rid of him till he wants to go. Everyone said he was my imaginary friend but he's not. Not imaginary and not my friend."

"And... so, where is he now?" Addilyn wanted to know, looking around her as if she might spot him and chuckling humourlessly at her idiocy.

"I don't know. I never know. He just comes and goes."

"And makes you eyes glow."

"And makes me count too."

Addilyn took a deep breath; she hadn't a clue what to make of Marcia, and she really wanted to get upstairs and close her door on the world. But she couldn't leave the girl when she was so obviously growing more distressed.

"Marcia, we'll have tea one evening this

week and you can tell me all about Daji, okay? But for now, I have to get – "

"No! I won't!" Marcia began to cry. "I *won't* tell! "

"Well, how can I help you if you don't tell me?" asked Addilyn, reasonably enough she thought.

"That's what *they* said," blubbered Marcia. "And then they grew scared and threw me out. So I won't ever tell, not you, not Josie, not anyone! "

"Tell me what?" Josephine Hodgson came up behind the child. She hadn't walked particularly quietly but Addilyn hadn't heard her approach. "And why are you upset, sweetie-pie?"

Marcia said nothing, just looked at her feet again.

"She – er – she stubbed her toe," explained Addilyn. "I think it hurt a bit, but I'm sure it's getting better now, eh, Marcia?"

"A bit," conceded Marcia, and Addilyn admired her for her quickness almost as much as she didn't admire her for her readiness to lie.

"Well, let's get you indoors," said Mrs Hodgson, putting an arm around her and herding her like a stray sheep. "A nice hot chocolate is excellent for healing toes!" She turned back to smile at Addilyn. "Thanks," she said.

For what? Addilyn thought, but didn't say it. Instead she just watched while the woman led the little girl to her own front door, guided her inside and shut out the world just as Addilyn wanted to do right now.

Four

Dathan Greenwood loved his wife dearly, but sometimes her quietude and acquiescence drove him crazy. They were young, after all, and married for only seven months and while it wasn't her first marriage it *was* his first, and he intended it to be his *only;* but he craved a bit more spice. Lena was a great support in his work, she also loved to come along and cheer when he was playing pool in the local; she was a shoulder to cry on, an ear to bend, and someone whose opinion mattered to him. In almost every way she was the ideal wife – but, dammit, she was so boring in bed!

She wouldn't try anything new; she wouldn't try anything adventurous. If he suggested something even one degree east or west of the norm, she would not only refuse point blank to do it but she would also refuse point blank to do *anything* and he would be left frustrated with her mumblings of how kinky he was as a background noise to his dreams.

It wasn't even as if he were asking her to something unmentionable – there was kinky, even erotic, then there was downright perverted and the latter he had no interest in whatsoever. But a little experimentation between two adults who loved and trusted each other – who were man and wife, for

Chrissakes – was nothing to get in a paddy about and certainly not anything to be afraid or ashamed of!

But Lena wouldn't entertain anything outside of the missionary position and the occasional cowgirl, and even this latter he had to beg her to do. He loved Lena, he really did, but the idea of getting a lover had crossed his mind more than once and now it seemed to be the only way to save his marriage; his heart and soul belonged to Lena and Josh but unfortunately his libido was in need of another.

"Dad! You missed the ball *again*!" Joshua's voice broke into his musings that had so occupied his attention that he had let yet another ball fly in between the makeshift goalposts that he and his stepson had erected only ten minutes ago on the back lawn.

"Sorry, Josh!" he grinned sheepishly. "I wasn't concentrating. Now I am; so try and get it past me *now* if you can!"

Josh lined up the ball and thwacked it towards Dathan who caught it deftly with gloveless hands and if it stung he didn't show it. Instead he poked his tongue out at Josh, who stuck his tongue out in return and then both of them doubled up with laughter.

They were still laughing when Lena opened the back door and called them in for tea, a puzzled expression masking a delighted one that indicated that she was both happy and relieved that the two lads she loved more than life itself were getting on so well.

*

Addilyn had had an imaginary friend when she was younger but she hated her; she hated her so much that she didn't even bother to give her friend a name. The friend was dark-haired, wore blue, had the ugliest face that anyone could ever imagine – or at least that six-year-old Addilyn could ever imagine – and was liable to go off on a strop at the least thing. If Addilyn wanted to pour out her troubles, the friend wasn't listening; if she wanted to play I-spy, the friend didn't like the game; if she shouted at her the friend shouted right back. Addilyn spent more time hitting her imaginary friend than the heavyweight boxing champion of the world did his opponents, but it made no difference: the friend was still beastly to her.

Of course, she realised as an adult that that was nothing more than frustration at being blamed for everything even if it were not her fault, and the subsequent inadequacy that she was inevitably bound to feel as a result; as a child, however, it compounded on her self-consciousness – if an imaginary friend hated her, what chance did she stand with a real one? Consequently, Addilyn grew up a loner. She had friends that were a little more than mere acquaintances, but no-one that she would trust with more than a few basic details about herself; thus she suffered in silence through a childhood that was less than kind to her through juvenility and adolescence which offered her nothing better, and became an adult who was self-sufficient, capable, careful and alone.

And it was alone that she made her way to Keswick the following day, hoping that the same sergeant was on duty who had grilled her on the day of the woman's demise. She wasn't so much after an apology as an answer to her question: why did you change your mind?

It was a grey day, but dry; there weren't too many dry days in Cumbria during the winter months – there were quite a few during the other seasons too – and the road was quiet. She glanced occasionally at the lake that resembled a sheet of grey slate to her left, beyond skeletal trees that awaited the spring and permission to bloom, but mostly she kept her eyes on the road, still a little apprehensive and suspicious, as was her wont to be.

As luck would have it, the policeman who had questioned her *was* on duty and, even luckier, he was about to take an early lunch break and he invited Addilyn to join him as soon as he saw her, and she didn't think it was because he found her attractive.

"So is this by way of an apology?" Addilyn asked as she sipped at her coffee. They were sitting in a small bar lounge in a pub a little way off the main market square which was comfortable and cosy.

"Well, it's a pretty poor gesture if it is," said Police Constable Kaden Taylor sheepishly. "I was going to claim it on expenses..."

"Then I shall go carefully," smiled Addilyn. "As it's my taxes that will ultimately be paying for it!"

PC Taylor chuckled, then sipped his own coffee, an awkward silence ensuing during which he tried to work out how to explain whilst Addilyn waited because she had nothing to say. The arrival of a couple of plates of sandwiches sided by crisp green salad made for a temporary distraction, then once more they were left alone and PC Taylor began.

"I suppose an apology is in order," he admitted. "Especially in view of the outcome."

"You *were* pretty harsh," agreed Addilyn. "I felt guilty even though I'd done nothing."

"I honestly thought that woman was murdered." PC Taylor was introspect; Addilyn wasn't sure if it were a comment aimed at her or if the constable were thinking out loud.

"I suspect you still do," she remarked at length.

"They said it was a heart attack," shrugged Taylor. "Who am I to argue?"

Addilyn hesitated, then: "If it helps, I don't think it was a heart attack either," offered Addilyn.

"She had such an expression on her face..." Taylor's mind was wandering again. "She looked terrified, horrified, as if she had seen something, like her impending death..."

"Maybe she did..."

"Of course, a heart attack is pretty frightening, I suppose, but somehow I don't think it was a feeling that frightened her, more like something she saw." Taylor paused then. "You don't think it was natural causes either?" he asked, as if it had just dawned on him what Addilyn had said.

"No, I don't."

"You didn't say that when I was questioning you."

"I didn't need to; you were saying it vehemently enough for both of us."

"You must have seen the look on her face though..."

"I did and you asked me that already. I said I thought she looked shocked but that as far as I knew that's what dead people's faces looked like when they had a heart attack. I didn't want a murder charge hanging over me."

"Did you see anything else?"

"Like what?"

"I don't know – maybe some*one* else?"

"No. I wasn't really looking. I was trying to decide whether it was worth attempting mouth-to-mouth or... then I was afraid I'd get it wrong and cause more damage if she was alive, and then I called you lot."

"You're trained in CPR?" Taylor sounded impressed.

Addilyn shrugged. "Only the basics, but they don't teach you how to react when you see a dead body. All that I'd learned went flying out of my mind on wings of panic!"

"Well, if it's any compensation, there was nothing any amount of CPR could have done to help her."

"Thank you."

"But you lied to me in the interview? "

"Yes, I lied to you in the interview. At first it was because I wasn't sure what had happened myself, later it was because you were really beginning to frighten me and I just wanted out." Addilyn paused and smiled sweetly at him. "And if you say anything to your superiors about it, I'll wholeheartedly deny it. Your word against mine, they won't pursue it. On the contrary, you might well find yourself up on a charge of incitement to commit perjury."

Taylor regarded her for a moment with an expression of curiosity, then: "Don't be so defensive," he said. "I'm not going to say anything; the Sarge would have my guts for garters if I did. He's most emphatic that I leave the case well alone."

"Reason for suspicion in itself," offered Addilyn.

"I thought so too." Taylor looked at Addilyn, cocked an eyebrow, and ventured after a moment: "Is there anything else you failed to mention to me during the interview? Any details that you – er – might just have remembered?"

"Like what?" Addilyn wondered, non-committally.

Taylor shrugged. "Anything at all. Any*one* at all. Look, I know you said you didn't, but maybe you'll remember something."

"Maybe I will," Addilyn conceded, getting up from her seat.

"You're off, then?" asked Taylor.

"Yes, I have things to do." She put her jacket on and fished her car keys out of one of its pockets. The car park where she'd parked wasn't far from here. "And I can always get you at the council offices, right?"

"Most of the time, but – " Taylor fished in his own jacket pockets until he found a small notebook. He wrote on a page, tore it out and offered it to Addilyn. “Here, this is my mobile. You stand a much better chance of getting me on that, during working hours or at any other time.”

Addilyn took the slip of paper and put it in her top pocket. “Thank you for lunch,” she said.

“My pleasure,” smiled Taylor. “Maybe something hot next time?”

“There's to be a next time?” asked Addilyn.

“If you remember anything,” nodded Taylor. “Absolutely!”

“And if I don't?”

“Careful, Miss Mackenzie. You're letting your defences slip...”

“Fine!” Addilyn spat the word out as she zipped up her jacket angrily, walked away from the table and out of the bar.

“*Shit*,” said Taylor to himself. He didn't spit the word but reluctantly swallowed it like a sour pill.

*

Addilyn was disgusted with herself. She had never been the flirty sort and to have asked stupidly if there were to be a 'next time' was just plain childish! It was no use trying to persuade herself that she was being sarcastic, or even funny – she knew herself and she knew she meant she *wanted* there to be a next time, which was totally ridiculous because she didn't know the man and he certainly didn't know her! Well, if he *did* contact her somehow, sometime, with an invitation she would turn him down point blank; no need to put herself through all that hassle again just to have yet *another* chunk prised out of her self-esteem. And she supposed that she liked him well enough to save him the bother too.

It was such a shame, because Addilyn thought that maybe she had love to give, and companionship too; she couldn't see herself as a mother because she was afraid that she had inherited her own mother's level of parental competence, which was to say: none whatsoever. But she could hold her own in an intelligent conversation on a variety of subjects, and she knew she was patient and understanding because with her own problems she had to be. And she would certainly be faithful; if she could find someone to love her in spite of all her hang-ups, she'd cling to him for dear life – and no doubt drown him in the process. No, better to keep her distance after all, Addilyn decided; that way nobody – especially she herself – got hurt.

As soon as she'd got back from Keswick she'd telephoned Don Gittins; the window was boarded up at the moment and although the front office floor was now clear, Don didn't think she should return to work because the boards let in one hell of a draft and she'd probably end up catching pneumonia. Of course, he'd still pay her – it wasn't her fault she couldn't work, after all – and, yes, he'd ring her when the window was all done. Addilyn had offered to do work at home if need be, and had assured Don that she was only half an hour away should he need her for anything, and then she bid him goodbye and went upstairs to turn on the hot water for a bath before letting Shadow out for a moment, then making a sandwich and a cup of Lady Grey tea. She actually fancied a glass of wine, but she never allowed herself to drink before 6pm except on her birthday and on Christmas Day, so she contented herself with the hot sweet tea along with a full bath scented with mandarin and patchouli bubbles.

The front doorbell rang.

Addilyn swore. It was the only time that her OCD didn't bother her hardly at all, when she was in the bath, and she valued the time to relax because she had very little of it. Usually her mind was preoccupied with both what she was doing and the nagging, intrusive thoughts that condemned her to forever count everything she came across. Only here in the sanctity of her bathroom could she really wind down and, just for a moment, forget that she was anything but ordinary with an ordinary mind that didn't play tricks on her, and now that sanctity was disturbed and she was darned if she were going to answer that door.

It rang again and then was quiet.

Addilyn settled down to enjoy the rest of her bath.

*

"I wasn't ignoring her on purpose, Mrs Hodgson, I was in the bath!"

It seemed that Marcia had taken her evasion of the doorbell personally and had complained to her foster mother about it. Of course, Josie Hodgson had taken it as personally as any mother would, foster or otherwise, and Addilyn understood Josie's reaction as perfectly as she didn't understand Marcia's. Okay, so the girl was prone to being bypassed and Addilyn knew how that could affect a person, but wasn't this taking things a bit too far.

Yeah, about as far as counting how many chocolates you eat in a given sitting, her brain told her.

"But I tell you what," she continued, as she handed Mrs Hodgson a mug of coffee and Marcia a glass of milk, "What say I take you out for the day tomorrow, Marcia? Show you one of my favourite walks, so you can appreciate the mountain views?"

"Oh, can I, Josie?" Marcia's eyes lit up and for once it was natural.

"I don't see why not!" beamed Mrs Hodgson. "You will look after her, won't you, Addilyn?"

"Of course I will!"

"Good." Mrs Hodgson took a sip of her coffee and put it down on the table in front of her. "By the way, Addilyn, did I tell you about the fence at the back? No wind but..."

They were friends again and the episode of Marcia's exclusion from her flat forgotten. Addilyn only wondered what revelations tomorrow – with any luck – might bring.

FIVE

As luck would have it, the day was a bright one, with sunshine bathing the cold, frosty morning. Marcia had been on her doorstep at the agreed time of ten o'clock on the dot – apparently she'd wanted to come earlier but Josie had been insistent that any earlier would be a bit rude – and now she, Addilyn and Shadow were walking towards the start of the walk that Addilyn had meant to take a few days earlier. Not only did she want to show the girl one of her favourite views, but also she wanted to see if there were any reaction to the place where the woman was killed (by whatever means) on the part of this 'Daji' that Marcia claimed overcame her periodically.

Marcia told her about how Josie was the best cook in the world and how Larrilee made her laugh. Sometimes when Josie had told her off for something, Larrilee would poke his tongue out at his wife when she wasn't looking and Marcia had to muffle a giggle because she didn't want to get him into trouble. It was quite evident from Marcia's chattering that Josie was the disciplinarian while Larrilee was more permissive, and this didn't surprise Addilyn in the slightest; she would have assigned the roles exactly that way herself.

They came across the pathway not far

along which Addilyn had come across the woman but Marcia didn't so much as flinch, and neither did Shadow, although Addilyn herself took a quick glance towards the darkness of the trees as if expecting to see a pair of golden-glowing eyes there. She chose not to mention anything about the occurrence as she wanted Marcia happy and therefore possibly prone to talking openly, not unhappy and possibly nagging to go home.

Marcia continued her narrative about the Hodgsons, about her favourite tea of beans on toast which she was never given before because *they* thought it was a poor man's meal. *They*, it emerged, were an upper class couple who lived in a four-bedroom house in the south lakes, with a plethora of money and a total absence of tenderness, either towards Marcia or towards each other. Marcia's days were spent in grandly-furnished rooms eating delicious steaks or travelling around the local countryside in a sporty Maserati Quattroporte with never a cuddle or a kiss or even an assurance that her foster parents actually cared anything for her. Addilyn suspected that these money-hungry idiots were only after the allowance paid for looking after foster children; they didn't need it by the sound of it, but weren't the rich people generally the ones who hankered after any money they could lay their hands on?

Addilyn was beginning to think that Marcia's childhood was proving to be as miserable as hers had been, and she regarded the girl skipping along in front of her – Shadow just ahead with a twig in his mouth – with a sad smile. No wonder the poor thing had mental problems, she thought; why is it that people find it so hard, not just to care but also to *show* they care? She shrugged, and the thought that there would be no shortage of affection from the Hodgsons warmed her heart; she was beginning to take to this little chatterbox with the bouncing pigtails and usually pale-blue, smiling eyes.

They climbed slowly for the next hour, taking in the sight of the fields on the side of the fells and the little white dots that were sheep, their coats thick and woolly against the cold of winter. Marcia seemed to be enjoying it, opting to take the stepping stones across the river whilst Addilyn walked towards the footbridge with the intention of leading Shadow across it before the dog decided on a more direct route and proceeded to swim across the water towards a delighted Marcia who watched and clapped her hands with glee. When they approached the scree, Marcia climbed it like an expert and Shadow slipped only once; Addilyn soon caught up with them – her legs were longer and stronger than Marcia's and longer than Shadow's – and together they topped the peak of the scree and looked over at the river below as it snaked its way to the lake in the distance.

Here, the sun shone weakly on the water, a pale yellow sparkle on a flat glass of silver-grey, and there was no wind to speak of which was why Addilyn frowned as she saw the waves on the distant lake grow and grow to almost impossible proportions. For a few moments the waves lashed at the shores of Derwentwater and then swelled as they appeared to come closer than the distance of the lake should have allowed. Closer and bigger, and Addilyn could see nothing around her except a white haze, as if a sudden fog had fallen and shrouded everything around her in a white veil. She tried to turn her head but could not. Across the distant lake was a gigantic wave racing towards her, a sound like deep thunder accompanying it, the top of it foaming with cream faces that seemed to be snarling. Her heart began to hammer in her chest, her breath caught in her throat, panic engulfed her and then all went black.

When she came to, Addilyn was on the ground, with Marcia kneeling beside her, crying.

"It wasn't me!" the girl wailed. "It was Daji! It was *Daji*!"Marcia

Addilyn looked about her, shook her head to clear it, petted Shadow as he licked at her face. “How long was I out?” she asked.

“A few seconds, I think,” said Marcia. “Hardly any time at all. I saw him go into you but he soon left. I think you're too strong for him.”

Addilyn tried to recall the experience she had just endured, but the memory of it was fading fast. She tried to force herself to remember, but the harder she fought to bring the images to the fore, the faster they receded to be forever lost in her subconscious memory. She gave up trying and instead got unsteadily to her feet; as far as she could tell, she was unhurt. She checked herself for cuts and grazes, shook her arms and legs and when she was satisfied with her self-appraisal of fitness, she turned her attention to Marcia, whose eyes were wet with tears.

“No crying,” said Addilyn, not unkindly. “We find a place to sit and have our hot drinks and then I think you'd better tell me all about this 'Daji', whoever he is.”

Marcia nodded and a small smile crossed her lips, and Addilyn had the distinct feeling that the little girl was relieved to be able to share her burden with someone who would actually listen.

*

Josh Greenwood hated lying to his mother.

Well, he hated lying to either of his parents, but especially to his mother who, up till quite recently, was the only parent who had any time for him. He was lucky insomuch as his maternal grandparents were amazing, but he was totally ignorant of his paternal grandparents who, it seemed, thought about as much of him as did his natural father who hadn't even as much as set eyes on his son. His mum had told him that his father had 'headed for the hills' when he learned that she was having him, which meant that he ran away from his responsibility as a father just as he ran away from any responsibility in life. His father would never amount to anything, his mother told him, and they were better off without him in their lives. Growing up, Josh wasn't so sure about that, but now that his mum and Dathan had met and married, Josh forgot about his father and was happy and content with his dad instead.

Josh hated lying to his mother but he just had, when she'd asked him if he'd gone out alone on New Year's Eve. Not in the evening, he was too young for that and besides New Year celebrations were nothing compared to Christmas, but during the day, when the nice policeman said a poor lady had a heart attack. But he hadn't been there, he said, and although there'd been a young lad there, it wasn't him. And it hadn't been; not in the strict sense anyway because he hadn't gone there of his own volition and he didn't remember hardly anything at all about it. So he tried to console himself with the assurance that he hadn't told an out-and-out lie because he hated to do that.

As for the policeman, Josh didn't know whether he'd believed what he said or not. Apparently the woman had whispered something about a young boy with glowing eyes, but it seemed that no-one knew anything about that. Not surprising, his mother Lena had said, it probably didn't happen because it certainly wasn't mentioned in the newspapers. No, it wasn't, the policeman had agreed, but somehow he hadn't seemed very happy about it.

*

Addilyn poured the extra milk she had thought to bring in a small pop bottle into Marcia's tea so that it wouldn't be too hot for the little girl to drink; in contrast, hers was steaming and both were very sweet because energy was essential even on easy climbs like this one. While she sipped hers, Addilyn watched Marcia gulp hers down to quench her thirst and then she took a deep breath and said: "Okay."

"You're ready?" asked Addilyn. "Only if

you're ready."

"I'm ready."

"Go for it then."

Marcia smiled a little uncertainly and the conflict within her between the relief at being able to share her secret and the fear that she would lose someone else because of the truth was almost palpable. Addilyn smiled at her and whispered: "I'm not going anywhere, I promise."

Marcia nodded and seemed to make up her mind. She gathered her thoughts and then she started.

"It started a few years ago," she said. "One day when I was unhappy, I was crying because my mummy gave me away and I didn't want her to. I was in the back of this car with strangers and I felt lonely and I was crying and then I heard the voice saying to cheer up."

"And that was Daji?" asked Addilyn.

"Yes," replied Marcia. "But I didn't know his name then, or what he was. I was just happy to have a friend and he made me feel good."

"Feel good? How?"

"I don't know, he made me laugh. He said silly things about people."

"Like?"

Marcia considered for a moment, then: "The first time," she said, "Was the morning after mummy gave me away. I'd stayed in a place like a hospital, only it wasn't a hospital, there weren't nurses or doctors but there were large wards and more children were staying there. We were having breakfast, bread and butter and a boiled egg, and he said that the girl next to me was called Emma and that she talked funny because her daddy slapped her in the mouth and broke two of her teeth."

"And that was funny?" Addilyn wasn't much impressed with a potential friend who could find humour in someone else's pain.

"Oh, no, that was horrible!" Marcia mirrored her sentiments without knowing it. "I said, Emma, I'm sorry about what your daddy did, it wasn't nice of him. She said, no-one knows about that, I didn't tell anyone not even the orthities so how do you know? I said, I dunno I just do. I wasn't going to tell her about Daji because he was *my* friend."

Addilyn inwardly smiled at Marcia's pronunciation of 'authorities' but didn't show her amusement lest the girl interpret it as a sleight on the merits of her story. "So Daji knew something that this girl had kept secret?" she asked.

"Oh, he knows about everyone's secrets. I think he can read minds."

"Really." Addilyn thought about that and her initial suspicion resurfaced. "So your friend makes fun of people's secrets?" she asked.

"He just told me things, I don't even know why."

"And that's what he does? Tells you things about people?"

"Oh no, not any more. He began to tell me other things about grown-ups and I didn't understand what he was trying to tell me. Once I asked a grown-up about what Daji'd said to me and the grown-up shouted at me and used swear words too. I was crying and Daji left me for a bit. Then the grown-up said sorry for shouting and Daji came back and he never told me anything else again."

"Why did the grown-up say sorry to you?"

"I don't know. I think maybe Daji told him to."

"He went into the grown-up and told him to say sorry?" Maybe this Daji – whatever he or it is – has morals after all, she thought.

"I think so. When he came back Daji said sorry too. He said he realised he shouldn't have told me such secrets and that he wouldn't do it any more. I thought he wouldn't make me laugh any more and I was right. He only came to me sometimes after that, not very often and even less now."

"So..." Addilyn had no idea where she was going with this; it obviously wasn't a case of OCD or any related problem and was bigger than she could handle. However, she seemed to be the only one that Marcia would speak to about it, and so if only for the little girl's peace of mind she decided to continue. "How do you know Daji is a man?" she wanted to know.

"He's got a deep voice," answered Marcia. "He sounds like a man."

She was well-read enough to realise that that was unusual; imaginary friends weren't usually male and adult. "Have you ever seen him?" she asked.

"With my eyes? No, never. But I see him in my head. He's small and black and a bit ugly too. I never said so but he probably knew anyway. "

"And where is he now, do you think?"

"He was here, but he's gone now. He's gone more time than he's here these days."

"Where does he go when he's not with you?"

"I don't know where he goes, perhaps back home where the mouflons are."

"And where *are* the mouflons?" Addilyn wanted to know. If this were another symptom of a mental problem, she was most surprised at the intricacy of it; however lively Marcia's imagination, it was almost unbelievable that she could have subconsciously conjured up such a fantasy world as she was describing now.

"They live where Daji lives."

"Where Daji lives? When you were home at Josie's and Larry's, you said it's where *you* used to live."

"Probably Daji was answering you, not me."

"Oh? He answers for you sometimes?" Classic shifting of the blame.

"He – he kind of puts the answers in my mouth and I speak them. People have said that before, that I answer their questions with funny answers. I don't remember doing it but I did ask Daji once and he said it was the only way he could say what he wanted to say. By making me say it for him."

"And you don't mind?" You shouldn't, thought Addilyn, not if he's the classic escape goat.

"I didn't mind until I got shouted at. After that I asked him not to say anything not nice and he said he wouldn't. He didn't really say much at all after that. He visited me but I think it was because he felt he had to, like he wanted to be friends still but not best friends. Like he found another best friend to replace me."

"And how did that make you feel?" She was sounding like a therapist and she knew it.

"Sad to start with. But then I got used to it. And now I have Josie and Larrilee and you and Shadow, and I'm not sad any more."

"Well, I'm pleased to hear it! So, could you

tell me about Daji's home now?"

"Addie, I'd really not talk about him any more." Marcia was playing with her empty plastic cup and it was obvious that she was nervous. "I'm still frightened that you'll hate me now that you know about Daji," she explained. "Everyone else does, so why not you?"

"Because I'm not everyone else, Marcia, that's why." Maybe she'd been correct about the clinicality of her questions. "So don't ever think that talking to me about Daji will spoil our friendship, because it won't." She paused for a moment, then: "But I wouldn't say anything to Josie or Larrilee just yet."

"Larrilee says I have an imaginary friend. Josie doesn't but Larrilee caught me talking to Daji one night when I was in bed. Larrilee came in to put my light off and he heard me and asked me about it. I told him it was my friend Daji and he said, oh right you have an imaginary friend. He didn't seem to mind. But I didn't want to tell Josie in case she sent me away too. She's the boss, I think she is anyway, so she could do it even if Larrilee didn't want her to."

Addilyn doubted that Josie would send the girl away, but she knew from experience that some people coped better with slight abnormalities in their children than others and so silently applauded Marcia's decision. Even now, the young girl was learning just as she had that any relationship was tentative, and that if you didn't adhere to stereotype, you risked being shunned.

"One more thing, Marcia, then we'll forget about it for today?" Addilyn was desperate not to push the issue but there was one more thing she really needed to know.

"Okay."

"Why the water? Why didn't Daji talk to me? Why did he make those big waves?" Addilyn was thinking of the ones in her dreams, the ones which now resembled what she had just witnessed to such an alarming degree that she didn't think it was coincidence.

Marcia didn't reply in words but she began to pick up pebbles from the ground and count them. She formed piles of three pebbles all around her and then she separated one pebble from the other two in each pile until there was a pattern around her alternating two pebbles – small gap – one pebble – large gap – and so on until the circle was complete and it started again.

Addilyn stared at the stones for a moment, and then she shrugged. It didn't make any sense to her, but she decided she'd pushed the girl as far as she dared for the time being. If she wanted to bring her out again to discover more, she would have to make sure these were fun times for Marcia as well as inquisitions.

“Come on, she said, we′ll take a slow walk back and then we′ll stop in the tea rooms for an ice cream. Do you like ice cream?

“I love ice cream!” declared Marcia with a big grin, and she caught hold of Addilyn′s hand and held it all the way back to familiar territory.

*

That evening Don Gittins rang her and asked her if she could return to work the following day and Addilyn was delighted to oblige. She needed normality, she needed routine, she needed familiarity.

What she didn′t need started when Josh Greenwood came through the front door two minutes after she′d opened up the following morning.

SIX

"Hello," said Addilyn. "Wasn't expecting you till Saturday!"

Josh grinned and looked embarrassed.

"You still off school?" Addilyn continued with a smile as Josh came into her 'office' area (as she called it) no doubt wanting to know how his order was coming along.

"Back next Monday," Josh replied. "Not looking forward to it one bit."

"Oh, they're the best days of your life!" smiled Addilyn. "Or at least they're supposed to be, but between you and me I hated mine!" She paused, then: "Don hasn't started on it yet, what with the window and everything..."

"That's all right, I just came to give you a fiver. Helped Dad yesterday and he paid me for it."

"That's nice of him. What were you doing?"

"Not so much what I did as what I said."

"Oh dear. I won't ask."

"It was just, they had a barney and when he went out to the garden he was chatting to a neighbour and saying what a soddin' ewer mum was. She overheard him. I think she came out to give him another earful, but when she heard what he called her, she went inside in tears."

"Josh, this is a family matter, I think. You

don't need to tell me the details." Addilyn was so relieved she was able to suppress her chuckle at the Cumbrian insult.

"So instead of telling her that yes, he did call her 'a soddin' ewer', I explained he said 'a straight arrow', it was just his accent. He has a bit of one."

"That was clever of you, Josh," Addilyn observed. "And kind."

"I like Dathan, he's a dad to me. I *love* Dathan in fact. So does mum. I didn't want them falling out over something stupid. So I made it up, I told her a lie, and she seemed happy with it." Josh handed Addilyn the crumpled five pound note that he had just extracted from his jeans pocket. "People always seem happy when you lie to them, don't they."

It wasn't a question and Addilyn didn't bother to answer it. She wrote out a receipt for the five pounds and handed it to the lad with a sympathetic smile. "I doubt your dad meant what he said anyway," she reassured him. "You did the right thing, so don't be too hard on yourself."

"Yeah, I suppose." He folded the receipt and stuffed it in his pocket. "Be back Saturday, then."

"I'll be here."

"D'you think he'll have started on it by then?"

"I'll nag him to. I promise."

"Cheers."

Josh walked over to the shop door and opened it. Halfway through he turned back. "You see, mum can be a bit hard to live with sometimes," he said.

Then he left.

*

When Addilyn arrived home that evening, Marcia was waiting for her. She was sitting on the bottom step of the flight that led up to Addilyn's front door and when she saw the car, she jumped up and started waving as frantically as if she hadn't seen Addilyn for ages. Addilyn smiled in acknowledgement, but she couldn't help hoping that this wasn't going to be a regular occurrence; not only did she savour time alone which it seemed she was going to get very little of, but also she didn't want Mrs Hodgson believing that she was trying to step in and take over. Maybe she should have a word with her landlady, tell her – what? I'm sorry your foster daughter is spending more time talking with me than you, but she doesn't think you'd understand about her being possessed by a creature that causes tidal waves and lights up her eyes? Putting it that way, it was so fantastic to be almost funny, but then again if she were to write down her OCD symptoms and consequences, they would read as a outlandish comedy beyond belief. There were more things in heaven and earth...

"Addie!" Marcia rushed up to her as she got out of the car. The girl threw her arms around her waist and rested her head on Addilyn's stomach and for the first time Addilyn realised that Marcia was, for her age, rather short. She wouldn't grow up to be a policewoman or a model, she thought idly, and if people thought that sizism no longer occurred in the recruitment process for these and similar job roles, they could think again; there were plenty of ways for potential employers to get round '-isms' and sound politically correct to boot.

"Hello, Marcia," Addilyn said as she ruffled the girl's hair and reached over her to lock her car door. "What haver you been up to today?"

"I've had a visit from the headmaster of my new school!" Marcia sounded excited. "I start next Monday officially, but I'm going in tomorrow just to look round."

"Lovely!" smiled Addilyn. "That'll save you from getting bored around here."

"Are you off work on Sunday?" Marcia asked. "Josie said you worked Saturdays."

Then she probably told you I didn't work Sundays, thought Addilyn, but she knew the child was trying not to sound too impertinent. "No, I don't work Sundays," she replied, "And if you're free I thought we could go out again, that's if you'd like to, of course." Once more wouldn't hurt, thought Addilyn. She's at school after that and will no doubt meet kids her own age and then I'll be forsaken for a group of juniors!

"I'd *love* to!" squealed Marcia. "Where'll we go?"

Addilyn chuckled. "How about we go into Keswick and I'll show you round, maybe have our lunch at Crow Park? There's a lovely caf□ there; there are caf□s all over Keswick, see what you fancy when the time comes."

"Fantastic! I'll tell Josie you said yes!" Marcia ran to her own front door just as it opened and Josie Hodgson looked out and, upon seeing Addilyn, waved. "Addie said yes!" Marcia hugged her foster mum with the same fervency as she had Addilyn, and Addilyn recognised that the unbridled love and affection the girl had to give, just as she had once possessed. Luckily Marcia had found people to receive it, something that Addilyn had not, and now she wondered if she'd retained any of that emotion or if she'd filed it under F for Forgotten – or maybe F for Frightened.

"Thank you, dear," said Mrs Hodgson. "I'd love to take her out walking but my old legs aren't as strong as they used to be. Same with Larry's."

She's wondering if she did the right thing, Addilyn thought, just as I predicted. Trouble is, I don't think she did, not now. "Oh, I can do the walking bit, and a pleasure," smiled Addilyn. "After all, you do everything else!"

Mrs Hodgson waved again then disappeared with Marcia into the house.

Addilyn turned and began to climb her stairs and almost fell back down them when PC Kaden Taylor stood up from where he had been sitting on her doorstep for God knew how long.

*

PC Taylor was now seated at a table in Addilyn's kitchen, having been scolded for giving her a fright and hanging about her flat like a stalker, nursing a hot cup of tea whilst dunking a chocolate biscuit. "I love it when they melt in my tea," Addilyn had confided with a grin, as she handed him the biscuit barrel for him to help himself.

Now she was just wiping the work surface clean from tea drops, and while her back was turned the constable gave Shadow the biscuit he wanted and the dog was gone with it into the living room before Addilyn joined Taylor at the table with a puzzled expression on her face. "So, to what do I owe this unexpected visit?" she asked, conscious of the fact that she'd almost said 'pleasure' before deliberately changing it to something that Taylor would not interpret as any kind of come-on.

"It was a heart attack," replied Taylor, and for a second Addilyn was reminded of the novel '1984' by the worn-down, resigned way in which Taylor stated it.

"Okay, it was a heart attack," said Addilyn. "Was it so important that I needed to know that?"

"They said her heart just gave out, one of those things. But the look in her eyes, before I closed them... she saw something that caused her heart to stop. It wasn't just one of those things."

"Okay, if you say so. But why tell *me?* Police officers don't usually discuss the finer points of cases with the general public! That you saw the need to come here and wait for me to specifically inform me of your change of mind indicates that you believe I am somehow personally involved!"

PC Taylor sighed, took a sip of his tea, then looked Addilyn directly in the eyes. She wanted to avert her gaze because his eyes were too brown and too intense and too deep but she wouldn't because she never backed down first. "I don't know how, but I know you saw something too."

"Well, it couldn't have been so bad because I'm still here," observed Addilyn flippantly, as she was wont to do in a defensive situation.

"So you did?" Taylor sounded almost shocked to have his suspicions confirmed.

Addilyn shrugged. "I saw a kid in the trees; a boy, I think."

"Anything unusual about him?" asked Taylor.

"Like what?" retorted Addilyn.

"I have a feeling you know bloody well 'like what'."

"Constable Taylor, if you're going to sit in my house and insult me, I suggest you leave instead." Addilyn got up and carried her mug to the sink where she placed it without rinsing it out. She leaned on the edge of the sink and looked out at the land beyond the shared back garden which neither she nor the Hodgsons used very often; she wished he *would* go but it wasn't his accusations that bothered her.

"I apologise." Taylor got up and walked over to her. "Look, Miss Mackenzie, I don't know why but you dislike me, I know." He paused to gather his thoughts, then: "And of course I don't want to be in your way. This was an unofficial visit anyway, Like I said, as far as everyone else is concerned, it was a heart attack. And I'm not disputing that. I'm merely disputing the cause of it and the only reason I came here was to find out if maybe you had seen what I think *she* saw before she died because not only did that look in his eyes strike more terror into me than even my headmaster at primary school, but also because she whispered your name as I bent over her to check if she were dead."

"She did?" Addilyn turned to him. "But I didn't know her, she didn't know me – at least I don't think she did."

"It wasn't a woman's voice, it was a man's," replied Taylor. He let his gaze remain on Addilyn's face for a moment, then he turned and made his way towards the kitchen door. "When you're ready to talk, I'm ready to listen," he said, and then he left.

*

She was having a lazy evening; no Taylor, no Marcia, no Josie or Larry, no anyone except herself and Shadow who was curled up on the settee at her feet, eyes half-closed, dozing but never sleeping. For her part, Addilyn had changed into pyjamas and slippers and had a throw wrapped around her as she lay on the settee reading a book with some documentary on Tudor England on the television for background noise; she had never been able to concentrate in utter silence

– even when she took exams at school she found it essential to hum to herself – and now, although she didn't exactly hear what was being said about Henry or any one of his wives, she would miss the commentary should it be turned off.

Her book was engrossing; a nice horror about devil worship and greedy humans, her favourite genre. She would happily read just about anything; books, to her, were worlds in which she could lose herself and share with their characters the adventures within the pages. She had gone whaling, she had sat in a courtroom to hear an innocent man found guilty just because of his colour, and she had gazed with doe-eyes on the owner of the mansion alongside the teacher who worked there. She had lived a thousand lives, seen a hundred countries, tens of alien worlds, and one trickle.

One trickle? She blinked and stared at the tiny rivulet that was tumbling down the left-hand page as if it were a virtual special effect – except she wasn't reading about water.

Shadow stirred and began to growl deep in his throat, a low warning sound that suggested that someone (or something) had just entered the room. Addilyn sat up and looked around, but there was no-one there and nothing looked different. She looked back at her book whose pages were now bone dry and she chuckled somewhat nervously at her silliness; she didn't get spooked because she wouldn't allow herself to get spooked and she lay back down after taking a sip of her coffee which had been sitting on the table for a while and therefore had gone cold. She settled to read some more and advanced another paragraph before there was a loud crack, a crash and she heard water streaming from above.

Addilyn swore as she realised that her boiler – or at least a major water pipe - must have burst and, sure enough, when she got up and walked into the small hallway off which the bedroom and bathroom were situated, she noted that the floor was wet by standing in a half-inch of water and soaking the soles of her slippers. She swore again, then went to turn the stopcock off so that at least her carpets would be saved.

As she passed through the sitting room she did a double-take.

She was lying on the sofa reading her book, Shadow at her feet dozing contentedly, the woman on the television explaining how Anne Boleyn had been a pawn in an ambitious game of politics and power. Slowly she crept up to herself and looked over her own shoulder at the book, which was opened at several pages earlier than the one she had reached when it started trickling. For a while she just watched the scene with incredulity, when suddenly Shadow stirred and began to growl quietly, and Addilyn on the sofa noticed that there was a rivulet of water trickling down a page of her book.

She – Addilyn with the soaking slippers – looked up to see the origin of the leak, and spied a small crack in the plaster above a second before the entire ceiling collapsed and water rained down on her in gushing waves of freezing cold. She cried out in shock – terror, maybe – covering her head as if that gesture would protect it from the deluge, and she was knocked to the floor with the sheer force of the torrent which, just as suddenly as it had started, then completely ceased.

She dared to open her eyes.

She was lying on the floor beside the settee, her book having fallen off after her. Shadow was looking at her curiously, as if he were trying to work out why she should be on the floor, and he followed her from his place on the soft cushions as she dashed through to the hall which was perfectly dry to inspect the boiler which was perfectly intact.

Shaking her head in a futile attempt to clear it, Addilyn failed to notice the half-dozen numbers on the wall that had been drawn with water from somewhere but which were now condensing into nothingness.

*

Sometimes Don Gittins closed up early on a Saturday, either if the shop was quiet or if he had a lot to do in the back room, and Addilyn sincerely hoped that this was going to be one of those Saturdays. She had hardly slept the previous night, jumping at each and every little sound that came from the flat, swearing that she could hear water trickling only for the sound to fall silent when she sat up in bed to better listen. Even Shadow, curled up beside her in a love-spoon position, was restless, and it was this that convinced her that it wasn't all her imagination. Either that or her restlessness was rubbing off on the dog who was acting out of sympathy.

She had re-enacted the scene over and over in her mind, her natural defences desperately seeking some logical explanation, even clouding details in order to pull it into the realm of possibility. Her brain had almost convinced her that it was nothing but a dream, but not quite; it had considered an out-of-body experience, even a dual timeline theory that really belonged in a science fiction story, but had settled on the dream as a most likely – and comfortable – solution. In dreams, anything could happen and the action therein needed no further justification other than it was that – merely a dream; she wanted to believe it but she couldn't – there had been something more. She didn't know what, but it was there, niggling away at the back of her mind.

Trade was slow, as she'd expect for this time of year, so she anticipated an early closing as she'd hope. No-one came in that morning, and she was able to report with a smile that Don had started on Josh's coaster when the lad came in later that afternoon to pay a further deposit on his dad's birthday gift. She had to admire the way he was working to pay for something which would hopefully show Dathan Greenwood just how much he was loved and appreciated, and she idly wondered if anyone would ever think enough of her to do something like that. Maybe, her inner voice responded, but you have to let them in first. Well, as that wasn't very likely to happen, Addilyn thought, she supposed that she would just have to go on buying things for herself.

Apart from him, however, there were no customers. There were a few window-shoppers and several phone calls – now was the time that orders came in for wooden garden furniture – so she ensured that Don was busy for the next three months but not so today. She took him a cup of tea after Josh had left, more to see how the coaster was coming on. She was pleasant surprised; Don had already started to engrave the decoration on a beautifully cut and orbital-sanded slice of dark oak log, the colour of the wood more reminiscent than lighter alternatives of medieval castle timbers, which would complement the coat of arms perfectly. He was etching by hand; one of Don's main claims to craftsmanship – and rightful justification of the high prices he (usually) charged – was the fact that every single creation that left the shop was hand-made with minimal assistance by machinery. Don loved his art, and it showed in his finished pieces; he was also damn good at it, and that too showed in his finished pieces.

"You have the patience of a saint," she remarked.

Don smiled. "Take your time and get it right first try, saves you a lot of hassle later."

"Josh is going to be delighted with it."

"I hope Dathan will be too!" Don put down his work and reached for his mug of tea. "I see he came in again today," he remarked.

"He's paid half of it now," replied Addilyn. "I still can't get over how little you charged him."

"He's a good lad, Josh. He's been messed about a lot, deserves a break."

"He mentioned that his mum was sometimes hard to live with..."

"Oh, I daresay. She's a bit of a martyr, that one. Lovely girl, don't get me wrong, but sometimes a man needs less than perfect, know what I mean?"

"Not really."

"Angels can be boring."

"Oh. Yes, I see."

"Anyway, don't you go mentioning that to anyone. I just didn't want you to think Lena was mistreating the lad or anything. Her standards are high and they're hard to live up to sometimes, that's all."

Addilyn nodded and put out her hand to take Don's mug which he was just draining.

"Thanks," he said. "When you've washed them, just lock the front shop and call it a day. It's nearly four anyway."

"Okay," Addilyn smiled. "I'll see you on Monday then."

"Monday it is," replied Don.

*

She was home before 5.00pm and was rather surprised that Marcia was not there waiting to greet her. Maybe Josie Hodgson had warned her not to make too much of a nuisance of herself, especially in view of the outing tomorrow, but Addilyn was curious to find that she actually didn't mind that much.

She climbed the outer steps slowly, and as she inserted her key into the door lock, she hesitated before throwing it open and being attacked by the only male she thought would ever be happy to see her arrive home.

She let Shadow out and after dropping her bag inside the door, she joined him at the side of the house and took him through the bushes along a makeshift pathway that led from where her car was parked into the adjacent field which she knew would be empty at this time of year. Later on, she might have to block the path because she didn't want Shadow worrying the sheep that would be there come early March; but for now the field was hers and anyone else's to exercise their dogs in, so long as they cleaned up after them.

Climbing the steps again, she felt the same trepidation as she had twenty minutes ago, but when Shadow entered the flat with his tail wagging deliriously, Addilyn took the plunge; after all, dogs were great sensors and if Shadow didn't think there was anything amiss, there probably wasn't.

The evening passed uneventfully and Addilyn fell asleep on the sofa, so tired was she after the previous night's lack of sleep. She awoke to the alarm on her mobile phone which she had set a couple of days before and wished that she could go back to bed for a few hours. But she knew she had to drag herself to the bathroom and get herself ready – heck, she'd settle for awake right now – for Marcia's sake, and besides, she would sleep again tonight if she was as tired as she foresaw she would be.

She'd just managed to gobble a couple of slices of hot buttered toast and gulp down a mug of coffee before Marcia came bounding through to the kitchen. The little girl ran up to her and hugged her waist, then suddenly gasped. Addilyn held her at arm's length, noting the look of alarm on her face. "Is it Daji?" she asked gently.

"No," said Marcia. "I just barged straight in without knocking. I am so sorry!"

Addilyn chuckled; if that was the extent of the problems today, she could handle them.

Famous last words, her inner mind teased her.

She dismissed its provocation as paranoia.

SEVEN

Parking her car wasn't as easy as Addilyn had anticipated, probably because the day was the best of the year so far. The sky was cloudless, and although it was chilly, the sun's light was strong and the ground was dry. In the distance the fells were covered in snow and their tops glistened like freshly-formed diamonds. Everyone in close proximity to the popular market town was out and about on such a day and so there were spaces in the car park only at the furthest distance from the town centre.

Marcia didn't mind, that was for sure; it was if she had never been for a day out. She glanced around her at everything, pointed enthusiastically at the fells that surrounded the town, looked in every shop window with sounds of glee and generally gave the impression that she were in Santa's grotto rather than in an ordinary Cumbrian town in coming up for mid- January.

"We'll go and see the Moot Hall," Addilyn was saying. "And then we'll take a walk down to the lake while it's still nice. Forecast says it's going to stay dry but this is Cumbria!"

"What's a moot hall?" asked Marcia.

"It's where the moot would gather to debate, usually something legal. Historically, that was what the debaters were called, a moot."

Marcia nodded, satisfied. Her attention was now turned back to the shops as they walked through an arcade that would lead to the market place. Many of the shops sold fell-walking gear – cagoules, sturdy shoes and boots, walking sticks of various lengths and thicknesses – but Marcia seemed as fascinated by these as Addilyn suspected she would the sweet shops and bric-a-brac shops that they would pass on the way to the north-east shore of Derwentwater.

When they reached the end of the alley where the pavement opened out onto the traffic-free market place, Marcia made a small squeal of delight. She ran up to the assembly hall that was now a tourist information office topped by a clock tower and a clock that had famously only ever had one hand as far back as anyone could remember, and up a short flight of steps to where the entrance to the presently closed tourist office was situated. Addilyn grabbed her mobile from her handbag and snapped a couple of photos, then Marcia skipped down the steps on the other side and followed Addilyn around the back of the hall and to the right where they entered into an oniomaniac's dream – or nightmare, depending on how you looked at it.

It was coming up to noon and Addilyn

figured on having lunch at around one; most of the local eateries were open – indeed Keswick was another town that never slept much – so they would have their choice of venue according to what Marcia fancied at the time. It was her day after all, Addilyn mused, although she was beginning to enjoy the place anew in the company of a little girl who seemed to be seeing it all for the first time. They stopped off at an ice cream shop, then continued down the slope, under a pedestrian subway and out into a car park. Marcia dropped a ten pence into a wishing well and wished aloud that everyone in the world would be happy, then carried on to the gate on the right which led to the open grassland that was Crow Park and that led down to the water's edge.

"Oh, wow!" was all that Marcia said, and instead of glancing this way and that with excitement, she simply stared ahead as if in a trance then visible relaxed and faintly smiled. Addilyn smiled with her; she had had the same reaction the first time she had seen this panorama too and even now on the umpteenth viewing her breath caught in her throat at the awesomeness of nature's landscaping skills.

Behind her, a couple seemed to be having an argument and she fought the impulse to turn around.

"But you know how much I like it," said a

man.

"Well, I don't!" The woman was adamant. "It's not natural!"

"Who cares about natural? Let's do unnatural for a change!"

"Look, I am *not* talking about it here! We came here for a nice day out, not for a discussion on – "

"Hi, Miss Mackenzie!"

The sound carried across the grassland just as the argument was getting interesting and Addilyn was a little disappointed that she wouldn't now discover what the subject of the allusive discussion was, but she turned to the caller of her name to see Josh Greenwood standing waving at her and she smiled and returned the gesture.

"So who's *that*?" The woman whom Addilyn surmised was Lena Greenwood demanded of whom she also surmised was Dathan Greenwood.

"I don't know!" replied Dathan. "It's Josh who waved at her, not me!"

Josh came over to where his parents were standing as if facing off, the contentiousness between them almost palpable. Marcia had come towards Addilyn and was now holding her hand tightly; obviously this show of hostility was upsetting the girl, probably because of past memories, Addilyn reasoned.

"Come on," she said to her. "We don't

need this aggravation. Shall we go find somewhere to have lunch?"

Marcia nodded and Addilyn turned to lead her away, when Josh passed in front of them and stood red-faced gazing at each of his parents in turn as if he couldn't believe their appalling behaviour.

"Mum, Miss Mackenzie works at the furniture shop in town," explained Josh.

"Furniture shop?" repeated Lena.

"That's right," said Josh.

"You met her in a furniture shop?"

"Yes."

"And what exactly would you be doing in a furniture shop that you should need to make her acquaintance?"

Addilyn was about to step forward and answer that, mainly because she didn't like the way the conversation was heading, but Josh quickly spoke out.

"It's nothing important," he said. "I just went in to have a look at something."

"At what?" asked Lena.

"Nothing much, just a – "

Addilyn decided that enough was enough; Josh was struggling and even if she wasn't as adept as he was at making things up on the spot, she realised what Lena was implying and her reputation meant more to her than a birthday surprise. But she didn't have the chance, because Lena turned on her husband

and attracted an audience that comprised of everyone within hearing distance.

"She's your fancy bit!" she accused, sounding almost satisfied. Then she turned to grab Josh's arm. "And you're in on it with him! I don't fucking *believe* it!"

Addilyn, shocked and indignant, was about to go and put her right on that score but Marcia was yanking on her arm urgently. A quick glance over her shoulder at the girl revealed to her two glowing eyes and a shaking hand whose finger was pointing to Josh who had obviously broken away from his mother's grip and was now running towards the shore.

"You just never give up!" he was yelling, and Addilyn didn't need to see his face to know that he was crying. "You just never leave him alone!"

Addilyn felt sorry for the boy but she needed to get away from here right now. She squeezed Marcia's hand and was gently pulling her away but the girl was having none of it and stood her ground stolidly.

"Help him!" she screamed, but too late. Josh jumped over a large boulder and, instead of landing safely the other side of it down by the water's edge, somehow caught his foot and dived head first towards the ground. A sharp crack sounded then, echoed as if someone had placed a microphone on the boy's head. As for Josh, he was lying stock still.

"Oh, dear *God*!" Lena rushed to where her son was lying prone on the muddy lake shore and Dathan had taken his phone out and was ringing for an ambulance. When he had terminated the call, he went to Josh and Lena but the woman stood up and fixed him with a stare that would have positively shrivelled him had looks been able to kill. "*You* did this!" she shouted as people began to back away from the scene, morbid curiosity giving way to embarrassed discretion. "*You!*"

Dathan opened his mouth to protest, but Addilyn had seen and heard enough. She turned on her heel and stormed back up towards the gate and the theatre that was situated opposite it, silently praying that Josh would be all right. She supposed she might have stayed, at least until the ambulance arrived, but then again she wasn't exactly popular with Lena right now even if she hadn't done anything to warrant the woman's suspicions. Besides, she had Marcia to think about; she didn't want what happened to totally ruin the little girl's day out.

"Time for lunch," she said with a forced smile. What she really meant was 'time for a talk'. "What do you fancy, Marcia?"

"I don't mind," said Marcia. "Perhaps some sausages and mash?"

"I know the very place," replied Addilyn, and she guided the little girl back to the road towards the town, happy and relieved to have something to do.

She didn't know what all that had been about, but she *did* know that she didn't want to be a part of it.

Except for the bit with Daji. For some reason, she really wanted to be a part of that.

*

There was a great mound of mashed potato on Marcia's plate, surrounded by a foot of grilled Cumberland sausage and topped with onion-flecked gravy. Addilyn didn't think she would be able to finish a meal that big, let alone a small girl; for herself, she had chosen a baked potato with cheese and now she was adding more butter from the little plate in the centre of the small table. They never put enough butter on baked potatoes, she thought, as she counted how many dollops she put on with very little interest.

Marcia took a scoop of mash and shovelled it into her mouth. When she'd swallowed it, she paused before saying: "Daji is sorry he couldn't save Josh."

Well, that saved trying to find a discreet way of introducing the subject, Addilyn thought wryly. To Marcia: "Save him how?"

she said as nonchalantly as she could.

"He knew Josh was going to fall."

"He set it up? Why?"

"No, he didn't set it up. He just knew it was going to happen."

"No-one just knows what's going to happen."

"Daji does."

"Is he God?"

"God?" Marcia thought for a moment. "I don't know. I'll ask him next time he visits me but I shouldn't think so."

"Oh?"

"Well, God lives in heaven with angels, but I've never heard of mouflons being there."

"Ah." Addilyn tried to repress a smile at the uncomplicated logic. What simplicity do children confer on their beliefs, she mused. She was just about to ask Marcia another question when she felt pressure on her shoulder and turned to see Dathan Greenwood – alone – standing behind her chair.

"Miss Mackenzie?" he said.

Addilyn wasn't at all pleased to see him. "Did you follow us?" she asked petulantly.

"No, I just saw you when I came in."

"How's Josh?"

"I don't know. The ambulance took him to the hospital. Lena wouldn't let me get in with her, said I'd done enough damage for one day." He shook his head. "I'm just so sorry for what she suspected about you. It's a cross between embarrassing and annoying."

"I think my sympathy would be more with your wife than with myself," observed Addilyn. "Either she has an inferiority complex, or you've given her reason to doubt you – either way it's not very nice for her."

"She's a stickler for tradition," sighed Dathan. "And that goes for all aspects of life and relationships. If it's not in the Bible, it's not allowed."

"And that's a bad thing?"

"It's very restricting."

"Well, that's not for me to know or for you to be telling." Addilyn smiled. "But I do appreciate your apology and I accept it. Now, I really think you ought to go to the hospital whether Lena likes it or not. Josh will want his dad even if she doesn't want her husband. And as well as expecting you to turn up, she'll be hoping you do, you know."

"You're right. I'm going."

"Goodbye, Mr Greenwood."

"Dathan."

"Addilyn."

"Lovely..."

*

Addilyn was almost relieved when it

started to rain because it left them little choice but to return home. It was well into the afternoon anyway and the sky was darkening, so the trip wouldn't be cut by that much if they went now anyway. It was just that she really wanted to be alone because there was a lot that was troubling her; but she hadn't rushed Marcia to finish her meal and afterwards she had taken the girl into the Puzzling Place on the way back to the car. Now, her conscience satisfied along with Marcia's curiosity, they were dashing the fifty or so yards across the car park in rain that was becoming heavier by the second and as they reached the car and got in, a sudden clap of thunder sounded as if as accompaniment to their slamming shut of the car doors.

The drive home was a wet one with the windscreen wipers throbbing fit to burst but still not enough to completely clear Addilyn's view of the road from the downpour. She hated having the wipers on because she found herself counting the beats and this detracted from her concentration. She tried to ignore the constant whooshing of the wipers but it was as if her compulsion antenna were on automatic; her brain counted whether or not she wanted it to.

"You're mad at me." Marcia's voice was small and Addilyn darted her a look before squinting back through the windscreen.

"No, no I'm not, sweetheart," said Addilyn. "I'm just having to concentrate on the road in this rain."

"I thought maybe Daji had upset you again."

"Not at all. I'd love to talk to Daji, but not just at this moment. Could he come back another time, do you think?"

"I don't know. He doesn't tell me, he just turns up."

"Would he visit *me*, then?"

"He might. Shall I tell him when he comes again?"

"Yes, please. I think I'd like that."

"Are you mad at *him*?"

Addilyn chuckled. "I don't rightly know," she admitted. "But I'm curious about him – and I'd love to know where those – "

Marcia screamed a second before the thud sounded. Addilyn slammed on the brakes and fought with the wheel as the car spun on the wet and slippery surface of the road. Luckily she hadn't been going too fast so it was relatively easy to get the car back under control, but still her heart was beating ten to the dozen in her chest . She checked that there was no other traffic then opened her car door and went across to where a body was sprawled on the grassy verge.

Please God, she prayed, *Don't let them be dead.*

The body groaned and its left leg moved. Then its right. Presently it tried to sit up and slowly but surely succeeded. Its owner was smiling and looking half-sheepish, half-intoxicated.

"We meet again," slurred Dathan Greenwood.

Then he passed out.

EIGHT

Addilyn had explained it to the Hodgsons before Marcia attempted to, and during this time Dathan Greenwood remained bundled up on the back seat of Addilyn's car, just as he had been for the duration of the journey home. Marcia had had to help Addilyn get him there – he was a dead weight and she couldn't manage on her own, she'd tried – but while the girl thought it hilarious, Addilyn was extremely annoyed with the stupid man and had more than once on the way back contemplated ditching him on the side of the road and ringing the police anonymously. But her own stupidity got in the way and she brought him home; now she'd have to live with the decision.

She had been quite surprised at the Hodgsons' reaction; she'd expected a lecture on morality but of course they didn't actually know who Dathan was so they were only aware that at long last she had was courting a nice young man and that it was about time too. If Marcia followed the conversation, she said nothing; it was possible that it was all above her head or that she didn't care either way, but Addilyn had a sneaking suspicion that the girl was being tactful. She mentally shrugged; it didn't really matter what anyone thought because nothing untoward had happened, she had just helped out an acquaintance when he needed it.

Shadow wasn't impressed at all; first of all his human went out without him, and now she was bringing home funny-smelling male humans whom he did not recognise. He kept his distance as Addilyn hauled Dathan up the steps, going into the field on his own and coming back when he had finished, running up the stairs and into the flat without looking back. When Addilyn finally got Dathan into her flat, she shut the door and turned to Shadow. "We got a visitor, boy!" she informed him with a smile, but Shadow just growled and left the room.

Plonking Dathan on a chair, Addilyn went into the kitchen to make some strong coffee. When she reappeared, Dathan seemed to have taken at least one step towards consciousness as he lay sprawled out and moaning loudly.

"Welcome back to the land of the living," said Addilyn as she put the coffee down on the table in front of him.

Dathan looked at her as if she were an alien, then shut his eyes again and moaned some more.

"I have no sympathy for you," she remarked. "You know what it is, you know it will go away eventually and you know how you could have avoided it."

"Thanks." Dathan sat up very slowly and

reached for his coffee. “Dear God alive, my *head*!”

“You should thank God alive that it's only your head. I almost ran over you.”

“My head feels like you did.”

Addilyn chuckled in spite of herself. “Well, you better be getting yourself back home soon,” she said. “You don't want to get into even more trouble with your wife than you are already.”

“Yeah, well, maybe I should just leave her be for a while. Let her temper cool.”

“Whatever you think best. But you can't stay here all day – I have plans.”

“Oh, yeah? What plans?”

“I – I have to do some work, work from home. To take into work tomorrow.”

“What kind of work do you do at home for a furniture shop?”

“It's not just a 'furniture shop', it's hand-made wooden furniture, more like works of art.”

“And what *was* Josh doing there? It's hardly a young boy's scene!”

“I'm afraid I can't say.”

“Oh?”

“Please, don't push it. It's nothing bad, just a secret. For now, anyway.”

“I don't like secrets.”

“Yes, well, you'll have to like this one because I won't talk.” Addilyn walked back towards the kitchen. "I suppose you want breakfast – "

She got no further. Dathan, moving quicker than his alleged headache should have allowed him to, had cleared the settee in one easy leap and was now holding Addilyn tightly around the waist with one arm while tickling her with the other. "You sure you're not ready to talk?" he teased.

Addilyn wasn't usually ticklish, wasn't now as a matter of fact, but the physical contact felt so good that she pretended she was. "No, stop it!" she squealed delightedly, although she didn't want him to. "I can't talk! I *won't* talk, I promised Josh!"

Dathan stopped tickling her but he didn't let her go. He stood behind her, his arms wrapped around her waist, his head resting on her shoulder.

"You'll find out at the end of the month," she said. "And that's all you're going to get out of me."

"We'll see about that." Dathan turned her gently to face him and Addilyn made no attempt to stop him or to put any distance between them. Her heart was beating fast in her chest and she was aware that she wanted him. She was also aware that it was because he belonged to somebody else, but it wasn't because she wanted to take him off his wife; indeed, the very fact that he was spoken for made him more attractive to her – that way there would be no commitment, no deep-felt emotions, just raw passion with no ties.

"Dathan, please..."

"No need to plead, Miss Mackenzie. This is going to be a pleasure."

It felt wrong, Addilyn realised. Dathan Greenwood was married, and quite apart from being unavailable long-term which she was okay with, he was someone else's husband and if she found out it would hurt her and Josh, which she wasn't okay with. But with his arms around her, his face inches from hers, his warm breath on her cheek, the very smell of him, the closeness, the anticipation, it all felt so *right...*

"I take it you're a willing participant?" he asked breathlessly, his lips only an inch from hers and closing in, his eyes sparkling as he watched hers.

She wanted to say 'yes' but she couldn't. Panic enveloped her as she realised that she could not physically speak, and that she couldn't even nod her head in assent. Dathan pulled away and was regarding her now with an expression that bordered on terror, his eyes wide, his lips parted, his brow furrowed in a frown of incomprehension. Addilyn tried again – just to call his name, nothing more – but Dathan was running for the door, now out of it, she could hear his footsteps on the stairs outside and then he was gone and it was eerily silent.

*

What just happened? Addilyn asked herself after a moment or two of trying unsuccessfully to understand Dathan's sudden change of heart, and also unsure if she were alluding to the bit where she felt paralysed or Dathan's strange, questioning look and subsequent rather hurried departure.

You escaped by the skin of your teeth.

The voice wasn't loud, just audible, but Addilyn wasn't sure if it were external or internal; the latter made more sense that the former as she knew she was alone, but then she wondered why she should regard hearing voices inside her head as anything like sensible.

And escape what? she wondered irritably; the only thing she'd managed to escape as far as she could see was feeling wanted and desirable...

You almost made the biggest mistake of your life, not only by lusting after another woman's husband but also by setting yourself up for a lifetime of regrets and self-recrimination.

I doubt if one fling would lead to years of remorse.

It would if you'd known the consequences.

And what were the consequences?

It doesn't matter now; they never happen.

You're going to be a annoying little sod, aren't you.

Sometimes it's unavoidable, but I do try.

Well, let me get myself comfortable. If we're going to talk I don't want to do it here gazing at my closed front door with my jaw dropping to the ground. Mind if I get myself a coffee?

Get a tea. It's better for your health.

*

Addilyn made tea whilst looking out of the kitchen window. The fells beyond were beautiful, especially if you were in a contemplative mood as she was now. Her tea-making actions were automatic – she had done it so many times that she fancied she could do it with her eyes closed – and she pondered the ludicrous situation she was in now, leaving that which she had been in not half an hour ago for later consideration. One thing at a time, she thought; after all, she didn't want to burn out the old grey matter right this minute – she hadn't got that desperate before and didn't think she'd quite reached that level of depression yet.

So, to the conversation she was having

with herself, or with some part of her brain, and to what it might be...

If this was a kind of intrusive thought, it was one such as she had never experienced before; it was more of an intrusive conversation than a single thought, for heaven's sake. So maybe her mind was getting worse. What started out as relatively harmless Obsessive Compulsive Disorder was now developing from the neurotic to the psychotic, and she was going insane. But surely that couldn't be? After all, she was aware that what she was experiencing was not normal and surely the periods where she gave her intrusive ideas some semblance of authenticity were so few and far between that for the most part she, not the disease, was in control. It was a bloody nuisance, that was for sure, and it caused much anxiety and even more frustration and annoyance, but in no way was she ever unaware of her own participation in the imaginings that were defined by the stupid condition.

Of course, it might not be imagination at all, but the taking up of residence by something as yet unknowable (she had her suspicions); either way, the best thing to do was to see it through.

She carried her mug of tea into the sitting room, placed it on the table, lay down on the settee, got comfortable and closed her eyes.

So why me? she re-instigated the question-and- answer session.

Have you noticed how you're talking to me freely, with no uneasiness? That's because your intrusive thoughts, they have immunized you against anything out of the ordinary, or if not immunized at least prepared you. Whether or not you realise it, you are constantly expecting something to pop into your head, knowing that you can cope with it.

Are you an intrusive thought?

I hope not. But it's hard to ask permission, so I just leave if I'm not welcome.

You're Daji.

That's what Marcia calls me, yes.

Did Marcia have OCD before she met you?

No. Marcia was a mistake. I wasn't so skilled when I first came here, and I misread the signs. She needed help, but not the type that I could give her. So I made sure that someone would –

The Hodgsons.

Yes, someone who needed her as much as she needed them. And, as luck would have it, I found you in the process. Agreeable outcome all round, I'd say.

Are you responsible for the glowing eyes?

Yes. I can't help it. It is my essence and it has to exit somewhere. It chose the route, I had little to do with it.

So what **are** you?

Something I doubt you could conceive of, for the time being.

Fair enough; I'm too exhausted to disagree. Besides, I still think I'm going mad.

No, you don't. You're afraid because you're accepting of something so out of the ordinary that anyone else would say you were mad.

Well, that's for sure.

So look upon it as their loss, your gain – I wouldn't choose anyone who was so narrow-minded.

Thank you.

Welcome.

Addilyn sat up, took a sip of her tea then settled back down again.

What are 'mouflons'? she asked.

I made them up for Marcia, Daji explained. *Planted an idea in her mind. I made a whole world up for her, a world where she could escape to and be happy in. It's very colourful.*

So I've seen. Marcia drew one.

It was the least I could do after I'd caused her so much anxiety. I honestly didn't realise that she wouldn't be able to cope.

Because she's a child?

More because she hasn't the capacity which she hasn't got because she's a child. There are adults who have the same level of intellectual proficiency – or rather lack of it. I need imagination, but I also need experience, belief, and trust that what I am doing is what should be done. All that and of course the ability to carry it out.

Carry what out? Addilyn was almost relieved that Daji wanted something of her; it didn't compute that whatever he was would give something for nothing.

That which will prevent what otherwise is inevitable.

Ask a stupid question, Addilyn thought, and then realised that Daji probably heard – if that was the right word - that. She decided to change the subject. So what of the dreams I've been having? she asked. Of water, of tidal waves? Are they relevant?

Yes, they were a warning.

We're going to get a tidal waves here in North-West England?

No, not as such. That was just my way of describing it, the end of the world. As in Noah and the flood. I didn't know else to express it to Marcia. She had been learning about Noah so I thought it would be a concept she could understand. I was wrong. I'm still learning.

The world's going to end in a great flood?

It's going to come close to ending but that's not a definite inevitability. There is a projectile coming, from the stars.

A projectile? You mean a comet or a meteor?

Think about them and let me look. Addilyn did; Daji paused and then: *Yes,* he told her, *that is what it is, an asteroid.*

When?

A year yet.

How do you know?

I know.

And why are you telling me?

Because you're listening. And now you have to make the others listen too.

*

That night Addilyn dreamed.

The tsunami began, not on the horizon where the deep blue of the sea met the golden glow of the setting sun, but in the sky where sunlight radiated outwards onto a pink cloud background and then out further onto a cornflower blue canvas. In the beauty of the sunset, one dark, ominous cloud stained the otherwise clear tapestry with a glaucous foreboding, which after a few seconds suddenly mushroomed into a billion raindrops which coalesced as she watched into a celestial tidal bore.

Tossed in the ethereal eagre, creatures of all sizes and shapes tumbled within the swell, surfacing, sinking, resurfacing. There were two of each, as befitted Daji's illustration of Noah's Ark, including a pair of mouflons, which Daji probably meant to signify the totality of the forthcoming destruction; but then there were people, a bearded man who was naked, clenching a bottle in his hand, another looking as if he were reaching out for the bottle – it hardly seemed feasible that any of these beings would survive because the buffeting they were being subjected to would surely kill them long before any Araratian sanctuary was reached.

Yet the water sparkled; like a myriad of diamonds, droplets were flung from the mounting wave which now approached her in a torrent of shimmering silver, atop which not Marcia but she, Addilyn herself, was riding, as if attempting to outwit the deluge, to survive its apocalyptic menace and suddenly she was seeing things from atop the giant wave, experiencing the ride, catching glimpses of a sad earth covered in a dark grey mist from which wailing skulls and whip-wielding arrow-tailed demons occasionally emerged, attention returning to the precarious-ness of her balance which equilibrium was being threatened with every yard advanced in the course of the seismic cataclysm.

These were dreams the like of which she had never experienced before. They were full, so full, that she had problems keeping up with them, yet she found she was taking in every detail, like watching a film and noticing every single action and every single word from everyone on the set, main cast and extras. She kept a hold of them only by designating variations of her OCD to each of them, which somehow allowed her to recall them so much more easily, and when it appeared that the dreams had acted themselves out, she relived them again and again in her mind trying to understand until she could try no more.

Then her brain gave up and she slept; even Daji could not awaken her which was most fortunate because any more input would have either driven her literally insane or killed her.

NINE

Kaden Taylor was exasperated; as much as he loved his brother and was happy to hear from him, he was also aware of how dramatic he could be. Timothy was in the sort of profession that effused drama, but Kaden knew that Tim liked to expound a little – okay, a lot – and a lot of what he said had to be sifted for exaggeration and embellishment.

"So, you spotted a UFO," said Kaden, imagining his brother's sour expression with a cruel amount of relish. "Well, you must keep your eye on it. That is your job, after all, and let me know what develops."

Timothy harrumphed. He knew fine well that Kaden believed him – Kaden was rather susceptible to believing anything out-of-this-world or other-worldly almost to the extent that he wasn't susceptible to taking his own life on Earth seriously – but he wished that Kaden wouldn't call everything a UFO. Back when they were younger, Tim would point out stars and planets to his kid brother and he would gasp and declare that "wow, it's a UFO!" and he'd never really grown out of it. If something could possibly (however improbably) have a supernatural or surreal cause, that was the angle that Kaden would view it from first before dumping it all together as boring when it transpired as conventionally explainable.

"Well, it might be something!" Kaden continued.

"Probably one of the usual culprits not acting quite as we expected it to," said Tim. "But, as I asked you and the reason for this call, are you going to be my best man or not?"

"Haven't got a choice," replied Kaden. "You don't have another brother so I have to say 'yes'."

Tim chuckled; he knew that Kaden was thrilled. "Okay, baby brother, thanks." He paused, then: "You really should come and visit some time. Been a long time since we saw you."

Kaden knew that 'we' referred to his brother and his intended, Darcy, and he also knew that it really had been one heck of a long time since he had visited his brother, but then his brother hadn't visited him either. Okay, so it was easier for him to go to Wales than for Tim to come up to Cumbria owing both to their jobs and to their other commitments – chiefly relative, of which Time had Darcy and Kaden had nobody – but it was bleak in that part of Wales that housed Tim's home county of Montgomeryshire, or whatever it was that modern geography called it. "I'll try and get up next holiday," he said.

"Okay," said Tim, knowing he wouldn't. "Take care, Kay."

“You too, Tim, love to Darcy. Bye.” Kaden ended the call and put his mobile back on his desk.

If he’d realised that he wouldn’t ever speak to his brother again, he might not have felt more excited by the prospect of a UFO than of being a best man; but Kaden didn’t know so the UFO maintained its precedence.

*

The following day Addilyn dragged herself out of bed and back to work with the reluctance she would have shown at taking a bath in sulphuric acid or accepting the wedding proposal of a handsome man who assured her he had no ulterior motive except to make her happy for the rest of their days. She was vaguely aware of something in the back of her mind (which she knew to be Daji) although it never interrupted her work or even her thought processes, but rather afforded a sense of reassurance that she was not alone which was rather comforting; she only wished that it would help her to relax and sleep.

Don Gittins joked about how tired she looked, but she knew that he was genuinely worried. She assured him that it was just anxiety following all that had happened recently, and that she had medication which she was sure would work soon; white lies but ones that she could live with if it meant that Don would stop worrying, would stop reminding her that she looked as drained as she felt.

Luckily, the week was quiet; orders were coming in by telephone but there were still very few shoppers who actually came into the place. January was being its usual self – cold and wet and misty – and it would be another few weeks before it would start getting busy. She had asked Don if she could help out back, that she felt guilty taking his money for no work done, but he assured her he was happy to just have her answering the telephone, looking after the administration and making 'the best tea this side of the Kirkstone Pass'; this latter, she knew, was an exaggeration but she accepted the compliment with grace, because God knew she didn't get many, unless you counted a drunken man trying it on with you.

Thus Addilyn struggled through the week, and although she talked with Daji, they covered nothing more regarding the forthcoming catastrophe. Daji had on more than one occasion enquired of her as to when she was going to start advising the authorities that they should act, but she explained back that she had to formulate some kind of plan first, that to merely walk into a government building of any sort – police, council, even a trip to London to visit an embassy or the Ministry of Defence (if she was even allowed in the latter, that was) would result only in her being deemed insane and treated accordingly; then she would be powerless to do anything. Daji sensed her fear and her frustration and so remained quiet. Daji, it seemed, was tactful as well as wise.

It was almost time for the alarm to go off on Saturday morning when Addilyn bolted awake in a flood of perspiration and with a scream, and she could have sworn blind that some sort of laser beam blast had tried to kill her.

*

When PC Kaden Taylor reported for work that morning, his stomach did a double-flip because he would have recognised the expression on each of his colleagues' faces anywhere; after all, he had employed it enough times when he had had not-so-good news to impart.

"What?" he asked shakily.

"Sit down, Kay," his sergeant advised.

"Just tell me," snapped Taylor. "I'm not a child."

"Your brother Tim's dead," said the sergeant. "I'm sorry."

Taylor sat down, heavily. “How?” he asked.

“I don’t have all the details. I suggest you take a couple of weeks’ compassionate leave and go and see his partner. She’ll know more than I do.”

“I don’t need two weeks,” said Taylor, getting up. “Just one will be fine.”

“Take two,” insisted the sergeant. “One to visit your brother’s girlfriend and one at home wondering what the hell is wrong with the world.” He patted Taylor on the back as Taylor passed him on his way out. “Believe me, I’m talking from experience,” he smiled sadly.

Taylor nodded but said nothing; he didn’t trust himself to speak.

*

“God, you look rough,” remarked Don Gittins when Addilyn walked through the back entrance to the shop. “Bad night?”

“Very,” replied Addilyn, “But I’ll be fine. A good strong coffee...”

“Don’t make me one,” said Don. “I’m off out now you’re here.”

“A commission?” asked Addilyn.

“No, just doing my Good Samaritan bit. Sorting out the broken window case without having to resort to the authorities – the chap’s offered to pay what it cost me plus compensation and I'm inclined to accept. I'll bring you back the details so you can record it in the books."

"And get his daft story about aliens, eh?" Addilyn chuckled in what she hoped was an authentic way, but actually she was hoping Don *would* get the story so that she could hear it later.

"Hah, aliens shmaliens!" grunted Don. "Too much grog, pure and simple."

"Oh, well, listen to his tale anyway; it might amuse you!" Addilyn turned to her computer then as if it mattered not a jot whether Don Gittins got or didn't get the story and she was glad of the distraction when the front door bell announced a prospective customer. She looked up with a smile and had to work hard not to allow it to falter, however, as she saw young Josh enter the shop and she prayed that she wasn't blushing as hot as she fancied she was.

"Hi, Addilyn." The boy sounded as sheepish as Addilyn felt; this was probably embarrassing for both of them.

"You're up and about quick!" smiled Addilyn, noting the rather large bump protruding from the right side of that lads' forehead. "Shouldn't you have that head bandaged?"

"I took it off. People were staring at me."

"Yes, they would." Addilyn had meant the remark to be silent, but realised too late that she had voiced it. "So how are you feeling?" she asked brightly, to change the subject.

"I'm fine. I've come to pay another fiver."

"Under the circumstances, it could've waited, you know."

"Under the circumstances, dad's lucky he's still getting it."

"Oh, you have to forgive adults, they can be pretty stupid at times."

"You think they were being stupid?"

"Oh, no – no, I didn't mean – "

"I don't think they were being stupid either. I think they were being *moronic*."

Addilyn had to laugh at that. She took the five pound note that Josh was holding out to her, fished from his jeans' pocket by the look of the crumpled paper money, straightened it out, put it in her desk drawer and printed him out a receipt. Handing it to him, she looked directly at him.

"Adults *are* moronic," she said earnestly. "Parents especially. But don't let it get you down. They both love you very much. You're not the problem."

"I hope not. I mean, I know I'm not dad's *real* son – "

"Of course you are. Just as there's a difference between a father and a dad, there's a difference between an offspring and a son.

In every sense of the word that matters, you're Dathan Greenwood's boy and he loves you."

"How do you know?"

It was a simple question, innocent even, but Addilyn's stomach lurched. She could not possibly let on that Dathan had visited her, even if nothing – nothing *much* – had happened; God knew, the poor kid was confused enough.

"Experience," replied Addilyn confidently. "Plus, it shows." She paused, then: "And if there are any other problems, remember that your credit is good here, at least for as long as you have that bump on your head!"

"Thanks."

Josh smiled as he turned to leave but it was a sad smile and Addilyn's heart ached for him.

*

FIVE SCIENTISTS IN FATAL ATTACKS; IS THERE OR IS THERE NOT A CONNECTION?

Kaden Taylor didn't usually buy newspapers – he had a perfectly good mobile with internet access should he ever want to wallow in the depression that was World News – but the headline grabbed him, particularly in light of his brother's recent death. Tim had been a scientist too, on loan from the University of Cambridge, he helped to work the telescope at the Spaceguard Centre in south central Wales, interpreting and analysing results from both the Schmidt camera and the robotic camera. He also enjoyed taking children around and explaining what he did; Tim was naturally enthusiastic about his job and didn't have to make an effort to make it sound interesting. And he loved kids, hoped to have his own one day, but that wouldn't happen now; for Tim, nothing would happen now or ever again.

Taylor returned to his reading – Tim wasn't the only one who wouldn't be doing anything ever again...

In the past two days, there have been reports of the deaths of five scientists – Dr Timothy Taylor of Cambridge University, Dr Hillary Johnson of NASA, Professor Adrian Hall of Pan-Starrs Hawaii, Professor Olivia Wetherington of the University of Arizona and Dr Raphael di Caro of the ESA – under very strange, but seemingly unconnected, circumstances. Although some sources have suggested a common theme, others have opined that 'science' is too general a concept to be readily accepted as a conjunctional link, and even those who have pointed out that there were all associated with space or astronomy are not at present being taken too seriously.

Taylor harrumphed to himself. Okay, to

anyone who didn't know the inner circle so well, these employees of various scientific institutions might be regarded as unconnected in any way other than they were scientists – possible astrophysicists – as the article suggested, but when you substituted Spaceguard UK for Cambridge, the NEO Program for NASA, Spacewatch for Arizona, and the Optical Ground Station Tenerife for the ESA , they began to have very close connections indeed to the remaining undisguised establishment in Hawaii. And the author of the article suspected as such, Taylor fancied, and he read on:

However, it is interesting that these scientists all worked in similar departments within their named establishments, and although we are prevented from further elucidation by a legal data protection measure, this reporter is going to propose a theoretical – and it is *purely theoretical – scenario.*

Oh, I bet you are, thought Taylor. Nothing like the feeling of power when you cause a nationwide panic; and one which you cannot be touched for either, because you've covered all the bases and stated that it's only a hypothetical situation, even though you know people aren't going to heed that part of it.

The thing was, though, having made the connection himself, he wondered if it wasn't right and proper for the masses to know what was coming. It may, of course, turn out to be nothing but coincidence and if that were the case, the panic caused would have been pointless, but it wouldn't actually hurt anyone and it might even make some people look closely at their lives and to make changes, which was usually never a bad thing. On the other hand, though, he knew people and he knew that in such a panic, a lot of them would be out to get whatever they could; belief in imminent death tended to totally remove consciences and morals. Thinking about it from that angle, people *could* well get hurt and there wouldn't be enough police officers or even moralists to stop that.

Taylor sighed and put the newspaper down, careful to hide the story; it might be a futile gesture but he wanted to do his bit not to spread the hysteria, even though he was sitting in his own house and there was no-one else there to see it. Or maybe it was a case of out of sight, out of mind; if it were, it wasn't working: Taylor was still thinking about the prospective predicament when he went to make another cup of coffee and when his mobile rang before he had time even to put the kettle on.

*

"I am NOT doing *that*!"

Lena stormed out of the bedroom as if Dathan Greenwood had suggested something so licentious as to be immoral, and Dathan watched her go with a sigh and a shake of his head. It was like being married to an old-fashioned Quaker, he thought; give her a bonnet and dump her in a field somewhere and she'd be a dead ringer. Then he chided himself for his cruelty – Lena had self-respect, and if it were a little OTT, it was her upbringing that was to blame, not her. So did he have licence to blame his upbringing on wanting to do what he'd proposed? He'd have to have a word with his parents next time he saw them if he did!

Dathan took a step forward, then paused. Would it do any good going after her? he asked himself. Or would it be better to let her cool off a bit? He really wasn't in the mood for another showdown – God knew they were pretty frequent these days – but then again he didn't like leaving her upset. He was about to go downstairs when he heard her talking to Josh.

"No, Josh, I am *not* okay!" she effused. "Your stepfather has just asked me to – "

Oh, I'm the *step*-father now, Dathan thought.

"Well, never you mind what he asked me to do," Lena was saying. "Just know that at least your *mother* has some self-respect!"

Dathan was at the top of the stairs, and Josh was at the bottom.

"Dad?" the boy said.

"It's a grown-up thing," Dathan said absently, wanting to get into a discussion with his wife rather than with his son right now.

"It's a *pervert* thing!" came Lena's voice from the kitchen.

Dathan skipped down the stairs, brushed past Josh with a quick wink and a smile, then entered the kitchen where the argument travelled to Josh's ears with a familiarity that the lad didn't want to get accustomed to.

"Lena," Josh heard his dad say, "It really isn't that much of a deal, but if you don't want to, okay, that's fine!"

"'Okay, that's fine'?" reiterated Lena in a mocking mimicry of his reassurance that for some reason caused Dathan's hackles to rise, "'*Okay, that's fine'*?!"

"Lena, please..."

"Don't you dare!"

Josh heard soft footsteps on the kitchen floor: his mother was moving around the table, obviously away from his stepdad who had asked her to do something she didn't want to do; sexually, Josh assumed. He wasn't a kid any more after all and he *was* a growing male and if Dathan had those thoughts sometimes Josh was mature enough now not to hold them against him because men, Josh knew, were *men*.

"I meant, it's not that important, Lena, and if the suggestion was offensive to you, I'm sorry."

"Yes, sorry I couldn't oblige, no doubt!"

"Lena, what the fuck is *wrong* with you? I only suggested doggy, for Christ's sake!"

Josh had heard enough now; understand your parents' sexuality was one thing, but hearing about it in detail was something else. He turned and padded quietly up the stairs to his room.

"I know what you suggested, and it's evil, Dathan Greenwood! And I'm surprised you had the audacity to ask, because that means you believed I'd consider it! Why, I never knew you thought so lowly of me!"

"I know, I'm sorry, I don't think lowly of you. It's just that I'd like to try other things now and again."

"Like giving it me up the *ass*?"

"Lena, that's not what I meant and you know it!"

"No, Dathan, I don't know what you meant, except that maybe you expect me to do it because *other* women do it! Women like that Mackenzie tart...."

"Lena, I have never had anything to *do* with Addilyn Mackenzie!"

"Maybe not, but you'd like to, wouldn't

you!" Lena snorted derogatorily. "Yes, I bet *she'd* let you do doggy!"

"Almost any woman would except you," muttered Dathan.

"I cannot believe you just said that!" screeched Lena, and Dathan took a double-take at the woman he had married but who had changed so much in eight short months. He oepend his mouth to say something, but Lena just scowled and pushed past him rudely, entering the hall where she grabbed her jacket from a coat peg affixed to the wall and leaving the house, with a demonstrative slamming of the front door as if to accentuate the full stop to their conversation and, Dathan feared, to their marriage.

And then he heard the screeching of tyres and the screeching of a human being and he somehow just knew that there was indeed a full stop to his marriage. He opened the door hesitantly, peered round it and, upon seeing his wife's broken body lying on the top of a red car that had been unable to brake in time to avoid her and where she had ended up after being flung twelve feet into the air, he shut the door again and sank to the floor.

"Dad?" Josh tried again.

Dathan said nothing but he didn't have to; opening his arms to his stepson, the tears streaming down his face, Josh knew as well as Dathan had that neither of them would ever have Lena in their lives again.

What he didn't know, what Dathan didn't know, was that Lena was carrying a baby girl which was why she was feeling so emotionally hounded.

What neither of them knew either was that the baby girl wasn't Dathan's and the guilt of that would have killed Lena almost as surely as the red car had.

*

Kaden Taylor pulled up outside the house and became Police Constable Taylor; the mess had been cleared up now, more or less, the driver of the car that hit the woman had been taken down to the station to make a statement, and the neighbours were returning to their houses knowing that there was no more morbidity to amuse and entertain them. Taylor's stomach churned because these people, whose lives were so boring that someone else's misfortune was the only diversion for them, had never really seen morbidity; neither had they sat on the opposite side of someone you were about to tell had lost a loved one; if they had, they would surely remain indoors when such events occurred praying to God instead of spectating. Not that he was sure it would do much good – Kaden Taylor, who had been brought up in a decent God-fearing family home, had seen too much to believe that someone overlooked the human race in a responsible capacity, and if God did exist, he was certainly leaving the earth to fend for itself against a growing contagion that was homo sapiens.

He got out of his car, checked the address and headed for the front door. He sighed deeply; he hated this aspect of his job.

*

"Dathan, no, I'm sorry," said Addilyn as she stood at her door barring his way in, "But you can't keep running here whenever things go wrong!" In truth she was rather annoyed at this intrusion; she hardly knew the man and yet here he was making a nuisance of himself again and any thoughts of being flattered had given way to thoughts of being taken advantage of.

"Lena's dead," wailed Dathan, the tears real enough, Addilyn thought.

"More reason for you to be at home!" replied Addilyn. "Where's Josh? You haven't left him there, have you?"

"I – I didn't think, I just wanted to talk to someone – to you." Dathan looked up at Addilyn with eyes that were red with tears and full of pleading.

Addilyn felt herself weakening. "Let me get my coat and I'll drive you home," said Addilyn. "I can get a taxi back later, let's see you and Josh right first."

Mumbling to herself and chiding herself for being such an idiot, Addilyn fetched a light jacket then escorted Dathan back down the steps and to his car. Dathan opened the passenger door and got in, sinking heavily into the leather with either relief or with resignation or more likely a mixture of both. Addilyn for her part got into the driver's seat and, finding the keys still in the ignition, belted up and started the car.

"Thanks for this," Dathan said quietly.

"It's the last time," Addilyn replied. "You and I are going nowhere."

"But I'm single now, and maybe after a fitting period of time..."

"Dathan, if you didn't have a young son waiting at home and no doubt wondering why his dad ran out on him at a time as devastating as this, I'd stop the car, get out and walk home. I'm doing this for Josh, not for you."

"I thought you'd admire someone who thought like you do."

"What do you mean, like I do?"

"You're hard, Addilyn. There's no sentiment where you're concerned. You're about as quixotic as a windmill. I wanted a no-strings-attached physical relationship and you seemed like the ideal candidate. You're attractive, intelligent, but above all you know how to keep your mouth shut."

"Well, I'm going to open it now and tell you that, coming from a man who has just lost his wife, those sentiments disgust me."

"What, you'd rather I was false?" Dathan snorted. "Oh, I loved Lena but things were far from ideal; once we married, she changed and the relationship had been deteriorating for months. Will I miss her? Yes, of course I will. Will I miss the arguments? No, not at all. And as for the sex life – "

"I really do *NOT* want to know!"

"No," sighed Dathan. "Neither did she, and that was a good chunk of the problem..."

*

PC Kaden Taylor was about to knock again when he heard the car pull up behind him and he turned to see Dathan Greenwood, the deceased's husband, slam the passenger door and stride purposefully towards him. Then his heart leapt when he saw Addilyn Mackenzie getting out of the driver's side and, lifting her handbag from behind the driver's seat and slamming the driver's door almost as loudly as Dathan had the passenger's door, follow the newly-made widower into the house. She paused at the door to give Kaden a sad smile and a shrug. Kaden invited himself in and followed her into the family sitting room where young Josh was sitting watching the television and seeing nothing on its screen. Addilyn crossed over to the boy and sat on the side of the armchair, opening her arms to Josh, who accepted the hug with gratitude. His erstwhile unreadable expression crumpled into a torrent of tears and Addilyn began to gently rock the boy while he cried; she lowered her chin onto his hair and just held him while he released all the tension, the anger, the frustration and the hurt.

PC Kaden Taylor tore his attention away from Addilyn – reluctantly because he had never seen her so tender, so caring – and looked at Dathan. "I'm sorry, mate," he smiled sadly.

"Why?" asked Dathan. "You didn't know her. You don't know me. Not well, anyway."

"I've just been through a bereavement myself – my brother. I think I know a bit what you're feeling."

Dathan was about to point out that the relationship between a man and his brother was nothing like between a man and his wife but he bit his tongue; his argument wasn't with this police officer, at least not right now, and besides Addilyn had been correct when she said he had a young son to take care of.

For the time being he had to play the good father, the grieving husband, and leave his plans on hold until such time as others considered his duty performed and he could start to live again. So instead he just smiled back and nodded, then got up and headed for the door.

"Dad?" Josh, his face tear-stained, looked over to his stepfather as if to silently question Dathan's leaving him for a second time.

"Son," said Dathan, and suddenly Josh was dashing over the room and flinging himself into his dad's arms, and Dathan finally succumbed to emotion and, dropping whatever mask he was wearing, whatever act he was performing, he burst into tears himself and led Josh out of the room without ever letting him go. Addilyn watched after them, deciding that if that had been an act on Dathan's part, it had been a good one. She and Kaden Taylor both heard the footfalls on the stairs and realised that the pair had gone to have some time to themselves.

"Let me give you a lift home." PC Taylor signed himself off duty and decided that he – and Addilyn for that matter – had outstayed their welcome. At these times, family needed to be together and that included his as well as Dathan's; he had things to do and he wanted to start doing them.

"Thank you," Addilyn replied, but she was

still watching the door which had been closed behind father and son, and, she fancied, in more ways than one.

Kaden got up and opened the sitting room door and harrumphed, indicating that he was ready to go and that she should exit before him. Addilyn snapped back to the present and smiled, getting up and going over to where he stood waiting. She left the room and when she opened the front door at the end of a short hallway, he took it from her and held it while she left the house. He hurried ahead of her and had the passenger car door open before she reached it and she got in with no comment. Kaden didn't mind; manners were inbred in the men in his family and there was no need for acknowledgment or gratitude.

He couldn't help being a little curious as to what Addilyn was doing there, though.

"This is the second time I've seen you in relation to another's death," he remarked not altogether casually when they were well under way. "Are you a jonah or something?"

"Twice is just a coincidence," replied Addilyn tartly. "If it happens again, then you can grow suspicious."

"That's a callous attitude, even for you," observed Kaden.

Addilyn noted the comment but let it go for the moment. "It beats bursting into tears and making an idiot of myself," she shrugged.

"Right now, I don't know how else to cope."

"You know I should take you to the station, don't you?"

"I assume from that, then, that you're not?"

"No, I'm not."

"Then I'm sure you have your reasons for not doing so."

"Yes, I do." Kaden paused then, tapping on the steering wheel his impatience at the herd of sheep that was crossing the country road and that would usually make him smile and thank God he lived in a place like this. Then: "Have you got a couple of hours to spare?" he asked. "And a pot of tea?"

"Possibly," replied Addilyn, her curiosity piqued in spite of herself. "Why?"

"Because, I think I you'll want to hear what I have to say," replied Kaden. "And I know I have to tell you!"

TEN

Sergeant William Gill hung up and shrugged, accepting that he would probably not reach PC Kaden Taylor today. Not that he was surprised; the man was still in shock over the death of his brother, and the sarge knew Kaden well enough to know that had there been anything worth reporting back, he would have reported it back. Evidently things went smoothly for him, or as smoothly as could be expected for a man who had been told a relative had died and then had to go out and tell someone else the same thing, and Gill wasn't worried. He returned to his office to finish his coffee and reread the statement made by the man who had subsequently had to be taken to hospital due to the dreadful shock of inadvertently but indubitably killing a person.

*

Addilyn had been listening to Kaden's story for only ten minutes and already she was thinking that a good strong glass of wine was more called for than a good strong brew of tea. What he was saying was fantastical but it also rang a bell with her because a lot of it made sense in light of what she had already experienced.

He had been aware of the rumour regarding glowing-eyed aliens, and although he didn't think that extraterrestriality were the explanation, he had in fact witnessed the phenomenon himself on two occasions, albeit only fleetingly. Addilyn poured them both another cup of tea from her one and only teapot before embarking on her own experience of what Kaden would soon come to know as Daji.

She began from the beginning and, idly fussing Shadow's ears as the dog lay across her lap as if he too were listening to the story, she told him the truth this time. How she found the woman lying dead on the pathway back at New Year and how she had seen the boy in the woods. She continued to relate the adoption proceedings on the part of her downstairs neighbours of the child who would be, for a while, Daji's host; but not wanting Kaden to pull the girl in for questioning, as it were, she quickly assured him that Daji was no longer resident in Marcia's mind but that instead he rented her own as and when he chose. And, yes, before he asked, she would try and summon Daji but he was not always at her beck and call.

Daji was not being accommodating. Or else merely calling for him in her mind wasn't the way to go about summoning him – Addilyn really didn't know. She wasn't going to go down and ask Marcia either; she suspected that she had already upset the girl by paying scant attention to her over the past week or so and she just wasn't in the right frame of mind for a confrontation. She tried again but still to no avail, then sighed, sat back on settee and hugged Shadow when the dog crawled up the front of her prone body for some fuss, as (he assumed) was the reason his human had lain back. He wagged his tail gently from side to side and closed his eyes, contented and happy.

"So where *is* this Daji thing now if not with you?" asked Kaden, still somewhat hesitant in believing he even existed, but also sure that Addilyn would not make up something so fantastical.

"I have no idea," replied Addilyn. "He seems to come and go according to his own schedule, whatever his schedule is."

"Indeed. He appeared when that woman was killed, he appeared just before that drunk driver crashed into Gittins's shop front, I wouldn't be surprised if he was there when young Josh had his accident or when Lena was killed."

"You think he's a portent of bad luck?"

"Well, trouble does follow him around, it seems..."

"Or he follows trouble," said Addilyn thoughtfully.

"Come again?"

Addilyn said nothing for a moment, then: "Well, think about it, Kaden: he doesn't *feel* evil and Marcia certainly wasn't afraid of him, so I don't think he's evil. The woman who had the heart attack – maybe it as because she saw the kid with the yellow eyes, just as the drunk driver said he did. Maybe Daji's not causing these things purposefully; these people were hurt merely because of their reaction to him."

"Then he should tone it down!" suggested Kaden.

"If he knew how," shrugged Addilyn. "I get the impression he's just a novice. When he told me about Marcia and showing her the flood to correspond to her understanding of Noah's Ark, and his inventing the colourful mouflon for her, it almost seems like Daji is *learning*, if you know what I mean."

"First contact, what the hell language do I speak?" chuckled Kaden.

"More or less," agreed Addilyn.

And then suddenly the furniture began to shake violently and Shadow, ears down, began to growl.

*

"That's two different men in almost as many days!"

Josie Hodgson was surprised because she

didn't think Addilyn was that sort of girl, and the comment wasn't meant in an accusatory way but rather in one of concern; for Addilyn to act out of character could only mean that she was in trouble, in one way or another – be it physically or emotionally – and for all her caring, it never actually occurred to her that they might be nothing more than friends who just happened to be of the opposite gender, and Larry said as much.

"Maybe there's nothing more in it than that," he concluded, lowering his newspaper and winking at Marcia, who was following the conversation with interest; but Josie was having none of it.

"Addilyn doesn't have many friends," she declared, busy with her feather duster and making the life of any would-be restrained arachnids most uncomfortable indeed. "She wouldn't suddenly make two friends, both of whom were young males, for no reason. Besides, I think one of them is in the police."

"I can't see Addilyn breaking the law sufficiently for a home visit," observed Larry. "Maybe speeding, a parking ticket, but nothing more serious than that!"

"Unless she started on the policeman trying to issue the ticket," mused Josie.

Larry chuckled. "Yes, I can imagine she wouldn't take that lying down." He folded his newspaper and winked at Marcia, who had gone back to her colouring; she was still drawing mouflons but today they were all blue, grey and black.

"Well, I think I might go and see her tomorrow morning," declared Josie. "Just see if everything's all right."

"Can I come too?" Marcia jumped at the chance to see Addilyn again; for a start, she wanted to ask her about Daji because the little presence didn't visit her any more and she wanted to know why.

"Maybe later," Josie said. "I want to see what's wrong first."

"Grown-up talk," explained Larry with a grin. "So that's you and me out of it!"

Marcia smiled and ran to Larry who happily lifted her onto his lap, while Josie turned to dish up more spider hell.

"You'll have to talk to her about your imaginary friend another time," he whispered, and Marcia sat up and stared at him in surprise.

"How did you know what I was thinking, Larrilee?" she asked.

"How what, sweetheart?" asked Larry. "Sorry, I was miles away. Say again?"

Marcia was about to expand on her question when the lamp on the table behind the settee began to wobble, followed by a house-wide tremor which lasted little more than ten seconds before it suddenly and abruptly stopped.

*

"What the hell was *that?*" Addilyn let go of Kaden's hand which she had unconsciously grabbed during the brief period of what she imagined a small earthquake would feel like, and stood up to walk over to the window and look out.

"I don't know," replied Kaden, looking at his now-empty hand as if he were missing what had filled it. "Maybe it's a minor earthquake in the Irish sea, we've had them before. Or heavy traffic?"

"Did you hear any heavy traffic?" asked Addilyn without turning from the window.

"Fracking then?"

Addilyn shrugged. "Well, there's nothing to see out here." She turned to Kaden. "I just can't help thinking it wasn't natural, though."

Kaden chuckled. "I was thinking the same but perhaps we're just spooking ourselves?"

"Maybe," agreed Addilyn. She sat herself down next to Kaden again, although she didn't offer him her hand."So where are we at now?"

"Daji refuses to appear, we feel an earthquake."

"You making the connection?"

"Would he?"

"Well, he hasn't done it before; usually he just takes up residence and talks to me – I suppose you'd say 'telepathically'."

"Hmm." Kaden lay back and linked his hands fingers behind his head. "Well, I need to get myself down to Darcy's."

"Darcy?"

"Tim's fiancée. God, Tim only just called the other day to ask me to be his best man. Now the reason I'll be going to church is to say goodbye to him. It just doesn't figure."

"These things never do; I've given up trying."

"You want to come with me? I'm betting Darcy will appreciate some female company. Tim told me her parents live abroad, so I doubt they'll be coming over just yet, maybe for the funeral but not right away."

"I'd be in the way," said Addilyn. "Besides, I have work to go to. I can't just leave Don in the lurch."

"You could phone him."

"I could."

"And you wouldn't be in the way. I'm not very good at things like that, being a comfort, knowing the right thing to say – "

Addilyn laughed.

"What?" asked Kaden.

"You think *I* know the right thing to say?" Addilyn chuckled. "I'm about as emotional as a tin can!"

"I don't believe that..."

"Believe it, it's true."

"Okay, well, would you come to help *me*? I don't want to do this alone, to be honest. Darcy will be crying, I will be crying – or feeling like it all the time, anyway – and *both* of us will be in need of someone sensible, someone not directly involved."

"Where does Darcy live?" asked Addilyn.

"Wales. Mid to south."

"Wow, that far?"

"It's only two-ten miles or thereabouts. it'll take about four hours to drive if we leave very early morning." Kaden paused. "You'd be doing me a great favour, Addilyn, and I'm sure Don Gittins won't mind. He's hardly up to his eyes in it just now."

Addilyn sighed. "Okay," she conceded. "I'll do it because, yes, you two'll need someone to do the arranging if you're going to be choked up about it all the time." She almost choked herself on the latter words. "I didn't mean –

Kaden smiled. "I know what you meant," he said, "And thank you."

Addilyn nodded, deciding to keep her mouth shut this time. She crossed the sitting room towards the kitchen where her handbag, and her mobile within, was lying.

"And, Addilyn?" Kaden said just as she was reaching for her bag.

"Yes?" Addilyn was rummaging through the bag and she didn't turn towards him...

"You *do* know the right thing to say sometimes!"

...which was just as well as he was bound to have commented on the smug grin of satisfaction that stretched across her face from ear to ear.

*

Addilyn thought it only fair to let the Hodgsons know that the upstairs would be empty for a while; at the end of the day, it was their property and they had a right to know the comings and goings of its occupant if it were outwith the usual routine parameters.

Kaden had decided to take his leave of her then, and they agreed that he would come for her the following morning very early indeed. He had proposed taking only his car but Addilyn begged to disagree; there might well come a time when they wanted or needed to be in different places at the same time, and that would be impossible with one car – whereas with two cars they could be either apart *or* together in one car while the other remained parked. Kaden saw the sense in it and he agreed; he furthermore assured her that Shadow would be more than welcome at Darcy's because he knew his brother liked dogs and assumed that he would have chosen a girlfriend who did too. Besides, Kaden had no choice – 'no Shadow, no Addilyn' was made very clear to him and he had to have her along.

Addilyn waved him off as he pulled out of the driveway then made her way to the bottom door which was the Hodgsons' and knocked quite loudly. It was hardly any time at all before Marcia answered and squealed in delight when she saw Addilyn standing there. Addilyn swooped her up in her arms, swore that she had put on a stone in weight since she'd seen the girl last, blamed Josie's amazingly tasty cooking, and was invited in by Larry for a cuppa. Josie, it seemed, was out shopping in Keswick and it surprised Addilyn that Marcia hadn't gone with her; however, over a hot, sweet cup of steaming tea that Larry made for them, he explained that Marcia had intended to come knock on her door almost as she, Addilyn, had knocked on the Hodgsons'.

"I'm sorry I've not seen you in a while," smiled Addilyn. "I've been rather preoccupied."

"We did notice," said Larry. "Or to be more accurate, Josie noticed. You know what she's like, a bit curious at times."

Addilyn chuckled. "I call it being diligent on my behalf," she said.

"Yes, well..." Larry looked as if he were searching for the right words to open a conversation about something and Addilyn thought she would save him the trouble.

"What is it, Larry?" she asked. "Spit it out. Do you want me to move out or something?"

"Dear Lord, no! Whyever would we want you to do that?" Larry sounded so genuinely shocked that Addilyn felt a pang of real appreciation.

"It's got something to do with that imaginary friend Marcia used to have but who's now gone away, hasn't it?"

"How did you – ?"

"Marcia mutters in her sleep. Oh, she may be talking to it for all I know, or she may just be pretending to, I know she missed it for a while, even though she didn't say anything. She was a lot quieter, a lot less bouncy than normal, and her drawings of those rainbow creatures all but stopped. Those she did draw she coloured in dark, sombre colours, as if she were reflecting her own sadness."

Marcia looked up but said nothing, as if discussing her while she were present was nothing unusual, but Addilyn noticed the hurt look in her eyes and determined to try and put things right.

You know you did nothing wrong, don;t you, she asked. What he wants doing is impoissible for an adult, let alone a child, and your age is the only reason he didn't stay with you longer.

Marcia nodded. He was with me last night, she said. And he told me I must never look at the stars,

So that's where he was, Addilyn thought. "Never look at the stars? she said aloud. "Well..." She stopped; that was probably the only way Daji could communicate the danger to the little girl and it was a message meant to save her. "Well," she said again, "Maybe he's right."

"This imaginary friend," said Larry. "He's not imaginary, is he...."

"No," answered Addilyn. "But just what he is, I have no idea."

"See, Larilee? I *told* you Daji was real!" Marcia sounded as triumphant as any child would sound having managed to get one over an adult.

Larry smiled at her. "Yes, sweetheart, you did, and I'm sorry I didn't believe you." He paused, then to Addilyn: "So what is all this about, do you know?"

Addilyn weighed up the pros and cons of telling Larry and the cons won hands down. "I haven't a clue," she said and realised what she'd said wasn't all *that* far from the truth. "I'm going away with Kaden for a while. He just lost his brother."

"Oh, I'm sorry to hear that." Larry said

nothing else, although Addilyn fancied he knew more about Tim's demise than he was letting on. No doubt he'd read the newspaper, and maybe he knew enough to put two and two together; Addilyn didn't know but she also didn't want to get into a long conversation right now and so she didn't follow up on her suspicions.

"Thank you, I'll pass your condolences on to Kaden." Addilyn stood up. "Right, well, I'd better go and pack."

"Can I come and help?" Marcia looked at her with large eyes that pleaded so vehemently that Addilyn hated herself for saying no.

"When I come back," she said, "I'll tell you all about it, and I'll bring you a present back, I promise."

"Is Daji going with you?" asked Marcia.

"I don't know if he 'goes' anywhere," replied Addilyn. "But, yes, I hope to hear from him!"

"Tell him hello from me," smiled Marcia, and then she turned her attention back to her bruise-coloured drawings and never so much as looked up when Addilyn stood to leave.

Larry walked her to the door. "She'll be fine," he assured her. "Just make sure you are too."

"I will," said Addilyn, and she opened the door. "Tell Marcia I really am sorry I can't spend more time with her just now. Things will be different when I come back, I'm sure."

"Will they?" asked Larry. "Because I get the distinct feeling that there is something going on here that neither of us are prepared to admit to."

Addilyn stepped out of the house. "Give my love to Josie," she said as she stepped outside.

"I will," said Larry.

Addilyn hesitated, then turned and hugged Larry hard before rushing up to her own flat where she let herself in and stood in the middle of the sitting room with tears streaming down her face because she couldn't shake off the conviction that she would never see Larry ever again.

*

"Ah, Daji, I wonder if you had anything to do with that tremor earlier?" Addilyn said to a ceiling that she couldn't even see. "And why didn't you come when Kaden was here? I'm sure he believes me but he would've been well within his rights to think I was a nutcase..."

Greetings.

Addilyn's eyes snapped open as she felt Daji's presence within her mind; it wasn't uncomfortable but Daji's sudden thought transference was akin to his having yelled right into her ear.

"Hello," she said, not at all unhappy to hear from him. "I could have done with you earlier!"

So I understand; sorry.

"I'm sure you had your reasons." Addilyn continued to stare at the invisible ceiling for a moment or two, then closed her eyes because she fancied that looking upwards suggested addressing the Almighty which she obviously wasn't; she doubted if it were actually sacrilegious, but some reason she felt a little self-conscious, and that surprised her quite a lot because she wasn't usually one for reverence. "I assume," she continued to Daji when she'd settled on lying sideways and staring at an invisible door, "That you're aware of what I intend to do?"

I am.

"And is it the *right* thing to do?"

I don't know. All I know is, you have to make people believe you so that they can stop it.

"People like those scientists who were killed?"

What makes you think they were killed?

"They're dead..."

You didn't say 'those scientists who died'; you said 'those scientists who were killed'. That suggests to me that you believe they were murdered.

"Well, from what Kaden told me, those scientists were likely ones who noticed something approaching the Earth. Very far away, but approaching nonetheless – maybe even on a collision course."

No 'maybe' about it.

"Great. Were going to be hit by a bloody great big asteroid or comet or something, and everyone who tries to do something about it is going to end up worm fodder. Pardon me for not being so enthusiastic about spreading the word, because it seems to me that telling people about it would endanger their lives, more or less condemning them to be murdered." She paused, and when Daji remained silent, she added: "And *I* know about it, which doesn't sit at all well with me."

Luckily, you'll be harder to believe. Those scientists knew what they were talking about – even Kaden would be given slightly more credence on account of his brother – but you won't. It makes your task harder but it also offers you a modicum of protection.

"So, what you're saying is: you want me to convince people by talking about something which I don't know anything about?"

You have someone to help you now; I am satisfied that you trust him and therefore I shall also.

"Two humans and a whatever-it-is-*you*-are

against the world?"

No-one said it was going to be easy.

"Indeed." Addilyn turned onto her other side and pulled the duvet up around her neck, thinking that the task ahead of her was all but impossible and wishing that she could just disappear back into the annuls of a boring life and forget all about it.

You can't do that, Daji informed her. *You have to make them stop it and I'll help all I can.*

"Thank you," said Addilyn drily. Then she snuggled up and got comfortable. "Well, goodnight, Daji. I need some sleep now; up early in the morning and a long drive tomorrow – so no dreams, please!"

But you need to dream!

"None of yours, I mean."

Ah, right, I understand. Yes, I can do that. Or I can not *do that, if you see what I mean, depending on how you look at it –*

"Good *night,* Daji!"

Goodnight, Addilyn. Pause, then: *Sorry....*

ELEVEN

For a lot of the journey, Addilyn was able to follow Kaden because the traffic at this ridiculous hour of the morning was almost non-existent; anyone with any sense, she reasoned, was tucked up warm and snug in bed with at least a couple more hours' slumber until they had to get up for work. But they – Kaden and herself (and Shadow) – had been up at 3.00am, met up at hers at 3.30am and hit the road at 3.45am, and the only one who seemed to be thoroughly delighted about it was Shadow the dog who was now in the back seat looking out of the side window and occasionally uttering a low woof at something only his sharp eyes could see.

The sun was threatening to rise above the eastern horizon but they wouldn't see it for some time owing to the mountains that lined the road to the left. However, a golden glow topped the mountains with a halo-like crown which colour reminded Addilyn of the glow in Marcia's and the unknown boy's eyes and soon it would be time to switch off the headlights and settle into a morning of motorway driving, followed by lunch and more motorways. Addilyn was beginning to wonder why she was even here; what Daji was proposing was nothing sort of ridiculous, as was this entire business, and if it weren't for Kaden's belief in her and other things that had defied any other explanation than that which was impossible, she would have passed the whole lot off as a bout of total insanity on her part. Or a dream, albeit a rather long one.

Addilyn's attention wandered back to Marcia, and she recalled the little girl's face at the sitting room window when she went out to her car earlier this morning. It was a strange time for the child to be up, and the expression on Marcia's face was a mixture of sadness and acceptance, as if she knew what Addilyn were attempting to do. Maybe there was a residue of Daji's presence still in her mind, enough to enable her to pick up the gist of what was going on, but there again maybe the child just couldn't sleep and she heard Addilyn's footsteps on the outside stairs and decided to see what the noise was about. The latter was a nice, safe explanation and Addilyn wanted very much to believe it, but she didn't; there was more to that child, she fancied, than met the eyes.

After another half hour of monotony, Kaden, in front of her, flashed his headlights and indicated left. Addilyn also indicated and pulled in behind him, waiting for him to walk over to her car with a carrier bag in his hand which turned out to hold a flask of hot sweet coffee and a buttered croissant each. She glanced at her watch; getting on for five – so they'd made pretty excellent progress, thanks to the deserted highways.

"We might make it by late lunchtime," commented Kaden when he saw her look at the time. "Depending on traffic."

Addilyn shrugged. "How much of a hurry is there?" she asked.

Kaden chuckled humourlessly. "Well, if it's the end of the world, I suppose you could say it was somewhat urgent," he replied. "But then again, if that were the case, *you* probably wouldn't."

"What do you mean by that?" Addilyn wasn't sure she liked that comment; for a start, it was too close to the truth for comfort.

"You strike me as one who doesn't suffer fools gladly," replied Kaden.

"No, I don't," Addilyn shrugged.

"And the majority of the human race are fools," continued Kaden, "So...." He let the sentence drift off unfinished, then: "Another coffee?"

"Better not, unless there's somewhere we can stop nearby."

"Transport caf□s will be open. You want us to find one?"

"Wouldn't mind."

"Okay." Kaden returned the flask and the wrappers of their croissants to the carrier bag, and took it back to his car. He waved at Addilyn before getting in and flashed the car's lights after. Then he pulled out into the road again and Addilyn followed, wondering if she actually knew what the hell she was doing.

*

Timothy Taylor's fianc□e picked up a cushion from the settee, then put it down again. She wandered into the kitchen and put the kettle on to make a cup of tea, then left the kitchen and two minutes later forgot about the kettle. She sat down heavily and switched the television on, flicking through the channels but finding nothing to inspire her at all. She let a film stay on the screen as background noise, but instead of watching it she flicked through the pages of a magazine that she had no interest in. Then she got up and went to the window that looked out on to a small front garden and the road beyond that. Seeing no sign of *any* car, let alone Kaden's, she returned to the settee, picked up a cushion, then put it down again.

*

They found a transport caf□ and stopped for a huge, greasy breakfast which both of them enjoyed immensely, not in small part because they hadn't discussed anything of any consequence while they ate. It seemed that

Kaden was preoccupied with thoughts of Tim and his intended – Darcy – and, as for Addilyn, she would quite happily have opted to forget about the entire Armageddon scenario but that was a little difficult to do

"So what's Darcy like?" Addilyn had asked by means of opening communication links with small talk whilst feeding pieces of sausage to Shadow who was sitting under the table and loving every minute of it.

"I only ever met her once," Kaden confessed, slipping some of his own sausage to Shadow. "And that was in a pub after Tim and me had downed more pints than were good for us. She's pretty, I think. Very pretty in a classy sort of way. Got quite a good job too although don't ask me what it is she does."

"She sounds impressive," commented Addilyn.

Kaden shrugged. "Doubt she's feeling impressive right now," he said, which remark brought the conversation to a halt for a while during which they ate without speaking.

"I like that dogs are allowed in," Addilyn commented after a few minutes to break the awkward silence between them. "It seems to be a good part of the country for our canine friends."

"Yes, I noticed," said Kaden.

"So do you like dogs?" asked Addilyn.

"Yes, I do. The only reason I haven't got

one is because of the stupid hours I have to work. It wouldn't be fair on the dog."

"And Tim? Did he like dogs too?"

"Yep, and he wanted one as well. But Darcy didn't think a dog would be conducive to their lifestyle. If there was one thing that Tim could fault in Darcy, it was that. Otherwise, he thought she was perfect."

"Everyone to their own," shrugged Addilyn, not wanting to step on Darcy's toes in front of her almost-brother-in-law. "I didn't have a dog either until Shadow adopted me."

"What happened?" asked Kaden.

"He belonged to the woman that died on New Year, the one we suspect was killed. Except I don't think she was, not purposefully anyway. I think she died of fright."

"Oh – how so?" Kaden put his knife and fork down on his almost empty plate and picked the remaining sausage between his fingers, feeding it whole to the waiting dog.

"I think she saw the kid's eyes," said Addilyn, noting Kaden's sudden interested attention. "Maybe even some sort of manifestation on Daji's part. Whatever she saw, I think it frightened her so much her heart gave up."

"So why did she utter your name?" Kaden wanted to know. "And in a man's voice?"

"I think that might have been Daji entering

her mind." Addilyn paused for thought, then: "Maybe *that's* what killed her, then," she sighed. "But I'm sure Daji didn't mean it to. He doesn't give me the impression of being in the slightest bit evil."

"You don't know what he *is*," Kaden pointed out. "Let alone what he's *like*..."

Addilyn shrugged. "There's a lot about this mess I don't know," she sighed. "I'm still at the 'can't-believe-it's-for-real' stage."

"Tell me about it! The only thing that is becoming *too* real for me is that Tim has gone."

"And that, no matter what she's like, Darcy needs us – or, more accurately, *you*. So let's finish up and hit the road, okay?"

Kaden nodded and smiled, but Addilyn knew the latter was forced.

*

She was very tempted, but she fought the impulse to see what Tim had written to his brother. They weren't very close so she supposed that there was nothing much in it except for a written confirmation of the invitation for Kaden to be his best man; the envelope was, after all, addressed and stamped so it was obviously intended for postage. She almost laughed now at the earlier suspicion that Tim had written it because he knew of his impending death;

loneliness and the circumstances had made her insecure and fearful, and she almost despised herself for it. She was self-assured and independent and this feeling of total helplessness was quite alien to her; moreover, she had been behaving like a moron for the past half-week, doing such absent-minded things ever since she'd been told about Tim and she couldn't wait for Kaden to arrive because she reluctantly had to admit to herself really needed someone here with her right now. She wasn't quite so keen on his bringing his girlfriend – Kaden had said 'friend' but Darcy wasn't stupid – and thought that maybe she could make the woman so uncomfortable that she would leave ahead of Kaden, who might end up not wanting to leave at all...

*

It was their intention to complete the journey from their present location near Lymm to Darcy's (Kaden still thought of it as Tim's) which was a journey of less than a hundred miles and for which Addilyn was most grateful. It wasn't that she disliked driving – it was okay but a bit of a strain on the old OCD and she'd actually been surprised at the start that she could focus on the roads sufficiently to be safe whilst still being aware of the numbers that presented themselves to her during any given journey – but she'd had enough for today, and probably for a week if she were honest. Also on her mind was the whole situation that she found herself in and the impossibility of it; she was still convinced she would awaken any moment and find it had all been a dream.

The going was good to start with but then they hit the rush-hour traffic just before they reached their destination. Level with Shrewsbury and just north of Welshpool the A-road that they were following began to fill up with cars but luckily the majority of them were travelling the opposite way; the towns of Wolverhampton, Chester and Shrewsbury itself were within commuting distance to the north and east, whereas to the south and east there were only small villages and the Brecon Beacons. It wasn't too bad though – worse than in Cumbria but nothing like in places like London and Birmingham – and presently Addilyn noticed Kaden speaking into his mobile and assumed (correctly, as it happened) that he was contacting Darcy to say that they would soon be there.

Darcy was standing outside the house when they pulled up, and the first thing that Addilyn noticed was that, for someone in mourning, she had taken exceptional care in her dress, her hair and her make-up. Darcy looked like a model; no, Darcy looked like a modern businesswoman and a successful one at that – she had the look of money about her, the appearance that money could buy. Addilyn glanced down at her fading jeans and then mentally shrugged; if people didn't like her, that was their problem, not hers. She also mentally fought to beat down the inferiority complex that was even now nagging her and telling her that she was a scruff and nowhere near in the class of this family, and even noting that Kaden wore jeans with holes in – not fashionable ones either – and a scruffy t-shirt didn't do much to assuage the feeling that she just didn't measure up.

As was the norm when she became anxious, she began to count and was still counting when Kaden opened her driver's door and offered his hand to help her out. She took it with a small smile and Kaden's questioning look expressed his confusion over Addilyn's trepidation; he was surprised that anything fazed this able young woman and Addilyn was surprised too. If she stopped to think, she might have wondered if she were not feeling a little too much for the young man whose hand she was still clinging to – a little too long, she told herself, you could have let it go before now – but she was too busy looking at Darcy and wondering how the hell she could compete with *that*. Then she wondered, as she closed the driver's door behind her and followed Darcy and Kaden up the few steps to the front door of the house, why she cared about competing – with Darcy or anyone else, for that matter.

*

As soon as they had entered the house, Darcy making it clear by her total …. of Addilyn that she wasn't pleased that Kaden had brought her along, Darcy crossed over to a stacked-up nest of tables upon which a white envelope was lying.

"He left you this letter," she said, handing the envelope to Kaden, on the front of which his name and address was printed in his brother's unusually (for a man) neat handwriting, a stamp placed neatly in the corner with meticulous accuracy. It was, Kaden assumed, a more detailed invitation for him to be best man and he said as much, to which Darcy replied that she had thought the same.

Kaden tore the envelope open, pulled out the single page and began reading.

"What does he say?" asked Darcy. "I didn't open it, although I'm sure you think I have."

"He was your soon-to-be husband," said Kaden, not really concentrating on what he was saying. "It would be within your rights to open it."

"No, it wouldn't," said Addilyn. "It has your name on the front, not hers."

Darcy glanced at Addilyn with a look that suggested the words 'down' and 'nose'; Addilyn smiled sweetly and Darcy turned on her high heel and walked out of the room with, Addilyn thought, an exaggerated swing of her hips. "May I ask what it says?" she called back in a voice that mingled indignity with resentment.

Kaden read the letter aloud:

Dear Kay

Remember the shed incident? Well, it's a case of role reversal now, so to speak. We weren't seen as I recall, but we would be in this day and age. All I can say is, work, brother, work quickly! At half seven in the morning on the wall, it'd be sad. Good luck, bro, and goodbye. I don't think we'll meet again in this world. Mine is not to reason why, mine is but to... to die; the doing is in your hands. I was so close to tying the knot too – but therein lies a tale.

It's all on you now, Kay-lee.

Timbo

PS: My will is in my desk drawer, top

right at the back. It's all yours; I love Darcy but I'm not stupid.

"What the bloody hell was all *that* about?" Darcy had come back into the room now and the contents of the letter had both confused and disappointed her; had Kaden read the letter's postscript, she would likely be more than just confused and disappointed, but the policeman had deemed it tactful to omit that particular point in the reading of it.

"I have no idea," said Kaden, and he was quite pleased at how offhanded he sounded. He knew very well what Tim was referring to, but apart from that it made about as much sense to him as it did to Darcy or, for that matter, to Addilyn.

"But he knew he was going to die!" effused Darcy. "How could he possibly know that?"

Kaden shrugged and looked to Addilyn for help but Addilyn merely shook her head. "I don't know, Darcy..." he began, but then he saw the horror dawning on her face and he thought he knew what she was thinking. "No, Darcy," he said. "I'm sure it wasn't that..."

"And I'm sure it was," interrupted Addilyn. "Unless of course Tim was a clairvoyant, and a bloody good one at that. Kaden, if you can remember what he was referring to, it might help you realise what made him do it..."

Kaden shot her an angry glance then turned

to Darcy. "Where is Tim's desk?" he asked.

"Desk?" Darcy re-iterated curiously. "Why, at his work, I suppose! I wouldn't have a desk here – it's a house, not an office."

Kaden thought of responding, but then changed his mind; it was better he drop the subject. What was he thinking anyway, getting out the will in front of Darcy only for her to learn that she wasn't mentioned in it? He wasn't thinking straight, he realised. He shoved the letter into his back pocket and forced a smile. "Put the kettle on, Darcy," he said mock-cheerfully. "I'm parched!"

"I only use a percolator," Darcy replied. "Coffee will have to do. And then maybe we could go to a lovely little restaurant I know; it's just down the road. I haven't eaten for twenty-four hours, but now you're here I feel a bit peckish!" She paused, then turned to Addilyn. "Of course, if you'd rather fish and chips, dear?"

"Why should I?" asked Addilyn.

"They seem more your scene," shrugged Darcy.

"And they are!" Addilyn sounded not only unoffended at Darcy's sleight but also quite cheerful. "I'll take good ol' fish'n'chips over a posh steak any day!"

"Thank the Lord for that," grinned Kaden.

"You too?" Darcy asked, somewhat disappointed.

"Me too," answered Kaden, although he hadn't quite meant the comment as endorsement of Addilyn's choice.

"Well, then," Darcy turned towards the kitchen. "I suppose I'd better get the percolator on while you go fetch them. Out of the door, turn left, immediate right and there's a takeaway some hundred yards along there on the right." She paused. "I won't join you, if you don't mind," she added. "I believe I have some smoked salmon and salad in the refrigerator which I suppose will have to suffice."

*

If his dad had one more, Josh swore he would either pour the rest of the bottle down the sink or break it over Dathan's head; the latter was looking a more attractive prospect at the moment, and God knew Dathan had imbibed so much he probably wouldn't even feel it.

His dad hadn't been sober since Lena had died; he supposed he should be happy that Dathan missed her so much, it proved how much he loved her, but he, Josh, had needs too and really the roles should have been reversed, with Dathan caring for a broken-hearted boy who had just lost his mother.

"Dad..." he began.

"I miss her!" Dathan sounded miserable and self-pitying.

"I do too!" exclaimed Josh. "But I don't drink myself into a stupor! Mum's gone, and there ain't no bringing her back. I need you to be a dad for me now, you're all I got."

"I know there ain't no bringing Lena back," said Dathan and he took another sip from the can of extra-strong lager. "I don't wanna bring Lena back. I wanna bring *Addilyn* back!"

"Addilyn Mackenzie?" Josh was shocked. His mother – Dathan's wife – had just left them forever and his dad was thinking about Miss Mackenzie. What the …?

"Addilyn fucking Mackenzie," repeated Dathan, punctuating the words by stabbing his finger into the material of the sofa seat. "I need to get her back afore she ruins it all."

"Ruins what?" Josh was confused, angry, horrified all at the same time. "Dad, I don't know what you're on about! Shit, I don't know who you *are* any more!"

"Don't fucking swear," giggled Dathan. "Naughty boy!"

Josh stood up and stepped towards his father, then forced himself to stop; if he took another pace he would deck his dad with a right hook, he knew he would. Better that he back off and let Dathan sober up, talk to him when he was *in corpus mentis,* so to speak, and God knew he was a far cry from that right now.

"I'm going to my room," said Josh abruptly, the disgust in his voice undisguised. "I'll see you later, dad, when you're sober."

"Dad?" Dathan laughed and it was an unpleasant laugh.

Josh continued up the stairs without looking back.

"I ain't your fucking dad," Dathan snarled.

Josh's heart leapt in his throat at the piercing words. He turned round to face Dathan, wanting to know if he'd meant that, needing to know that he hadn't.

Josh couldn't help but squeal when he saw the features on his dad's face; dark, ugly, angry and *evil* described what he saw but not adequately whilst not at *all* his dad's face was spot on....

*

If fish and chips tasted much better with vinegar, then they tasted even more much better with Darcy's disapproval, and Addilyn quite enjoyed her meal. Kaden tucked in too, while Darcy sat at the kitchen table and played with her salmon and salad, although Addilyn didn't see her eat any of it.

After the meal Addilyn went into the kitchen to wash up but Darcy pointed out the dishwasher and proceeded to load it with the .

Of someone handling highly toxic . When she'd switched it on, she returned to the sitting room and crossed over to the hall door.

"I'll ring and see if they have vacancies at the Royal," she said to Addilyn. "I've only got one spare bed. The Royal's just up the road and it's not expensive."

"Don't bother," said Kaden. "I'll take the sofa."

"Indeed you will not!"

"Indeed I will. I don't want Addilyn in a hotel, I want her here. Unless you want to check if they have two vacancies?"

Darcy slammed the telephone down onto its cradle – Kaden wondered why she didn't use her mobile that was sitting on the kitchen table – and strode back into the sitting room. "As you wish," she said tartly. "The bedroom's second left at the top of the stairs. The bathroom is straight opposite. My bedroom is the first on the left. Please don't walk in there by accident." She paused. "I'm going to have a shower," she continued. "I'll leave you two to talk about me while I've gone."

*

"I want to come too!"

Marcia didn't usually throw tantrums but she was getting very close to it now. All morning she had watched Larrilee packing a small briefcase with a couple of pairs of socks, some underwear, a couple of t-shirts and a pair of jeans that he wore when he did the gardening and which were more holey than whole; however, they were comfortable and comfort was what mattered at his age. He'd also popped a can of body spray in there, of the eternal favourite 'Old Spice' variety, but he hadn't bothered with a shaver or shaving foam which may have meant he didn't intend to be away for long but which may also have meant that he didn't expect to need it because where he was going, looking tidy was the last thing that was important. Now he popped a few days' worth of medication into a side pocket of the briefcase then he snapped it shut noisily.

"I'm sorry, Marcia," he said, "But no. I don't know what's going to be there to meet me when I get there and I certainly don't intend to take you into any danger."

"I'm not frightened," said Marcia glumly. "Only scaredy-cats are frightened and I'm not one!"

Larrilee put the briefcase on the carpet, then reached out for Marcia. She turned her back on him. He shrugged and walked to the door to the hallway where his coat was hanging and as he opened it, Josie came out of the kitchen, took in the scenario and nodded to herself: she'd expected it to play out like this. Her husband was going off on a whim, convinced that Addilyn would need him in the next few days, but he didn't know why, when, or where. Marcia wanted to go too, of course, but Josie would have put her foot down and prevented it even had Larry been willing to take the girl along with him. The silly old fool would be back in a day, maybe two, with his tail between his legs, admitting his foolishness, but for now Josie was content to let him live out his dream as he'd told it to her the night before last. When he did return, Josie was determined to rid the family of the stupid little imaginary friend Daji, who was responsible for a lot of the trouble even though it didn't exist. But let Larry have his moment, she thought; he'll be so much easier to handle when he learns the hard way...

"Marcia, come and help me make some fairy cakes," she said to the little girl who was peering over her shoulder to see if Larrilee would come in to see her before he went.

"In a second," replied Marcia, and she inched towards the hall door, suddenly afraid that Larrilee wasn't going to say goodbye.

They almost collided when he pushed the door open from the hallway and Marcia pulled it open from the sitting room; Marcia started to giggle and Larry's eyes misted over.

"I won't be long," he assured the girl as he

took her into his thinning arms and hugged her tight. “But I have to go. You understand, right?”

Marcia nodded but Larry doubted she did; Josie didn't either, but she let her husband leave with just a smile; she'd never been a one to cry at goodbyes and besides, the silly old fool would be back tomorrow.

*

“We're going to have to go to Tim's work after the funeral,” Kaden was saying as he leaned over the table to reread the note from his dead brother, which was sitting in the middle.

“They'll let us just walk in?” asked Addilyn, surprised. “I'd have thought there'd be massive security measures in a place like that.”

“There are,” replied Kaden. “I don't think, once we're in, that getting access to Tim's bit is going to be too much of a problem. as I'm sure I can find Tim's access details. But there's bound to be security cameras, night watchmen, that kind of thing. And, even with the hints in his note, there's always the fact that I for one don't even understand what the hell we're supposed to be doing.”

“Well, that makes two of us.” Addilyn paused, then: “But it doesn't need two of us, surely?" she asked. "Wouldn't one of us stand more chance of slipping by unnoticed? If of course you're actually serious about this whole ridiculous plan."

"I am and, yes, undoubtedly one would be easier, but I don't want to do it alone."

"Then *I'll* do it. And if I fail, then you can try."

"No dice," said Kaden. "We'll both do it. For all we know, it might need two. Until we know exactly what it is Daji intends, we can't make plans. And Daji doesn't seem to be conversing with you right now."

"He *has* been absent for a day or two," conceded Addilyn. "But I've learned to trust that when he's somewhere else, it's because he needs to be." She chuckled drily. "I only hope," she added. "That he realises that when we get to wherever we're supposed to get, he's with *us* is where he needs to be!"

"*If* we get to where we're supposed to get. We don't even know where that is!"

"I don't think Daji would ask it if it weren't possible, and he's bound to let us know somehow."

"Well, you have more faith in him than I do, that's all I can say."

"Yes, and it's frightening."

"What, that you find you need to put your total trust in someone?" asked Kaden.

"That I find I *can* put my total trust in

someone," replied Addilyn, and as she turned back to sorting through some of Tim's books which were piled around her on the carpet, she didn't notice Kaden's hurt expression that suggested that he wished it were him she trusted instead of a mysterious, unfathomable non-entity.

TWELVE

The day of Dr Timothy Taylor's funeral arrived, and it was bright and sunny. Kaden thought the weather most inappropriate but Addilyn surprised him by commenting that God was smiling because He had Tim back again, and although he didn't believe a word of it, he was touched that she would utter such words of comfort. He watched her with a warmth in his heart as she took Shadow out for his morning walk before getting ready for the church.

Addilyn had, Kaden realised, been a tower of strength over the past few days, even if she and Darcy didn't get on. Sure, Addilyn was making a bit of an effort to remedy the situation, but Darcy wasn't a willing participant in this and Addilyn, he knew, was getting tired of trying. In fact, he realised that if it weren't for him, Addilyn probably wouldn't keep her mouth in check at all, so he thanked God for small mercies and now tried to pull himself together more for Darcy's sake than for his own.

The church was crowded. Kaden had chosen a conventional churchyard burial for his brother because he just couldn't stand the thought of having nothing left of his kin save for memories, which, whilst precious, were not at all substantial. That he would probably seldom – if ever – visit his brother's grave was beside the point; at least if he *did* want to pay his respects, there was somewhere functional for him to talk aloud without getting strange looks only pitying ones. Darcy's preference had been sought but she'd been too busy glowering at Addilyn to offer any helpful input and so Kaden had chosen the hymns and everything else on his own too – well, not *quite* on his own, but if he'd told Darcy that Addilyn had had a say in the music, he was afraid she wouldn't even go to the funeral, let alone refuse to sing.

As it happened, Darcy couldn't have been more delightful, and even though he guessed it was for her guests who had for the most part been friends of both she and Tim as a couple, Kaden was extremely grateful and equally as relieved. What's more, Addilyn was perfectly-behaved too and now, as he sat between them listening to a story of Tim's life (a lot of the aspects of which he hadn't even been aware) he felt he could relax and concentrate on feeling sorry that he hadn't made the effort to be closer to his brother than he had.

Addilyn in the meantime was regarding Darcy will a pained expression on her face. Darcy was weeping so elegantly that Addilyn was sure the young woman was putting on an act, and she wondered if there had been a problem in the relationship before Tim died that made his supposedly future wife so unmoved by his passing. So some people coped better than others, she thought, she herself for one; she had long ago disallowed herself to be hurt by anyone leaving her, by erecting a wall over which no-one would ever be able to climb. She even worried about trusting Daji, and he was something she knew nothing about – but at least he wasn't human. It was human beings who hurt you, she realised; human beings who turned their backs on you when you needed them most and laughed at you when you said you loved them. So now Addilyn had sworn never to love another one of them again; the song might have spoken about being a rock, an island – but Addilyn was an impenetrable vault, her heart locked safe within where it would never be allowed to escape again, her head trained to a hardness that assured no more betrayal.

She felt Kaden's hand on hers and it wasn't until she looked at him that she realised that she was weeping. Luckily Kaden had assumed it was because of the funeral and Addilyn wasn't about to correct him; sometimes people who knew too much about you could turn their knowledge into a weapon. So she just smiled thinly, pulled her hand away and reached into her handbag for a paper tissue although she knew she hadn't brought any.

*

Larry Hodgson had withdrawn what he considered enough money to live on for a week, then walked towards the bus stop with the intention of catching a train down south on this fool's errand, the details of which were very vague but the importance of which was very marked.

It had been the dream – if it were a dream because Larry doubted it was – that he had had a few nights before during what was a fitful sleep during which he tossed and turned and thought he was burning up of a fever. It felt as if he were really living the story in technicolour with sound effects so like the real thing that he could have sworn they could be nothing but.

He was lying on the shore of a lake, the water lapping gently and lulling him into a false sense of security as he relaxed in the afternoon sun, his deep breaths accompanied also by the sound of birds singing. At first it was a lovely dream, and Larry *knew* it was a dream, yet it was so calming that he chose to remain in it until the ground began to shake, he decided he needed to wake up and found he couldn't.

It felt like he imagined an earthquake would, but instead of the sun going behind an ominous cloud as it habitually did in these sort of dreams, it actually got warmer. He'd opened his eyes at the first tremor, and was now shielding them from the glare of both the solar heat and light, and swore the disc was bigger than usual. Small waves formed on the lake and grew, fed by an invisible wind that did not chill, and as the shoreline crept closer and closer to Larry with the increasingly vibrant waves, he realised that he couldn't move. The water was only yards away, then only a matter of feet, then he felt the first wave lap at his legs and he thought he would probably drown.

The little orb shone brightly above him; not the sun, that was growing steadily by the minute, but the little bubble-like light which radiated a kind of calmness rather than warmth, assurance rather than illumination. When he looked at it, Larry dared to hope that he would come out of this alive.

Then a huge wave came crashing over him and he wanted to flail in panic, although whatever force was holding him down wouldn't allow him to, but nothing could stop the pounding of his heart which was thumping in anticipation of death. He closed his eyes to give up to the darkness, realising that there was nothing he could do, accepting that which he could not change, and he was about to slip into the void when a voice yelled in his ear.

"Wake up, you have much to do!"

Larry opened his eyes to see the little light bubble, obviously a vestige of his dream because it was silhouetted against the familiar wallpaper on his and Josie's bedroom ceiling. He turned over, thinking it must have been Josie who'd awakened him, but she was fast asleep, a steady, low snoring confirming that it hadn't been she. Larry rolled back over and pulled the duvet tight around him, shrugging off the dream as having too much of that honey-roast ham for supper the night before.

"Addilyn needs you!" squeaked the little bubble that was still on his pillow only inches away from his eyes.

Larry chuckled and told the dream image to go away.

Two seconds later he was on the floor, the pressure of the hard shove still tingling in his lower back, whilst Josie still gently snored.

Two hours later he was here waiting for a bus to God knew where.

*

The service came to a close after the second hymn; the first one at the start of the ceremony had been a lively one that Kaden had barely heard of but which had lifted his spirits upon the singing of it, and now the strains of *Amazing Grace* had just died down and Tim's coffin was being carried out to the churchyard through the side entrance of the church to the quiet, dulcet tones of Debussy's *Clair de Lune*. All three musical items had been Addilyn's choice, with Darcy choosing the entrance music and going for an aria from an opera Kaden had never heard of. He wondered if a love of opera was another thing he hadn't known about his brother, but a later remark by Darcy confirmed for him that his brother had hated opera but that she loved it.

Darcy preceded him in the procession following Tim, then he walked a pace or two behind with Addilyn at his side. Most of the fifty-strong congregation kept their heads bowed, with only the occasional tear-stained face stealing a glance at the coffin in sadness. Tim was, Kaden knew, a scientist who regraded all things mortal as a perfectly logical progression of things, as he had learned when their parents died; it would naturally follow, he supposed, that Tim's friends and acquaintances would feel the same, although to Kaden, even though he wasn't particularly religious – maybe agnostic at a push – it seemed almost essential that there was something else beyond this earthbound, trouble-filled, very unfair game of chance called life, in order for the universe to make sense. Otherwise, he would be forced to accept that your station in life, your comfort or discomfort, your celebrating or suffering, everything that the average three-score-years-and-ten threw at you, was mere inadvertence and you were at the mercy of only what happened, not at the mercy of something that *caused* it to happen, and that just didn't sit right with him at all.

Tim's plot was at the back of the churchyard, about halfway along a row of grave sites that had either been taken up already by deceased tenants or had been purchased in advance of the inevitable; whatever, Kaden thought illogically, at least Tim wouldn't be alone.

To Kaden's relief, only a handful of people followed the small cort□ge to the graveside, although why he should feel that way he didn't know; a sudden feeling of indignity had risen up for no reason at the thought of these people who weren't family trespassing upon such a private moment as the interment of his brother, even though these same people no doubt knew a lot more about Tim than he did, and had spent a lot more time with Tim than he had. He put it down to the mixed emotions of sadness, regret and guilt that he was feeling and totally ignored the hypocrite in him that didn't mind Addilyn being there.

The hole looked evil, there was no other word for it. It looked like a big, gaping, toothless mouth that was eager to devour the corpse within the pine coffin and that promised it would have no problem gnawing through the wood to reach the flesh and bones inside. As they lowered the box into the maw, Kaden stifled a sob but couldn't halt the tear that trickled down his cheek and he felt Addilyn's hand tighten on his in comfort and support. When it was his turn, he took a handful of the proffered dirt and sprinkled it on top of Tim's casket, regarding the plaque on its lid which heralded Tim's time on earth. Not long enough, thought Kaden, only four seven five three six five … what the hell?!

Addilyn gasped next to him and when he looked up to see her face, she was staring at the coffin in as much bewilderment as he felt.

"You see the numbers too?" he whispered while the vicar droned on about ashes and dust.

"I've seen them before," replied Addilyn, whispering back. "In my flat, when the boiler exploded, in my dream, at least."

"What do they mean? There are over fifty of them..."

"*Shh!*" Darcy elbowed Kaden in the ribs and shot Addilyn a look that would have rendered her a companion for Tim had they been capable of killing.

In return, Addilyn looked suitably abashed while Kaden looked merely annoyed, but he held his cool and allowed the graveside eulogy to continue to its conclusion, whereupon everyone turned and drifted towards the gate to exit the church grounds in a much less orderly fashion than that in which they had entered it. Just as Kaden and Addilyn had left the graveside arm in arm, Addilyn turned to Kaden and smiled, and, feeling her eyes upon him, Kaden turned to meet the golden gaze of warmly illuminated orbs.

"Forget the dead," she said in the voice of Tim Taylor. "Go save the living!"

"How...?" Kaden asked, flustered.

"How what?" asked Addilyn, herself once more.

"Later," replied Kaden, and he escorted Addilyn out of the churchyard without further comment or a backwards look.

*

Larry was on a coach to Cardiff, still not sure why. The weather was fine and the views for the first part of the journey were awe-inspiring, but Larry didn't want to admire them; he had decided to try and drift off to sleep in the hope that he would dream at least some of the answers to his plethora of questions so he got comfortable – or as comfortable as he could as the vehicle jostled along the country roads – and closed his eyes.

*

Marcia had never been so grateful for older foster parents because it was easy to get out of the house when Josie took her afternoon nap. Armed now with a carrier bag in which was a change of clothes, a book and her drawing pencils, and tucked inside her jeans pocket some money that she had borrowed from Josie's purse, Marcia was reluctant to leave without kissing Josie goodbye but, not wanting to risk waking the woman, she just slipped out the front door and began her quest to find Larrilee.

*

The wake was being held in the clubhouse of a nearby golf course of which Tim and Darcy were members; Kaden hadn't known that Tim played golf, yet another thing he didn't know about Tim. Darcy got a lift with friends – the funeral cars had done their job and now it was time for the slow black to go home – and, noticing her complete dismissal of her brother Kaden and his companion, a co-worker of Tim's offered his back seat to them, and although Kaden tried to strike up a conversation during which he hoped to learn something more of what had happened, his comments were met with short, sharp answers that indicated that it was a subject that should be strongly avoided and the majority of the eight-mile journey was conducted in total, somewhat awkward, silence. It was only when Addilyn commented on the beauty of the surrounding countryside that the quiet gave way to an enthusiastic agreement on the part of the driver, and the taciturnity soon descended again.

The main room of the clubhouse was offering a buffet both hot and cold and pre-paid drinks of all varieties and already people were milling around and helping themselves. Kaden wasn't hungry, however, and he headed straight for the bar and ordered a whisky and lemonade while Addilyn opted for nothing more ambitious than an orange juice. Kaden was glad that one of them at least was being responsible and he was equally as glad that it wasn't him.

When he had been served with the drinks, he looked round for Darcy but she was speaking with a group of rich-looking older men who may have been club members or seniors at Tim's work. He had been meaning to go and have a friendly word with her, but now decided against it and walked over to an empty table where he seated himself without even checking that Addilyn was following him; she was.

"So," she said, sitting down. "What happened?"

"Huh?" Kaden was watching Darcy with his lips tight.

"At the graveside," prompted Addilyn. "Did you see those numbers too?"

"Oh, that." Kaden sat up and shifted his concentration from Darcy to Addilyn. "Yes, I did," he said. "A great string of them. You said you'd seen them before?"

"In a dream I had, they were steamed onto the wall," mused Addilyn. "They evaporated before I really had a chance to notice them, but I remember briefly seeing them now."

"What do they mean?" asked Kaden.

"Damned if I know." Addilyn shrugged as she sipped her drink and looked round. "Nice place," she commented absently.

"We have to talk about it!" urged Kaden.

"Yes, we do," agreed Addilyn. "But not here and not now. Here and now is for remembering Tim. We can talk about it later."

Kaden nodded, reluctantly agreeing, and nursed his whisky for a while, watching as Darcy mingled with her doting crowd. It was obvious that she was immensely popular, and Kaden wondered what it was he was missing about her, but when he overheard a couple nearby mention that the charity takings from the funeral and wake was to go to the clubhouse, he (correctly, as it happened) assumed that it was more Darcy's money they were doting on than Darcy herself. He also thanked Tim for having the foresight to leave his brother in charge of his legacy rather than his fianc□e. He watched her with a renewed feeling of bitterness; Tim could have done so much better for himself, yet he had fallen for the good looks and the charm that was as on tap as any of the beer in the golf club's nineteenth hole, stupid bloke.

Then Darcy was crossing over to their table and Kaden got to his feet to greet her.

"Darcy..." he began, arms out to hold her.

Darcy accepted his embrace and kiss on the cheek, answering it with a kiss aimed about an inch away from Kaden's face in the style that made Addilyn laugh whenever she saw the gesture. Now, however, was not the time for mirth so she kept her expression sombre, smiling and nodding acknowledgement when Darcy glanced her way, but making no effort to move forward or infiltrate what she felt was a private moment between those who had been, in one way or another, closest to Tim.

"So when are you going home?" Darcy asked as soon as the pleasantries had been dutifully performed. "I need to sort out what

I'm going to do now."

Kaden shrugged. "Hadn't much thought about it," he replied. "Wanted to get today over with first."

"Well, just let me know tomorrow, then," said Darcy, and she turned on her heel to return to the hubbub of the wake and the admiration of the pecuniary benefactors, leaving Kaden to stare in disbelief after her.

"Well, of all the – " he started to say, but Addilyn was on her feet and standing behind him. He turned to look at her. "She really doesn't like me."

"I don't suppose I'm her favourite person either," chuckled Addilyn. "But just remember, today is for Tim, not for her." She leaned over the table and picked up Kaden's drink, hers having been finished, and handed it to him. "Come on," she said. "Let's leave the partying to the locals before you deck someone."

"That obvious, eh?" said Kaden, forlornly.

"Only because I recognise it and wholeheartedly sympathise," Addilyn smiled, then she linked her arm in his and walked him towards the back of the room where a pair of double doors was slightly open to let in the fresh air and the warm sunshine.

They stepped through the doors to the outside and to an umbrella-ed patio area where they sat alone and silently for a few moments, Kaden nursing his drink and Addilyn admiring the surrounding countryside that constituted the small golf course, each thinking their own private thoughts.

"So how long *are* we going to stay with Darcy?" asked Addilyn at length. She tried to make it a light-hearted query, but in truth she was beginning to tire of the pretentious woman and the false life she led, and now that Darcy had made it quite clear they weren't really welcome, they might as well discuss it.

"As long as we need to," replied Kaden. "We need a base to work from."

"I suppose." Addilyn shrugged but in truth she hadn't really thought of that. "And of course it'll depend on what we find at Tim's work."

"Exactly."

Addilyn hesitated, then: "Kaden, just what do you *expect* to find?" she wanted to know.

"I have no idea." Kaden didn't sound so much tired as downtrodden, defeated, and Addilyn fancied that Darcy's treatment of them had affected him more than he cared to admit. "But if Tim thought it was important enough to tell me about it and in the way he did, it's going to be pretty awesome. Tim was a scientist, his feet planted solidly on the ground. Whatever it is he wants me to know, it matters. And it matters enough for him to need me to do something about it."

"So what did that riddle of a note mean?" asked Addilyn. "Just what exactly *happened* when you were kids?"

*

If Tim caught him out once more, Kaden felt he'd throw the bat down and never play cricket again. He'd almost thought 'wrap the bat round Tim's head' but he'd managed to amend it to something less violent. He wasn't a bad loser, but having a big brother who was better at everything than you were could be quite harrowing and, if truth be told, he was a bit fed up of it. It was always "Tim did this" and "Tim did that" or even "Tim's is bigger" and "Tim's is nicer" and he was, even at the tender young age of seven, aware that his confidence was being eroded day by day; indeed, if what happened next hadn't happened, he could have grown up feeling insecure and useless.

But for once he managed to whack the ball so hard, it sailed clean over Tim's head, and in spite of his brother's being taller than him, even Tim jumping couldn't halt it in its flight clean over the tree-lined fence into the field where they were forbidden to go.

The trees weren't all that high, but they constituted an adequate enough cover so that no-one could see over them or through them into the four-acre meadow which belonged to the farmer, Mr Selsby, who lived in the farmhouse (which you could just see from Tim's and Kaden's bedroom window) with Mrs Selsby and their backward daughter Linda. Linda went to the same school as Tim and Kaden, but she stayed in the same class every time the new academic year came round; she was what the teachers called 'special needs' but Tim and Kaden knew she was backwards and that it was Farmer Selsby's fault.

Ernest Selsby was an ogre. Standing over six feet tall with hands as large as a family-sized frying pan and a beard that almost touched his waist, he was a formidable man. He scared almost everyone who met him and as both Ellen Selsby and Linda Selsby met him all the time, they were usually petrified. Ellen was a small woman, short blonde hair, pretty in an elfin kind of way, and not at all the kind of woman you'd think would fall for a man like Ernest Selsby, but then Tim and Kaden had their opinions on that: Ellen didn't have any choice because if she didn't marry Ernest, he would have throttled her with his bare hands. Linda was born backwards probably because Ernest Selsby hit his wife while she was pregnant and even though, whenever they heard the boys talking about the strange family, Tim's and Kaden's parents chastised them and said that Linda Selsby was 'just one of those things'. Kaden always thought that calling the girl a thing was worse than calling her father a would-be murderer, but Tim always went quiet and apologised because "Tim was more polite" and the entire matter would be closed. And Tim and Kaden were to stay away from the family, stay off their land, don't bother them.

So, this particular afternoon at this particular moment, when Tim and Kaden had to make a decision (did they climb up onto the shed and then drop down into the adjoining field to rescue their ball, or did they call it quits and go play something else) Tim was more inclined towards the latter – he would be, Kaden thought – but Kaden didn't favour the good two-shoes option because good was boring. Before his elder brother could stop him, Kaden had scrambled up the drainpipe and was sitting on the shed roof almost smugly.

"Kay..." Tim began.

"I'm just going to drop down and get the ball," said Kaden. "Then I'll shimmy up the tree and come back over. Mum and Dad need never know." He glared at his brother then as if daring him to turn tell-tale on him, then his expression softened. "You coming?" he asked.

Tim looked up at him for a moment, almost made a move before checking himself, then shook his head. "No," he said. "And if you're going to go, you'd best be quick. I'll keep a look-out down here and if mum or dad come I'll try and delay them, but just hurry up."

Kaden nodded and turned towards the field, a mere ten feet jump away. It looked empty, no sign of any of the Selsbys to be seen, no animals or crops. He wasn't going to damage anything if he landed heavily which he supposed he was bound to from this height, so he shut his eyes and let himself fall before a sudden jarring of his legs told him he had landed and he allowed them to buckle to break his fall and not break them.

He looked back at the fence to his left – to the right of the shed from their garden – but there was no sign of Tim. He thought his brother might peer through the trees, try to espy Kaden just to ensure he was okay, but if Tim were watching him, the cover of the dense foliage was an excellent shield against being detected.

Putting Tim to the back of his mind, Kaden looked around for the ball which was nowhere to be seen. He didn't think it had travelled all that far, but there wasn't any sign of it as far as he could see. He ventured further a little, thinking it might have landed in a hole or in the grass which was sparse and clumpy, stepping carefully, and he was so intent on watching out for any of the Selsbys that he didn't notice it before it cried out in a very tiny voice: "Ouch!"

Kaden stepped back unconsciously and looked down to where the sound had come. There was what looked like a little ray of sunlight catching on some buried tin or foil paper, and as he squinted to see better what had made the sound, the ray of sunlight moved.

Then it spoke. "You stepped on me," it said.

Kaden looked stupidly at the little light which was bobbing around on the ground like an iridescent bubble with a life of its own. Then he turned tail and bolted for the side of the shed where he scampered up using the fence then tree branches as a ladder, a scream stuck in his throat , his heart pounding fit to burst. When he reached the top, his cry of "Ti-i-i-i-i-mmm!" was enough for the older boy to scramble up the drainpipe to see what the matter was.

Tim had never seen his little brother so frightened. Kaden was sitting on the shed roof hugging himself tightly, trembling from head to foot, his eyes wide and terrified. He was trying to tell Tim something but nothing came out of his mouth other than a thick deep sound that reminded Tim of the way Linda Selsby communicated. Tim crossed over to him and held him by the arms, shaking him gently out of his shock – or at least trying to – and when, several minutes later, Kaden pointed a very unsteady finger towards the ground some yards away in the forbidden field, Tim looked but couldn't see what Kaden was trying to bring his attention to.

"What is it, Kay?" he asked, sounding genuinely concerned. "What frightened you?"

Kaden tried to reply but couldn't.

"Was it a spider? A mouse? A rat?"

Kaden shook his head.

"Well, whatever it was, it's gone now and you're safe. Let's get down before dad comes out and catches us."

Kaden shook his head again.

"What, you want to go have another look?" Tim sounded incredulous.

Kaden nodded.

"You're crazy, but – "

The rest of the sentence got stuck in Tim's throat as the ray of light floated upwards and into view. It hovered in the air for a moment, like a ghostly orb in full daylight, then it said "Bye bye" before it shot away like a flaming bullet. For a second or two, both boys stared into empty space, then turned to each other.

"Did you see?" asked Kaden, his voice still small but at least he'd found it.

Tim regarded his brother for a moment, then: "No," he said, "I didn't." And he climbed down the drainpipe and headed for the house without so much as another word.

*

"And that was it?" asked Addilyn. "He never mentioned it again?"

"Never," replied Kaden. "Until now, in that letter."

"Was it Daji, do you think?"

"I don't know. Daji doesn't strike me as something to be suicidal over, and that thing all those years ago sounded nothing like you describe Daji to be."

"Hmm, good point. So what about the role reversal bit? Does he mean that now he believes it but you don't?"

"Maybe, but then again maybe he means he saw something that I didn't."

"Do you really believe it was suicide?"

"I don't know." Kaden paused and sighed a deep, long sigh. "I don't want to think so. And if it was, that would mean the others committed suicide too, and *that* would beg the question: why? What was it they all discovered that was so bad that they chose to die? Or that their knowing about it resulted in their having to be killed?"

"Extraterrestrial life?" ventured Addilyn.

"Like the one you both saw when you were kids? It's the sort of thing that they all had in common."

"I wondered that too, but why die or be killed for it? I mean, if that were the case, that they'd discovered life, they would have told a hell of a lot of people in a very short time and there aren't any cases of mass suicide or mass murder."

"I guess we'll have to search for answers at Tim's work, then."

"Yes, and soon. That's what he said, work quickly. I think he meant, go to my workplace quickly."

"And what did he mean by half seven being sad?"

"I have no idea," said Kaden, "And my head's beginning to hurt just thinking about it. We'll talk about it later, but right now I'm going to get drunk. Can you manage Darcy if I'm out of it?"

"I can manage Darcy," affirmed Addilyn, but as it turned out, Darcy got legless too and later Addilyn had the downstairs of Darcy's house to herself while the pair of them slept like babies, and that's when Daji began to explain.

THIRTEEN

When Kaden informed Darcy that they'd like to stay for a few more days, her reaction was as they expected and Addilyn, who was considering moving out to a cheap hotel anyway, had her mind made up for her when Darcy informed her that Shadow would have to live in the car because he was "too smelly for a nice place like this". She moved into a little inn just not a mile from Darcy's house and when Kaden declared that he'd get a room there too, Addilyn told him it was pointless wasting money when there was a perfectly good residence available for him where he, at least, was welcome. Kaden joked again about her thriftiness and Addilyn acknowledged it, although she wasn't in the mood to smile. She bundled the few things she had into her carry-all and took Shadow to the snug little hotel room – well, 'snug' sounded better than 'cramped' and besides she was lucky that the place allowed pets – where she spent an hour imagining what she could happily do to Darcy before giving up on the exercise and instead taking Shadow for a walk over the barren hillsides where there was no-one visible for as far as the eye could see.

*

Larry got off the coach and stretched; he'd been on the thing for hours and it wasn't the most comfortable vehicle he had ever ridden in. He estimated they were about halfway to London because that would be the logical time for a thirty-minute stop and, although he had never been south in his life – his dad had been stationed on the south coast but he and his mother and two sisters had never travelled to visit him – he fancied that Birmingham was, if not distance-wise, at least time-wise roughly fifty percent of the journey.

He walked the length of the concourse towards the little shop and marvelled at the prices they had the nerve to charge; he thought living in Keswick was expensive enough, but these people took the biscuit! Her took a packet of them himself but refused to pay for a bottle of water. Instead he bought a two-pint bottle of milk and downed it while the shopkeeper got his change, then he returned to the coach, ate the biscuits while he watched other passengers new and old alight, then settled back down to try and sleep when they got going again before nature wanted her way.

He still held on to the hope that he would dream, but it hadn't happened yet.

*

They planned to visit Tim's work on the Sunday. Addilyn still held that it probably made little difference as stars tended to come out every night, not just during the week, and whilst Kaden agreed wholeheartedly with her, he said he'd prefer Sunday because that was the day that Darcy spent at home and he really didn't fancy spending all of it with her. Yes, he knew he could come and see Addilyn whenever he wanted, but that wouldn't be a good enough reason to avoid offending Darcy; and no, he didn't give a rat's arse about offending her but it might be better if he waited till he didn't need her house as a headquarters any more. And definitely no to believing Darcy had designs on him – she was used to better, and no, he didn't mean that Addilyn should put up with second best.

"You mean, you want to put up with me?" he'd asked at the point when the penny dropped.

"If you're willing to do the same with me, I'd be silly to turn you down," smiled Addilyn, and that's when they shared their first kiss.

Now Kaden had gone and Addilyn was lying on the single bed, fussing Shadow who was lying over her and trying to play a game on her mobile. She didn't play often as most games involved numbers and they just drove her crazy but this one was a general knowledge quiz and she could skip the questions she didn't like the number of.

She was just about to answer a question about Mary Shelley when her phone vibrated and the sudden shrilling that broke the silence of her room made her jump. Shadow was on his feet in seconds but as she answered the phone call she reassured him that it was only her silly nerves, nothing to worry about.

Which was more than could said for Josie Hodgson, who was frantic.

"*She's gone*!" Josie was wailing down the phone and Addilyn had to hold the phone away from her ear. "*She's gone and I don't know where!*"

Addilyn wondered why Josie had rung her, what the older woman expected her to do when she knew she was away. She could hardly go look for her.

"Josie, have you looked for a note?" asked Addilyn.

"*I don't need a note! She's gone to catch up with Larry, I'd bet my life on it!*"

"And where's *Larry* gone?"

"*I don't know that either! Both times I was asleep, and they snuck off! But wherever they are and for whatever reason, they're in it together and I have a feeling it's to do with you as well!*"

"Whoa, don't go blaming *me*! I'm hundreds of miles away and they're definitely not here!" Addilyn paused, then: "What do you mean, *both* times?"

"*Larry left yesterday, Marcia today. And, I'm not* blaming *you, Addie, but I can't help thinking it's something to do with what was going on, you know? Oh, I know I didn't say too much about it, Marcia and her Larilee seemed to have it all in hand, but I'm not stupid. I know* something *was amiss, just I didn't know what. I* still *don't know, I just think you* do."

Addilyn hesitated; she felt sorry for Josie – even though the woman wasn't the best person to take your problems to, she was obviously a little hurt that her husband and her foster daughter were leaving her out of things, keeping secrets. Yet could Addilyn she tell her? She didn't know all that much, and what she *did* know wouldn't be of much use to Josie; after all, it would worry her more than allay any fears she had for Larry and Marcia, and Addilyn didn't want to add even further to her distress.

"Josie, if they do come here," she said at length, "I will insist they contact you, or failing that I will phone you myself. In the mean time, I'd just sit tight; when Marcia doesn't find Larry, she'll be back."

"*If that DJ thing lets her*!" Josie sounded more resigned than petulant and she terminated the call before Addilyn could think of anything constructive to say.

*

Kaden had picked up his mobile when Darcy came in from the kitchen with a glass of wine for each of them, and he really wanted to refuse the alcohol but thought better of it. He wasn't planning to see Addilyn tonight – they were due to meet up tomorrow morning and all arrangements had been made – so there was really no need other than because he wanted to see her now that they seemed to be a couple.

And 'seemed' was the operative word, too, because nothing had been said after that first kiss, with Addilyn and he parting lips and then going on as if nothing had happened. Maybe nothing *had* happened and it was wishful thinking, or maybe Addilyn was so independent that she wasn't quite used to being one half of a couple, but Kaden thought there *was* something special between them and it was probably their present predicament and problems that was preventing things from developing any further...

"I do hope you two aren't serious," Darcy commented, pulling Kaden out of his reverie.

"About what?" he asked.

"About each other," replied Darcy, setting her drink on a small occasional table in front of her and turning sideways to face Kaden straight on. "She really isn't your type at all, darling," she continued. "And you're far too sweet for me to let you get hurt!"

"I think – with all due respect, Darcy – that whatever is or isn't happening between me and Addilyn is nobody's business expect mine and hers."

"Yes, I know, but you're at a difficult time, and you are more prone to the first sympathetic person that comes along."

Kaden so wanted to point out that that wouldn't be Darcy, then, but he bit his tongue and stood up. "I'm off to bed," he said.

"I know you weren't all that close to Tim, but it must've hurt you to lose him nonetheless." She paused, as if searching for the right words to say, then continued: "Kaden, please don't make a fool of yourself with that woman. She really isn't the sort you want to get involved with."

Kaden didn't sit back down – he liked having the taller height and subsequent psychological advantage of looking down at Darcy – but he wasn't going to go to bed and leaving it at that, either. "And what *sort* do you think Addilyn is?" he enquired of her.

"Well, she's a bit common." Darcy shrugged in a 'sorry-but-you-know-it's-true' manner and smiled. "Oh, I daresay she's a good friend – she has been very good to you during the past few weeks, I'm sure – but she's hardly, you know, *other half* material!"

"Whereas someone like you is?" Kaden tried to keep the tightness out of his voice but he was finding it very difficult not to sneer outright.

"Oh, I know what you're thinking," said Darcy, "And you wouldn't be the first. But I loved Tim and I showed it. In public, in private, I didn't care. And he loved it!"

Of course he did, thought Kaden. *A man is always attracted by a woman who obviously loves him. And she* is *a looker...*

"Addilyn, on the other hand, gives off the message that she'd rather be a million miles away, the sourpuss."

"She has trust issues."

"The only people who have trust issues are the ones who don't think enough of themselves to realise they're worthy of trust. There's obviously something wrong with her."

Was it that obvious?

"Anyway, that's just my opinion." Darcy stood up. "I'm going into town to pick up something for tomorrow's lunch. What do you fancy?"

"I'm fine, thanks," replied Kaden. "I'm out tomorrow, all day."

"With Addilyn?"

"With Addilyn."

"I'll save you some. You'll need cheering up when you get back."

*

The following morning Kaden was up early and round at Addilyn's just as she was taking Shadow for a walk. He fell into step beside her and they talked about their plans for the day. Upon returning to the hotel, Addilyn made sure that Shadow was watered, left the television on "to keep him company," she told Kaden, then they drove to a caf□ for a full English breakfast because they didn't know when they'd have the opportunity to eat again. When they'd satisfied their appetites, they made their way to and through Knighton to Tim's little observatory. The sun was trying to shine through the thick cloud layer and little blue spaces emerged to facilitate its breakthrough.

There was a tour just about to start when Addilyn and Kaden rolled up in Addilyn's car; so much for coming on a Sunday when it was quiet, they both independently mused, yet it did make getting into the place a lot less hassle.

Getting out of the car, they hurried to where a group of about a half dozen people were showing tickets to an academic-looking young man – jeans and trainers but well-pressed and well-scrubbed with a t-shirt and jacket that announced to the world (well, to Kaden anyway) that this was a fresh-out-of-university graduate who was most enthusiastic about the work he did. The latter observation was based more on his broad grin than his clothing, but Kaden's suspicions were confirmed when he hurried Kaden and Addilyn along without asking for their ticket. Thank the Lord for small mercies, he thought, and he checked his watch; thus, as he looked down, he didn't notice the brief flare of gold in the postgrad's eyes.

The centre was small, and Kaden could well imagine Tim being quite content here. There were several observation rooms housing differently-sized telescopes and, the postgrad explained, you were left alone to get on with your work and there were no bosses, just a team. They shared jokes, laughed and drank tea or coffee together (but never alcohol) and the atmosphere was conducive to good work through good peer relations and a relaxed workplace. And here on the left was the first of the offices – the door announced its tenant as DR TIMOTHY TAYLOR B.SC (HONS) MPHYS PH.D (ASTROPHYSICS) FRAS – and Kaden felt a surge of pride followed closely by a stab of guilt and then a wave of panic. He noticed Addilyn staring at the door and assumed that she, like him, was wondering when their chance to backtrack and let themselves in would arise. They'd need time, Kaden reasoned; there was a hooded keyboard to the left of the door which no doubt required some sort of password to persuade the mechanism not to sound an unholy alarm and of course they didn't have the number. Maybe it was disabled, Kaden thought, or maybe Tim had left the number somewhere and they'd not found it when they went through his things. Maybe, with the keys, you didn't *need* a passcode, you just unlocked the door and waltzed right in. *Yeah, right*, his cynicism mocked him.

"Er – no, Dr Taylor doesn't work on a Sunday." The postgrad was answering a question from a member of his tour group and he sounded a little tongue-tied. "In fact, Dr Taylor has left us."

"On to pastures new or pastures bigger?" This question from a big man who looked as if he were a business executive in his working time, and very probably the chief.

The postgrad cleared his throat and Kaden actually felt sorry for him.

"Er – he had a heart attack," he said at length. "He died."

A heart attack; now, Kaden mused, was that the story for the benefit of the tour group or for Tim's co-workers? He glanced at Addilyn, who nodded to indicate that she was thinking along the same lines. She smiled back briefly then returned her full attention to the postgrad and Kaden could only guess that she was taking in everything he said just in case something somehow helped them somewhere down the line.

The postgrad meanwhile was ushering people past Tim's office with embarrassed haste, but Kaden fancied that only he and Addilyn would know it for that. He began to lag behind and Addilyn followed his lead, and soon they were last in line and then some twenty feet distant and then, when the postgrad led the tour group outside to admire the view, Kaden reckoned that now was as good a chance as they were going to get and he doubled back to Tim's office, had a quick look round to ensure they were alone and drew a key out of his pocket. It fitted the door lock perfectly but then a hooded keyboard to his left started to wink brightly and the door wouldn't budge.

"Okay, so the key fits and that keyboard is flashing and I have a horrible feeling that we're being timed." Kaden sounded, Addilyn thought, totally stressed. "Now all we need is the passcode."

Addilyn regarded him for a second as he tried the key in the lock again, then she turned to the flickering keyboard mounted on the wall just beside the door. She hesitated then stepped forward and pressed five buttons in sequence, waiting for the alarm to sound and alert whoever was left here to their presence and their break-in.

Instead the spring lock on the door pinged open and Tim Taylor's office beckoned.

"What did you do?" Kaden was incredulous. "How did you – "

"Tim's note," replied Addilyn, standing back so that Kaden could enter the room first, then quickly nipping in behind him and closing the door quietly. "'Seven in the morning, it'll be sad' – I figured zero-seven-zero-zero-blue and it worked."

"I'm surprised you remembered it."

"I'm good at remembering things like that," Addilyn said, but did not add that she had been remembering numbers for every moment of the day for as long as she remembered.

Not that it was quite so bad now; it was funny, but when she was totally engrossed in something, it didn't bother her quite so much as when she was bored, alone; that's when it hit with a vengeance: *you think you're miserable, girl? You ain't seen NOTHING yet* and then the thoughts came and she had to count and wash, and wash and count, and sometimes it could be half an hour before the stupid thing could be ritually satisfied. It was crippling, more so because the reasonable – the *reasoning* – part of her knew that she was being silly, that no harm would come to her or anyone else just because her mind made illogical connections between totally random things, but then there was that part that asserted that she could never be certain about that, and she would cry and scream and wish to God that she were one of those people who didn't have to put up with this kind of frustrating *crap* at all…

"Addilyn, you in there?" Kaden's voice sounded as if from a long way off.

"What?" Addilyn snapped to in an instant, embarrassed. "Sorry, I was daydreaming."

"Not a good time." Kaden was riffling through some papers in the top drawer of his late brother's desk. "Stand by the door, would you, listen out for anyone coming."

Addilyn nodded and crossed over to the door, looking through the frosted glass for approaching shadows, listening intently for oncoming footsteps.

"If that keyboard has stopped flashing, which it must have done because I can't see any lights through this glass," observed Addilyn, "Then we *should* be all right. There's no reason for anyone to come in, at least while they have the public around, is there?"

"That would depend on whether he checks the tickets against the number of tourists," replied Kaden. "Hopefully he'll be too keen to get away home or back to work or whatever to bother counting them, but you never know." He pulled open a drawer and found a bundle of paperwork bound with string and a post-it note on the top file cover, marked

For the attention of my brother
with the very best of luck

and for some reason he shuddered. It was probably, he thought, because this was as if Tim were speaking to him from beyond the grave; or maybe it was because Tim knew he was going to die when he wrote it yet marked it for his attention rather than for Darcy's. Tim must have been sure that Kaden would come as soon as he heard, and of course he would, it wasn't that fantastic an assumption, they were brothers! But Tim, knowing that he was running out of time, had formulated a plan for his brother Kaden to follow through with no doubt whatsoever that that is exactly what Kaden would do, or at least *try* to do, and that rather humbled him. Tears began to well in his eyes but he didn't have time for sentimentality; he grabbed the bundle, closed the desk drawer and turned to the door.

The postgrad was standing in the doorway with his hands on his hips and with a questioning expression on his face, while the members of the tourist group were behind him straining to see what was going on and as pleased as punch to be treated to this unexpected extra-schedular show.

*

Josh didn't know his father any more.

It wasn't just the drink either, although God knew Dathan was imbibing more alcohol than Josh thought possible; but the more he drank, the sober he seemed to become, and then he got angry (he said) because the booze wasn't having the desired effect. Why his dad should want the drink to have *any* effect, Josh didn't know; Dathan Greenwood wasn't the only one suffering because Lena died!

But it was more than that, Josh realised. His dad *wasn't* his dad any more. Oh, the face was the same – maybe a little more haggard, definitely in need of a good shave – but the person inside his dad's body had changed. Sometimes it spoke to itself and it didn't sound at all like his dad usually sounded, and at other times it would cry and it was then that Josh thought his father had come back. But the tears didn't last long; one more glass and it was back to plotting and planning with whatever it was that inhabited Dathan Greenwood's body and Josh would go upstairs to his bedroom where he near enough lived full-time now and lie on the bed till he fell into a troubled sleep and just lately getting up and going to school was actually, if not a pleasure, then at least a relief.

*

"Can I stay at yours tonight?" asked Kaden.

Addilyn had slowed down after driving like a bat out of hell for the first couple of miles just in case anyone was attempting to follow them, and was now cruising almost as if she were out for a Sunday cruise with not a care in the world. Now she turned briefly to regard Kaden for the first time since they'd made their getaway.

"You want me to sneak you past the landlady?" she asked in reply. "You think I've had experience in doing that?"

Kaden didn't take her seriously because he could hear the jocular tone in her voice. "I'm sure you haven't," he said, "But I'm also sure it wasn't for the wont of a hundred or more lads trying!" He paused. "I mean, there must have been many boys who fancied you, not that you – "

"I knew exactly what you meant," smiled Addilyn. "You want to go through those papers without Darcy interfering, is that it?"

"Well, that's a part of it. The other part is that I want to go through them with you and therefore, as Darcy is unlikely to welcome you into her house with open arms, I have to come to you."

"It's a pity we didn't get on better."

"It is?"

"Well, not for me, but it would have been so much easier for you."

"Hey, don't you worry about me!"

"Why not? You worry about me, don't you?"

"After what happened back there, are you kidding? I don't think I'll *ever* need to worry about you!"

Addilyn chuckled; it hadn't been a big deal, not really, but she had twisted the poor graduate into such a tight knot that he was probably as relieved as they were when they left.

He had challenged their presence in Tim's office with an attitude that he had every right to adopt under the circumstances, but which immediately rubbed Addilyn up the wrong way (reasonableness be damned; when you were hypersensitive, you overreacted unreasonably whilst reasonableness on anyone else's part became unacceptableness on yours) while Kaden just smiled at the young chap with nothing else to say or do.

"What the hell do you think you're doing?" thundered the postgrad, surprisingly authoritatively for someone his size and build.

"This office is out of bounds!"

"Then you shouldn't have left it open!" retorted Addilyn.

"It wasn't open!" protested the postgrad.

"So how did we get in, then? These doors are protected by a four numeral plus one phonetic code; did you expect us to guess it?"

"No. I mean, I'm sure that door was closed when we passed it. And how do you know what code format we use?"

"You might well ask," replied Addilyn knowingly. "And you might well ask why you insisted that Dr Taylor suffered a fatal *'heart attack'*..."

"Why do you say that?" The poor postgrad was looking somewhere between terrified and puzzled. "Of course he had a heart attack!"

"Oh, don't worry, we're not going to tell." Addilyn walked up to the grad while Kaden began to walk past him. The postgrad put his arm out to halt Kaden's progress but Addilyn leaned forward and whispered: "We're part of it," she explained. "We know what really happened but we need to remove these files in case someone finds them, reads them, and talks. Now, make sure you increase your security because we don't want a repeat of what happened to Dr Taylor, do we?"

"No," the postgrad. "No, we don't." He paused. "Where exactly are you from?" he asked.

"Need to know information only," replied Addilyn. "And that you *don't* need to know."

And with that she walked out of the building to catch up with Kaden who had made a hasty exit while he had the chance and she was shaking like a leaf and wondering how the hell she managed – or dared – to pull that charade off...

"So how is Darcy anyway?" Addilyn asked, her reliving the whole episode convincing her with even more certainty that, somewhere along the line, Daji was somehow involved.

"She's okay," said Kaden.

"Been dissing me, has she?" Addilyn smiled to herself as she said it.

"No, of course not!"

"Liar."

"Okay, but I didn't take any notice. In fact, I defended you. But of course you don't actually care what she thinks, do you."

Addilyn realised that he really didn't know her that well at all; she also realised that the veil she had drawn over her hypersensitivity had done its job. Everyone thought she was a devil-may-care with a tough skin and beholden to nobody, but in fact she could be hurt easily because her raw feelings were barely covered by that veil because in reality it was very thin and its covering very tentative.

"I'm surprised she hasn't asked about the Will," Addilyn said to change the subject.

"So was I," agreed Kaden. "So I brought it up in conversation the other evening. It seems that Darcy didn't want to mention it because she's so sure that Tim has left everything to her and she didn't want us to be offended. She was going to sort it all out when we left."

"She's in for a shock then!" chuckled Addilyn.

"Don't be mean!" Kaden was chuckling too. "I'll give her the house, she's lived there for so long, it's her home. Money she doesn't need, but I'll arrange something anyway."

"Aw, you're an old softie!"

"So would you be if you let yourself."

Addilyn turned and stared hard at Kaden, but he was grinning at his flippantly-voiced observation so it was difficult to be angry with him for seeing through her disguise. Instead she sighed.

"You know me so well, it's beginning to frighten me," she said.

*

The knock on Josh's door was very gentle and had he been asleep he would never have heard it. As it was, he was reading a book and now he lay it down on the duvet; he called "come in" and waited for his father to fall into the room and start going on again about Lena and about how cruel life was and although he hated his father's being like this, the truth was that a bad father was better than no father at all – at least there was someone downstairs and that was reassuring even if Dathan couldn't have been of any use should Josh have wanted or needed him for anything; in short, it beat being alone.

Dathan looked rough. He was unkempt and he smelled of sweat, and Josh knew that he hadn't had a bath for at least a week, if not longer – although his deterioration hinted at something other than mere lack of hygiene. His breath smelled foul too, and he was now beginning to visibly lose weight. His eyes were sunken, he was unsteady on his feet, his skin was red, blotchy and becoming wrinkled. He looked twenty years older than he actually was, and the expression of pure terror in his eyes evoked a kind of sympathy in Josh that only a child could have for a parent who had treated them badly but who still represented, for them, all that they should have been but weren't.

"Dad?" Josh had to break the silence, because although Dathan hadn't said anything, Josh knew he wanted to. "What is it, dad?"

Dathan half-sat, half-fell on the bed beside Josh and the boy moved over to the edge of his single bed to make room for his father; they rarely shared these kind of moments any more and Josh wanted to make the most of it because tonight his dad seemed more like his old self and less like the thing he had become, and maybe, just maybe, tonight would be when he, Josh, discovered just what the problem was with with Dathan Greenwood.

"Dad?" Josh said again, but his dad wasn't listening. For the first time in weeks, Dathan had fallen asleep without a bottle in his hand and even though he really wanted to talk, Josh didn't have the heart to disturb him. Instead he lay back, repositioning himself so that he could throw one arm around his dad, then waited for sleep to come.

But when you spend so much time in your bedroom lying on the bed because there's nowhere else to go, nothing else to do, your tiredness dissipates and leaves you restless, tossing and turning irritably because *you* want to sleep but your mind doesn't, and night doesn't mean sleep any more because you've been doing that during the day and your body is totally confused...

"No! No! Leave me alone!"

The shouting made Josh start but he didn't move his arm; in fact, if anything, he tightened it around his dad in a protective, maybe also reassuring, way. His dad seemed to be having a dream, and not a very nice one at that, but Josh wasn't sure what he should do, awaken his dad or let him sleep, let the dream run its course, just tighten his grip to let Dathan know on some subliminal level that he was being cared for.

"I don't want to, no!" Dathan began fidgeting and Josh's grip tightened. "I won't do it, I won't hurt him!"

It seemed now that the best bet was to wake his dad up; even if Dathan wasn't afraid of nightmares, Josh was frightened enough for both of them. He shook his dad's shoulder very gently. "Dad, wake up," he whispered. "You're dreaming. Wake up!"

For a moment it seemed as if Josh's words had penetrated the dream, for Josh could feel his dad physically relax and his breathing became more regular, the shouting silenced as suddenly as it had roused. Josh too began to relax, and to allow himself to fall into a light slumber in which he too dreamed.

He dreamed that his dad was trying hard not to kill him.

FOURTEEN

The majority of the night was spent teeming through the wads of notes that Tim had left unfiled and unsorted in his office drawer (for him to find? wondered Kaden) and there was only the chance for intermittent naps before one or the other awakened and pored over more paperwork, wondering what the hell it all meant. He had to admit that Addilyn had a far greater aptitude for remembering numbers than had he – probably due to her little problem which for some reason she was loathe to discuss or even admit to, for that matter yet which Kaden thought was a very minor flaw in an otherwise pretty awesome character. He realised that he was getting in deeper but he couldn't help it; the more time he spent with her, the more she appealed to him.

As for whether the feeling was reciprocated, Kaden was fairly sure it was, but Addilyn was not a one to wear her heart on her sleeve.

"I used to," she'd told him once. "I allowed my emotions to show and people ridiculed me for it. Either ridiculed me or took advantage, and sometimes even both together. So now not only do I not show emotions, I also don't allow myself to feel too deeply and that way I don't get hurt."

Kaden had felt sad at that; Addilyn was missing so much due to someone or a few someones who obviously didn't know how to respect a fellow individual, and he just wanted to penetrate the forcefield and show her that certain emotions could be the best feelings in the world!

"Stuck again?" Addilyn's voice brought Kaden round from his musings and he realised that he had been staring at a page of numbers with a slight frown on his face which he now checked and turned into a small smile.

"No, just thinking," he replied. "But maybe you'd be better looking at these. Maths was never my strong point."

"You mean, I'd be better looking at them because they're numbers and my stupid brain seems to be obsessed with them."

"I prefer the way I put it."

"So do I."

The next few hours passed in more or less companionable silence, both of them staying awake as dawn approached, sometimes making small talk but most of the time just discussing any interesting points they might come across. Addilyn was sure that they were all interesting if they actually realised what they meant, whilst Kaden marvelled that his brother not only made a living understanding all this scientific gobbledegook, but was extremely good at it to boot.

Presently, as the sun began to lift itself lazily from its horizontal bed, Shadow proclaimed that it was time for a bathroom break by leaping onto the top of the papers and sending them flying off the bed to scatter like abandoned snowflakes on a carpeted lawn.

*

Marcia was relieved when the coach came to a halt but not for long because she suddenly realised that she didn't know how she was going to get out of the luggage compartment without the driver or one or more of the passengers seeing her.

It was sheer luck that the driver smoked, for it afforded her the opportunity to sneak into the luggage bay underneath the main body of the vehicle and there she had remained, only panicking once when they stopped about halfway for a break and for several people to get off. She had squeezed herself as far to the front side of the limited luggage space as she could, hoping that the suitcases belonging to those alighting would not be the ones closest to her.

They weren't.

The driver left the compartment open and as tempted as she was to get out and stretch her legs, Marcia remained put and made do with a half hour of fresh air instead. Then she was shut in again and the rattling and roaring restarted and now it was still and quiet in here with a lot of shouting outside and she realised that she was at the end of her coach journey and now she had to somehow escape unseen.

She was so busy plotting that she didn't notice Larry Hodgson step off the bus into the urban smog.

*

The bathroom break was a quick one and when they came back, they looked at the littered floor with a mixture of consternation, irritation and resignation. Kaden had wanted to clear it up straight away but Addilyn had gently led him out of the room, declaring that a breath of fresh air would do them all good, besides which the papers in a mess didn't really matter in view of the fact that they didn't understand them anyway. Now they were regarding the figure-, text- and diagram-covered sheets of paper with hopelessness and Addilyn had half-voiced her opinion that it was a waste of time because – when Kaden noticed a sheet with a string of numbers which lay alone, away to the left side of the rest. He picked it up and regarded it with interest.

"It says 'predicted co-ordinates'," said

Kaden. "It has a double underlined postscript which has a date of impact."

"Sounds like that might be something we were looking for," observed Addilyn, looking over his shoulder at the list of numbers and appreciating the aroma of Kaden's now-fading aftershave and his natural perspiration.

Kaden turned the sheet over. "It continues," he said.

"And someone put their coffee on it," observed Addilyn. "There's an entire chunk that's illegible."

"But surely someone will be able to work it out?" asked Kaden, rhetorically. "Tim did."

"So who do we take it to?" asked Addilyn.

"Who do we know with the expertise of my brother who wouldn't mind possibly being dead within a week or less?" Kaden asked her, glumly.

"Who do we know with the expertise of your brother who will not learn about the second bit because the safety of the world outweighs the life of one astrophysicist?" countered Addilyn.

"You're a hard woman, Addie."

"I'm a practical woman, and I need a shower."

And with that, Addilyn left Kaden staring at the incomprehensible sequence of numbers while she got ready for whatever the day ahead held.

*

As Larry Hodgson got off the coach, walked out of the station and regarded the plethora of red double-decker buses trundling along the road, he appreciated that he was in London and was quite happy about it; he would have been happier still had he known what he was doing there.

He took a leisurely walk to the end of the road – or was it the start? – and turned left. He crossed the road at a zebra crossing and continued to walk as if he knew the way to wherever it was he was heading.

It was a lot busier here than he had ever seen it up north, and there were many people sitting on the ground with paper cups or mugs in which to collect money, some even with dogs or children which he considered quite out of order. He might have thrown a copper or two into the beggars' receptacles but he wasn't sure how long he was here for and how much money he might need, and he'd more or less emptied his bank account of what little savings he had. Josie had the keys to the main account, metaphorically speaking; there was enough in there to see to their funerals and a bit over "just in case", as Josie would say, although she didn't know quite what the case in question was. But maybe it was just as well that she kept the serious accounts; Larry thought it a waste of money to spend ridiculous amounts on lavish send-offs and was an avid member of the 'give it to me now while I'm alive to enjoy it' persuasion. When he went, they could just bin bag him and take him to the landfill.

He eventually reached the train station which he cut through to get to the underground. He took the light blue Victoria line and knew he had to get off at Green Bank, wherever that was, but he didn't panic because it wasn't so much a feeling of being controlled than one of merely *knowing*. Plus he was certain now that Daji had something to do with this and he wondered if Marcia or Addilyn were having anything like as much fun.

*

"So where do we go from here?" asked Kaden as he donned his coat, feeling fresher now that he had jumped in the shower after Addilyn had finished with it. "And I mean literally."

"Well, I was considering going back to Knighton," said Addilyn, checking that she had everything, then turning off the bedside lamp and tidying up the papers that they had been poring over all night. "It's the only place

I can think of with people who would talk the same language as these figures do!" She waved the full envelope in the air for emphasis.

"You think we'd be welcome?" asked Kaden. "They might just call the police and then we'd be helpless."

"Maybe that would be a good thing. We could explain – "

" They wouldn't listen. Well, they'd listen – half-heartedly – then ring the police psychologist."

"Not a good idea, then."

"No."

"So where?"

"I have no idea. But maybe we should just get into the car and drive. We might end up somewhere we never knew we wanted to be."

*

The locks had been changed on Dr Timothy Taylor's office door, although it was a bit late now. Mollie Hathaway had just finished emptying all the drawers and cupboards (the science staff had already been in and taken what they wan and she didn't much care either; they were all far cleverer than her and all this science and space stuff was far beyond her.

But she wasn't so stupid as to not realise

that the secret compartment she'd found under the desk must house something pretty important. She could see white through the cracks of the little drawer that had been carved into the underbelly of the large desk right in the centre where the monitor stood, and she knew it was paper she was glimpsing, although she hadn't been able to access it at all.

So now she was off to tell Leslie, the young, quite fetching, newly-qualified PhD scholar who was here on a twelve-month trial basis and who made a welcome change to all the other boring old farts now that Timothy Taylor, God bless him, had left. Dr Taylor had been nice and she, Mollie, had always liked the way he had time for *all* the staff here, not just the ones with the high IQs; but now, only Leslie spoke to her, and if the pair of old coots that now constituted the senior staff had anything, he'd be ignoring her too by and by.

Which would be a pity, because she quite liked talking to Leslie, and by all accounts he seemed to like talking to the 25-year-old dizzily blonde bombshell with an IQ to match that was Mollie Hathaway, and she still harboured hopes and dreams...

*

"I think I know where we're heading," said

Kaden, about ten minutes into the drive.

"Good," replied Addilyn, putting down the papers with the coordinates on. "Because I've just noticed something about these figures."

"Oh?"

"You remember the numbers I saw on the gravestone at Tim's funeral – sorry to bring it up – and I think you might have done too?"

"I'm still battling that one; I'm not sure what I saw that day. But anyway, what about them? Do they match the ones there?"

"No, not match, but there's a pattern here. I don't understand it, but I notice it."

"And the numbers you saw?"

"Are the same as those I saw back home in a dream; I realise that now, I didn't make the connection before. But I think they're a continuation of the pattern. There are certain clues, such as recurring numbers and recurring relationships between numbers. Did you ever study thee Fibonacci sequence at school?"

"I doubt my school teachers could spell it, never mind teach it. My school wasn't the best but it was the only one I could attend."

"Well, it's just that sequence one, one, two, three, five, eight..."

"You add the last two numbers together to get the next? Yes, I've seen that but I never knew it had a fancy name!"

"Everything has a fancy name in the world

of scholarship. It's the way scholars make themselves sound good." Addilyn chuckled. "My school was a bit snobbish. You were taught all the academia you would need to go to University, but nothing that would help you in day-to-day-living."

"Oh?"

"I could sew a three-piece suit complete with lining for myself using the latest sewing machine, but I couldn't darn one of your socks."

"I throw my socks out if they gets holes in them."

"And that isn't about to change. Not only do I not know how to darn socks, I don't think I'd particularly like doing it either. Who wants to handle sweaty socks, especially if you have to hold them close to see what you're doing."

"I'd wash them first."

"Too right you would, because I wouldn't. Only holey things that are meant to have holes escape the dustbin if I get my hands on them."

Kaden smiled and regarded Addilyn whilst the road was quiet and he could risk a look at her.

"What?" she asked him.

"You seem in a good mood, that's all."

"I'm always in a good mood. It's just that today I'm in a *particularly* good mood!"

"What's brought that on?"

"Oh, undoubtedly the company."

"Me?"

"No, Shadow." Addilyn felt behind her without looking to locate the dog, who was lying on the back seat quietly dozing, and upon finding his tongue and being licked, she chucked him under the chin. "Of course you! And the fact that I worked out the numbers. And the fact that we're doing something about them."

"I still can't believe it."

"Believe what?"

"That we're embroiled in some plot to destroy the earth, that people around us are being murdered, that we have some sort of alien presence in our midst every now and then that seems to communicate telepathically. I mean, that kind of thing belongs in a sci-fi film, not as a part of the lives of a policeman and a receptionist!"

"And there was I thinking you meant you couldn't believe your luck in finding me! Oh, well, I don't suppose I'm *that* good a catch..."

"Shut up."

"Sorry?"

"You know as well as I do that you're an amazing catch, that I am absolutely gobsmacked to have found you, and that I intend to marry you as soon as we sort this mess out and if the planet survives!"

"Well, that's a bit of an odd proposal but,

okay, I think I can fit you in some Saturday afternoon for a few hours. I'd need to consult my diary as to when, though."

"Fair enough." Kaden paused, then: "Did we just get engaged?" he asked her with a grin.

"Yeah," smiled Addilyn. "I rather think we did!"

*

Leslie had dutifully reported Mollie's find to Dr Steven Calloway, who had taken over Tim's workload until Tim's successor had been decided upon. Leslie had playfully suggested to Mollie that, had it been a wad of paper money instead of boring old figures, they could have run off together; Mollie had been in seventh heaven while her imagination ran wild and she'd decided that if ever she won the lottery, she would hide it in Leslie's drawer, then hold him to his suggestion.

Steven Calloway was now reading the notes and examining the diagram that his colleague Timothy Taylor had produced, and slowly it dawned on him what the numbers were all about. He began to perspire, because if these predictions were correct, they were all in rather a lot of trouble...

He turned to Tim's computer; he would have to check the calculations, just to be doubly sure, before he took the matter to somewhere that could deal with it because it was essential that he was absolutely positive about what would prove to be probably the biggest revelation of the century – no, the millennium – no, actually it was probably the most important discovery in the history of the planet, although the dinosaurs would probably have disagreed had they had brains enough to think about it...

No time for jokes, Calloway chided himself, and he reached out to turn on the computer. Before he could reach the little switch, however, the monitor lit up by itself, and Calloway reasonably assumed that he had inadvertently jolted the machine awake from a 'sleep' or 'standby' mode. Obviously Mollie hadn't bothered pulling the plug, which upon reflection was fair enough; she wouldn't know whether or not they had saved or backed up any information from it – providing that she had even thought of that consideration – so he wouldn't mention it to her, at least not for the time being. She was a good little worker; oh, her head was in the clouds most of the time and she was trying to punch far above her weight with their apprentice Leslie Billinghurst, but with a job as boring as cleaning, his mind would have been away with the fairies too.

Calloway resumed the business in hand

and he pressed the 'enter' button on the keyboard to bring up the password log-in page. Everyone knew everyone else's password for the general site, but there was also a private section of memory in each machine for whatever private data the operator wished to keep there. Calloway wouldn't have tried to break the password code even had he been able to, but as his finger seemed to be glued to the keyboard, he didn't have the opportunity anyway.

Instead of Tim Taylor's workings, however, the rugged (or was it haggard?) face of a youngish man appeared on the screen and he was grinning like a loon, his teeth a dirty cream, his lips chapped and bleeding in places. Calloway was just wondering who the hell he was and what the hell he was doing on the monitor screen when a sudden surge of electricity made the lights flash and at the same time passed through the keyboard and into Calloway's finger. Thereafter it travelled rapidly into and through his body, and he could only react to the overdose of thermionically-charged current that was frying his insides and his outsides by screaming hysterically, which alerted the only other person inside that part of the building at the time.

A few minutes later, with his hair on fire and his skin red and blistering, Calloway mercifully passed from consciousness into the great unknown, and when Mollie Hathaway found him a minute after that, the man on the screen had advanced from grinning to laughing delightedly as though he considered the whole event rather hilarious.

FIFTEEN

The place was in a state of panic when they arrived, some young woman in absolute hysterics outside the main entrance being consoled by the young postgrad who was their tour guide the day before, and as they neared the entrance they could hear commands being barked out by a deep, old-ish voice which, by the sound of the responses of the commandees, was one Professor Bartholomew, although no clue had yet been given as to his first name.

"What's happened?" Kaden was asking as his police training kicked in and he took in as much as he could see for the time being.

The postgrad looked up, and although he recognised Kaden, he didn't mention it at that time.

"There's been another death," he said instead, not even attempting to cover anything up this time. "Tim's co-worker has been electrocuted."

Addilyn overheard that as she closed up on Kaden, but now she was dashing straight past him and into the building which smelled badly of smoke and urine. She put her hand over her nose and mouth and continued forward until she bumped into a short, stout man with a bald head and a beard who could have been a garden gnome as easily as he was a scientist.

"Out of my way!" he snapped irritably, and as Addilyn stepped aside, he brushed past her and hurried along the short corridor and turned into what Addilyn knew was Tim's old office.

Addilyn raced after him and when she turned into the office and saw what was in there, she almost gagged. She managed to keep her breakfast down, however, and merely whispered: "Oh, my dear God!"

"God had nothing to do with this," muttered Bartholomew, then he looked up as he heard approaching footsteps running towards the room. "Dr Billinghurst, is that you?"

"Yes," came a voice, followed momentarily by its owner's body. "And this is Police Constable Kaden Mackenzie."

Addilyn lifted an eyebrow at that, and when he had entered and acknowledged the professor, he glanced at her and shrugged sheepishly. He didn't want any connection made between himself and Tim just yet, and he was sure that Addilyn would realise the fact.

"Well, I don't know what to tell you, sir," said the scientist. "Steven was working in here – one of my colleagues left, you see, and he was just checking that our group records were up-to-date – and the next thing, his screams brought me running. Seems the computer somehow electrocuted the poor old chap, although I don't know how. As you can see, I haven't touched anything so the monitor is still on and it seems to be working perfectly."

Kaden glanced at the computer monitor and froze.

"I think he might have been chatting to someone," explained Bartholomew. "But I think there's some lag because that chap on there has been laughing for ten minutes now."

Kaden glanced over to Addilyn who was standing behind the computer desk.

"What is it?" she asked when she saw the expression on his face and the paleness of his blanched complexion.

"It's Dathan Greenwood," said Kaden.

"You know this man?" asked Bartholomew. "Is he a criminal of some sort?"

"I'm not sure," replied Kaden absently. "He may be involved..."

"Well, if you're not sure, that's going to be a problem, isn't it."

"Not half as big a problem as this," commented Addilyn, and she held up an electrical lead with a plug attached. "This is the mains connection. As you can see, the computer is switched off."

"I doubt that lag could cause a machine to

stay on when the power is cut," commented Bartholomew. "And who are you anyway, madam? I don't recognise you at all!"

"It's nothing to do with lag," replied Addilyn. "And I'm Addilyn Mackenzie."

"Related?" asked Bartholomew.

"Might as well be," responded Addilyn.

And before she could say more, police sirens sounded in the distance, getting closer by the second.

"Ambulance and back-up," said Kaden instinctively.

Bartholomew regarded Kaden with suspicion and was about to say something when Leslie Billinghurst stepped forward and gently suggested that they leave the police and the medics to it.

"The police and their wives," murmured Bartholomew crossly, and as he stormed out of the room, Kaden wasn't sure whether the old man believed him and disapproved of wives being present, or didn't believe him and disapproved of liars being present.

He quickly forgot about feeling guilty when the face on the screen stopped laughing and became deadly serious.

"Kaden Taylor and Addilyn Mackenzie," it snorted derisively. "Fancy seeing you two here!"

*

Josh Greenwood had often wished he lived alone, but now doing whatever he wanted whenever he wanted wasn't quite so appealing as it used to be. Oh, his dad was in the house, but about as much company as a brick; he stayed in his room and didn't, as far as Josh knew, even come out to use the bathroom. He seemed to be constantly asleep. Josh wondered if he were ill, but whenever he knocked his dad's bedroom door (which was locked and goodness knew when Dathan had fixed a bolt because none of the bedroom doors had locks before) he received a somewhat irritable "I'm fine!" followed by silence.

Dathan had never come to Josh after that night, and with the nightmare he had experienced on that occasion, he wasn't totally unhappy about that. He didn't really think his dad would kill him, not deep down, but Dathan had changed ever since Lena died and not at all for the better.

He had always been the loud one to Lena's almost mousy disposition, but she'd seemed to be happy for him to take the initiative and so that was okay. As far as Josh was aware, Dathan had been good to (and for) his mum, and although he had a wandering eye, that was the only part of him that wandered and he'd been faithful right up until – well, until that day he saw Addilyn Mackenzie and the Big Argument (as he always referred to it as) ensued; that was when he began going crazy.

Josh didn't blame Addilyn at all; she was quite a pretty lady and if he'd been older – heck, he didn't need to be older, he appreciated her just fine right now. But he'd heard arguments coming from the bedroom, arguments which suggested to Josh that things in that department weren't as satisfactory as they had been, and Lena sometimes confided in him that Dathan was suggesting preposterous sexual activities which she was repulsed by. Dathan had also sometimes confided in him that his mum was a bit 'plain' in bed, but Josh didn't want to know his parents' difficulties in that regard and the only thing their confidentiality had done was to engender a fear of inadequacy in that part of a relationship which he hadn't even experienced yet. Basically, Josh was terrified of sex before ever he gave it a go.

Josh had to remind himself that that day when Dathan came across Addilyn Mackenzie, his parents had already been throwing insults at one another. He was quite aware that it was normal for mums and dads not to see eye-to-eye all the time, and he also appreciated that Lena could be a little too paranoid on occasion, but he still couldn't shake the feeling that somehow Addilyn

Mackenzie was involved in whatever it was that was turning Dathan Greenwood evil.

Josh switched on the television set and then his x-box. He didn't want to think about adult things any more today.

*

"Right, I went along with your little plan," declared Bartholomew, as he sorted out papers on his vast desk that didn't need sorting at all. "And the only reason I did is because Dr Billinghurst endorsed your credibility. So you'd better tell me whatever it is you have to tell me, and it better be good. Otherwise those police officers will be making a return trip and you, P C Kaden Mackenzie, will not have a job."

"If we don't sort out this little mess," remarked Addilyn. "It won't matter."

"And I assume *you* are not a police officer, or his wife, Miss – it's not 'Mackenzie' too, is it?"

"Yes. No. I mean, I'm Addilyn Mackenzie."

"And I'm Kaden Taylor. I'm a real police constable. I'm also the brother of the late Timothy Taylor."

Martin Bartholomew looked up at that and Kaden fancied he had aged ten years in the past ten seconds. "Tim's brother, eh?"

"Yes."

"I didn't see you at his funeral..."

"I was there, Professor Bartholomew. It's just that I'm not – I don't socialise with the same people as Darcy does."

"Hmm, I don't think many people do. Darcy Allen is a catch all right, but she's an expensive catch and her pals are more for show than for friendship." Bartholomew paused, then: "Very well," he said. "I'll hear what you have to say; impress me."

*

She'd managed to slip off the coach unnoticed, but Marcia still didn't know what she was doing here, and the vast city which was so busy, teeming with all kinds of people, strangers who either ignored her or eyeballed her with suspicion, was frightening. She wished that Daji would come and keep her company and tell her what to do next.

"Hello, young miss," a voice said from behind her.

Marcia turned to see a tall policeman wearing a domed hat which made him look as tall as a giant.

"Where's your mum?" the policeman asked, then: "Or your dad?" he quickly added, politically correctly.

"My dad was meeting a friend but I

loitered and he must have gone on without me," said Marcia.

"Where was he meeting this friend?"

"Burlington House, Piccadilly."

"That's quite a way away. I don't think he'll go that far without you. What car does your dad have?"

"He came on a coach."

"I see. Well, I think he'll be along here somewhere looking for you. Shall we go and see if we can find him?"

"Wouldn't it be better to take me to Burlington House? Then his friend can phone him on his mobile. I don't know the number but his friend will."

"That might be an idea after we've looked for your dad..."

"Okay."

The surprise she felt at answering these questions in the way she did was eclipsed by the relief she felt at having Daji back. She knew he wouldn't be able to stay long, but it was nice to have him if only for a little while.

The policeman offered his hand to Marcia and she took it. She knew they wouldn't find her Larilee because he wasn't here. But to keep the policeman happy, Daji was telling her, it was better to let him think he was doing the right thing. So she was content to put her safety in the hands of the policeman and her destination and subsequent actions in the hands of Daji; all she had to do was go along with it and see what happened next.

*

Don Gittins hadn't noticed the change creeping up on the town until it was almost palpable.

At first he put the quiet down to the time of year – it was still too soon after Christmas to expect substantial orders – but the place seemed eerily silent, as if the inhabitants were staying indoors to hide away from something outside.

Addilyn Mackenzie hadn't been in touch, but he kept up-to-date with the news and a visit to her flat to make sure she was all right had resulted in the old lady downstairs informing him that she had gone down south with her boyfriend and her husband and daughter had traipsed after her. It didn't make much sense but at least he knew that Addilyn was okay. He'd keep the receptionist job for her; he could keep the business going himself for the time being, and when it got busier, he was confident that Addilyn would be back. Besides, if he were being honest with himself, he'd held a candle for her for a very long time, and one of the reasons he'd offered her a job helping him was so that he could see her most days. Not that she would notice him in that way – he was old enough (almost) to be her father – but he was content to admire her from a distance and having her well was far more important to him than having her present.

William Gill had likewise noticed the change, but in a different way.

There had been an increase in crime in the town, mostly related to what he could only assume was some kind of mass drug experiment. People were seeing aliens with glowing eyes, the police reports said, only one or two at first but now getting more frequent. Obviously these citizens had been drinking or smoking or sniffing and were hallucinating; he'd gone out himself to see these aliens, but of course they didn't exist. All he needed to do now was find the source of these recreational medicines and he would hammer the culprit good and proper.

Kaden Taylor hadn't been in touch, but with his brother dying, Gill assumed that he wasn't yet ready to return to work. It wasn't a problem; he'd keep Kaden's job for him because he was a bloody good police officer and Gill had even considered promoting him. For now, however, he'd let the young man grieve until he didn't need to grieve any more and *then* they would discuss the matter.

*

Larry Hodgson found the underground station with little difficulty, boarded the correct underground train with no difficulty at all and vaguely wondered where he was taking himself. He knew when his stop arrived and he knew what exit to take at Green Park station. He knew to turn left when he left the station and left again just past the Burlington Arcade.

All this he knew without knowing it and then he came to the entrance of the Royal Astronomical Society – which made perfect sense to him even without Daji's assistance – which was watched over carefully by two gentlemen, one of whom he would soon discover was the head librarian, the other of whom would shortly introduce himself as an officer of the RAS.

For now, however, they looked like guards and Larry wondered what story he would come up with that would allow him access to see whoever it was he was here to see.

*

They had searched high and low – well, the policeman had searched high and low and Marcia had just tagged along patiently – but the little girl's father was nowhere to be seen. He had paged his superiors, who agreed that taking her to where her father was heading was the best course of action, although the officer was quite surprised that any parent would go off to an appointment when he or she was aware that her offspring was missing and just expect them to have the sense to turn up. After all, it didn't matter how many times you drilled stuff into kids' heads – when the time came to use that information, common sense generally flew out the window and the kid panicked.

At least, that was his experience, but the little girl who was holding onto his hand lightly didn't seemed fazed at all. In fact, he had the distinct impression that she was the one comforting him with her easy grip, rather than the other way round.

She seemed to enjoy the ride to Piccadilly in the police car but not the seat in the back. She hadn't complained at all, but the look of utter disappointment in her eyes had melted his heart and he'd affixed the seatbelt very tightly around her in the front and warned her – with a grin – to keep her hands off the switch which activated the siren. Of course, Marcia flicked it – when she'd glanced at the policeman and received a nod of permission – and she laughed as they overtook everyone and had the roads near enough to themselves.

It wasn't very far but it took them almost twenty minutes even with the siren sporadically going off to aid their progress.

The roads were busy and there were a lot of one-way traffic lanes so they got to their destination via miles of itinerant detours.

When the police officer pulled up outside the Burlington shopping arcade, Marcia found herself looking for Larilee even though she wasn't expecting to find him. She didn't know where he had gone, but she doubted it was here. Maybe if she searched the local public houses...

"Larilee?" she suddenly screamed as she caught sight of him, simultaneously wondering what on earth he was doing here and thanking God that she wasn't in this strange city without someone she knew and trusted. It was all very well for Daji to look after her, but he had a habit of disappearing every so often without notice, and that wasn't very comforting at all.

She clambered out of the police car and ran towards him.

"Oh, there you are!" cried Marcia, running up to him with her arms open for a welcoming and welcome hug. "Larilee!" she shrieked again, genuinely happy to see him but no longer in charge of her own voice. "You haven't seen Uncle Erik already, have you?"

Uncle Erik, mused Larry; so was that who he was here to see? But the name meant nothing to him at all, so he was no better off; Uncle Erik *who*, he wondered.

"No – er – no, not yet," he replied, totally shocked to see Marcia but also relieved at the same time. He didn't like to think of her wandering around this huge city alone. Plus, if she was here, then Daji wasn't far away either, and that was rather reassuring.

"Good," Marcia was saying, "Because I wanted to see him too!"

And with that, she walked up to the librarian, smiled and asked him how his daughter Beth was after her fall from her horse at the weekend. While he was still wondering how the hell a little girl he didn't think he'd ever seen before knew about that, Marcia strode right past him through the library to a door at the back which she knocked twice then entered without being invited. Larry was close on her heels, realising that he needed to take advantage if the opportunity created by the attention-diverting tactic that he had no doubt they owed to Daji, and the next thing he knew he was facing a very important-looking, middle-aged man with a monocle who was sitting behind a vast oak desk. He had been reading but now he looked up at the two newcomers with a mixture of annoyance and curiosity.

SIXTEEN

Dr Martin Bartholomew hadn't said anything for five minutes, which was the length of time since Kaden had completed his narrative. He appreciated that the scientist would need time to digest it all, but he wished Bartholomew would just say *something*, even if it were to express total disbelief at what he considered a load of science fiction claptrap.

He shot a glance at Addilyn who just shrugged. Neither of them knew what was going through the scientist's mind, so they could do nothing but wait. Even Leslie Billinghurst, who was more prone to suspending credulity than Bartholomew by virtue of his younger age if nothing else, had found it hard to swallow when Kaden had given him the low down outside, but then again Leslie Billinghurst had started to suspect something fishy as soon as he'd been ordered to lie about Timothy Taylor's absence, both from work and from the world at large.

Now they were all standing, sitting or leaning in silence, all eyes on Martin Bartholomew as the most senior member of staff to see what he would do next.

He stayed silent for a minute longer, then let out a long sigh.

"Well, I suppose it had to happen one day,"

he said.

Kaden glanced at Addilyn and they'd both visibly relaxed at the confirmation that Bartholomew seemed to believe them.

"I saw the figures," Bartholomew continued, looking at Leslie Billinghurst, perhaps because he thought the young man was the only other one present who would actually understand his reasoning. "The first set are most definitely co-ordinates and the second set is a sequence of equations that describe the course for a projectile that might wish to land on whatever it is out there. But the second set is incomplete. Without them it would be impossible to send up anything in time."

"Couldn't we work them out again?" asked Billinghurst.

"No time. Obviously Tim had been working on these for a while and they are based on a launch within the next fourteen days, the window necessary to ensure success. Of the launch, that is. The missing figures are alternative values depending on what day that launch is."

Addilyn and Kaden exchanged glances again. Both knew all too well that you didn't just launch a spacecraft when you felt like it; there were a million and one things to do on the theoretical side before ever you began to even build the thing. Fourteen days was simply not enough.

"So that's it, then," said Addilyn.

"Not necessarily." He picked up the telephone receiver from the old-fashioned telephone that he insisted on keeping on his desk, as if in rebellion against modern mobiles which were ergonomical but hardly attractive. "I'm going to phone a friend of mine, Dr Erik Croptom, at the RAS. I need some advice and some justification for what I think I have to do."

Bartholomew dialled a number and waited only a couple of seconds; the phone at the other end was answered almost immediately. Bartholomew proceeded to outline what Kaden had told him without preamble, then concluded with: "There you have it, Erik. Laugh if you like but I think it might be genuine."

"*I seem to be ahead of you,*" said Croptom. "*I have two people here who are telling me a similar story.*"

Bartholomew covered the mouthpiece, and to Kaden he said: "There are two people with Dr Erik Croptom now who apparently corroborate your story to a quite high degree."

"Who are they?" asked Kaden.

Bartholomew asked the question.

"*An elderly gentleman named Lawrence Hodgson and his daughter Marcia. It's funny, but the young girl seems to know more than the old chap.*"

Bartholomew relayed the information.

"Okay," said Kaden. "Well, tell him to tell them that we'll take it from here. There's little they can do. I wonder why they were even involved in the first place."

"Back up?" suggested Addilyn. "In case we failed?"

Bartholomew was about to relay what Kaden said again, then he handed the mobile to Kaden.

"Here, you talk to Erik directly," he said. "I now have things to do other than act as a conduit for your messages." He got up from his desk and gestured for Kaden to sit in his place. "I always knew this day could come, but by God I never thought it'd be in my lifetime..."

"Can I assist?" asked Billinghurst.

"No, thank you, Leslie," Bartholomew replied. "It's just calculations, which it would be awkward for two to share. Then I must contact Jodrell and see what they can do. We have to confirm what Tim seems to have known, and if he's right, we have to stop it."

"Do you think those other scientists – the ones who died – knew about it too?" asked Billinghurst.

"You mean, were they killed?" asked Bartholomew.

Leslie nodded.

"But that suggests an underlying intelligence." It was more a warning than a disagreement.

Leslie nodded again.

Bartholomew sighed and nodded.

"Undoubtedly they were murdered, my dear boy," he said at length. "But at a time when the whole world stands to suffer, a handful of lives don't really matter, do they...?"

*

Kaden was beginning to regret using his car and didn't blame Addilyn for refusing to drive one little bit. The traffic was ridiculous in this city where feet and wheels vied for space on the road, of which there was very little for either. One-way systems sent him to the moon and back before he got to where they were heading, and by the time he pulled up outside the impressive archway of Burlington House, his nerves were in shreds and his temper frayed.

Outside waiting for them were Larry, holding tight the hand of Marcia. She was giggling about something and generally giving the impression that she was very happy to be with her Larilee again; she also gave the impression that she didn't really understand what was going on and was oblivious of the potential future – or rather, the lack of one.

While Kaden was positioning the car where it would create the least obstacle, Addilyn got out and hurried over to where the old man and his adopted daughter were standing. Marcia turned when Larry lifted his hand to wave and she saw with much surprise and not much less glee who was coming towards her.

"*Addilyn*!" Marcia almost screeched the name and ran into Addilyn like a junior scrum half, nearly knocking her off her feet. "I've missed you so much!"

"And I missed you too," Addilyn replied, managing to keep her balance and hugging the little girl as if they had not set eyes on each other for years. Then she looked over Marcia's head to Larry. "Hi," she smiled.

"Hello, lass," Larry Hodgson smiled back. "Fancy seeing you here."

"Fancy you *being* here," Addilyn commented. "Do you know what's going on?"

"I have a fair idea. I don't understand the details – I'm as technically minded as a banana – but if you mean … well, yes, I'm aware of that."

Addilyn nodded and understood; Larry knew the seriousness of the situation but he didn't want to worry Marcia, who had been operating under Daji's control – and protection – since she'd left home. Even now she wasn't as shocked as she should have been to find herself here and Addilyn silently thanked Daji for maintaining the security.

You are welcome, said a voice in Addilyn's head. *But we must hurry.*

"We have a fortnight," muttered Addilyn, and seeing Kaden's querying expression she shrugged and added: "Sorry, thinking out loud."

You have a fortnight to get it off the ground, Daji continued, *but I do not have a fortnight before...*

The explosion cut him off short, and Addilyn, Kaden, Larry and Marcia, along with everyone around them, looked to see where the sound had come from.

*

"Now, where did Timothy keep his – ah, I see."

Martin Bartholomew had been talking to himself this past half hour while he used Tim's computer to verify this, compare that, estimate the other. Timothy Taylor's data was correct but it wasn't complete. There was a section missing that looked as if someone had cut out with a pair of rusty scissors; either that or Taylor had put a hot cup of coffee on top of them and he didn't think *that* was very likely. It looked like deliberate sabotage and if he'd seen Kaden's copy he would have been sure of the fact because the dirty ring mark and missing section that was identical.

As he was concentrating on a particularly complicated equation, he heard the door open but he ignored it for the time being; it was probably Leslie Billinghurst, either with another offer of assistance or, more helpfully, a strong cup of coffee.

"I won't be a minute," he called over his shoulder without turning. "I just need to express these equations."

There was no reply but suddenly the chair he was sitting in was lifted and turned in one graceful movement and he was sitting facing a man with a face like thunder who was also grinning insanely. Bartholomew recognised him as the chap on this very computer monitor after Steven Calloway had been killed.

"We desperately need to talk," growled Dathan Greenwood.

And even though he wanted to scream, Martin Bartholomew found that he had no voice.

*

It turned out to be nothing.

At least, it turned out to be nothing associated with the matter in hand. They would later learn that it was a microwave oven exploding in the restaurant over the road – someone decided to try and microwave with silver foil covering a dish – and no-one was hurt, apart from the junior cook who took a dent to his pride.

Addilyn, Kaden, Larry and Marcia were now sitting in a nearby caf□, the three adults drinking coffee and Marcia with a banana milkshake which was so thick that she could stand her straw up in it.

"I honestly thought that was the RAS," Kaden said with a nervous laugh.

"So did I," agreed Addilyn. "I suppose we're going to have to learn that not *everything* bad that happens is anything to do with this." She paused, then: "Still, I hope there were no casualties in that restaurant."

"We'll read about it tomorrow, I'm sure," said Kaden.

"I'm still not sure what's going on," said Larry. "I've got an idea but I don't have the whole picture."

"Maybe it's better that way," sighed Kaden.

"And besides, now isn't really the time to talk about it," added Addilyn, casting her eyes to where Marcia was still amused by the erect straw in her milkshake.

"Oh, don't mind me," Marcia said, turning to Addilyn and smiling sweetly. "Daji explained it all to me a long time ago."

"Well, I wish he'd explained it all to me!" Addilyn erupted.

Kaden shot a glance at Addilyn which warned her not to attract attention to their little group. He added a smile and a wink to convey that he wasn't annoyed, just concerned.

"So what did he tell you?" he asked the child.

"That something is coming that could possibly destroy our planet and that we must stop it," replied Marcia, simply. "That's what you and Addie are doing, and all the clever men you've been visiting. Daji is helping too so I'm not worried because I know you can do it."

"Is that all?" asked Addilyn.

"That's enough," said Marcia. "I couldn't understand about all the deaths and the betrayals and everything else."

Addilyn and Kaden realised immediately that Daji was speaking now.

"So we stand a good chance of succeeding?" Kaden sought reassurance because it would be a comforting thing to have.

"Succeeding at what?" asked Marcia. "What are trying to do?"

"It seems that your little friend has gone again," observed Larry.

"He didn't want to reassure us because he

doesn't know whether or not we can pull it off," sighed Kaden.

"Or else he knows humans well enough to realise that they get lazy and careless when they think they're going to win," pointed out Larry. "But I'm more concerned with us. It seems that whoever has knowledge of the imminent danger gets removed."

"But it's also anyone who can do something about it," said Addilyn as the idea suddenly crossed her mind. "They were all scientists, people who knew what they were talking about. We all know and we're all still here."

"We're also the only ones to have Daji," pointed out Kaden. "If his protection is somehow removed..."

"So," said Larry. "Essentially, this little creature or whatever he is, by getting us involved he's actually putting us in potential danger. Even Marcia."

"Yes," said Kaden. "But he's also helping us. We would never have got as far as we have without his help."

"Do you think he knows who is trying to stop us from saving ourselves?" asked Larry.

"I would have thought so," said Kaden. "But I can't be sure. There are too many unknown factors. I don't know who's trying to stop us. I don't know what Daji is, I don't know if they're even linked, although it stands to reason they will be."

"Then you two *are* in danger," said Larry, "And so are Marcia and I."

"We're in danger anyway," said Addilyn. "At the end of the day, if this thing goes ahead, we'll all be – "

"Yes, quite," Larry interrupted her, lest Marcia started understanding too much. "So, what can I do?"

"Nothing, Larry," said Kaden. "You've done enough. And you have a wife at home and a little girl here who need to be looked after."

"I'm not so little!" commented Marcia.

"No. No, you're not," Kaden smiled, not adding that he thought it would be a pity if she never got any bigger...

"Right, well, we'll be going then," Larry said. "I'll take the lass back home and we'll wait to hear from you."

"I think that'd be for the best," confirmed Kaden. "Er, are you okay for money?"

"Enough to last," said Larry. "At least until we get back."

The old man stood and Kaden stood with him.

"You tread carefully," said Larry and offered Kaden his hand to shake.

Kaden was about to take it, then he stepped forward and took the old man in a bear hug.

"I do hope I get the chance to know you

better," he whispered.

"You will," smiled Larry; but while his voice declared it, his eyes clearly shared their doubts. Then: "Come on, Marcia, we're going to get a bus back up to Josie," he smiled, offering her his hand which she took happily. "And tomorrow I'm going to take you both shopping for new clothes!"

Addilyn and Kaden watched them go, then sat back down again.

"Shopping for new clothes," sighed Addilyn. "When there might not be any time to enjoy them..."

"Well, why not!" said Kaden. "There won't be any time to use unspent money either..."

*

There wasn't even a sound to alert anyone that there might be something wrong.

And the fact that he was wishing there were probably said more about him than he realised.

Dathan Greenwood was having fun, that was for sure, but he wasn't *enjoying* having fun. That little piece of his mind that he still retained, independent of whatever it was that controlled the vast majority of his brain, knew that what he was doing – what he had done, what he would no doubt do in the future – was not right, was in fact utterly *wrong*, but – oh, boy, the feeling he got as a reward for completing a mission was better than climaxing while doing certain things to someone that Lena would never have allowed! They were just to damned good to let go, so he went about doing these things, knowing that they were wrong, but anticipating the almost immediate reward much more keenly than dreading the eventual retribution.

When people were scared of him, he felt powerful. No-one had ever been scared of old Dathan Greenwood. He was a bit of a lad, but generally speaking he was harmless because he didn't have the brains to be anything else. He had a high sex drive and a low ambition. He could be found in the pub a million times more often than in the library. And while he wouldn't hardly lift an arm to help someone unless there was money in it, he found lifting an arm in order to get a beer glass to his lips absolutely no problem at all. It was these characteristics that made Lena think she had a right to dictate their partnership, as if he should be grateful that he had her and Josh. But he'd loved Josh far more than he'd ever loved Lena, and if he thought about it, Josh was probably the only reason he stuck around with Lena for as long as he did. He was a crap husband, then, but a pretty awesome dad.

Martin Bartholomew was visibly shaking and Dathan liked that he must look threatening, a force to be dealt with. He had spent thirty-seven years being told what to do, put upon by Lena for the past decade (and not even something a little out-of-the-ordinary at bedtime for his trouble) and by and large made to feel like he didn't matter. Now, though, he mattered a lot. When he walked up to someone, that someone took notice of *him* and he supposed that that feeling was almost as great as the physical one that always followed the successful completion of one of these 'missions'. He hadn't ever failed one either – being a bully seemed to sit well with Dathan – but he had idly wondered what would happen if he did, just on one or two occasions. Would the pain be as excruciating as the pleasure was immense? He shrugged mentally; it didn't matter because he didn't intend to fail.

Who it was controlling him, Dathan had no idea, and when they weren't controlling him he realised that he didn't like that they did, but when they did, he liked that they did even more. Sometimes, he thought, it was much better just to sit back and go with the flow; he didn't have a mind for much more consideration of problems than that anyway, which actually was probably one of the reasons he had been chosen, although of course that idea had never crossed Dathan's mind, nor would it in a month of Sundays.

Dathan was now lowering his head so that Bartholomew could see his eyes. He had an hand on either side of the old man, leaning on the arms of the chair so that the scientist was trapped and couldn't get out of the chair unless Dathan let him up. Which obviously Dathan wasn't about to do. The man tried to call out, but no sound came out of his throat. Dathan had ensured that he couldn't speak, at least not right then. When he wanted the man to speak, he'd be able to speak, but for now he was content to play around with the old sod and put the fear of – whoever – into him.

For a few minutes, he kept the old man frozen to the chair, then stood up straight so that Bartholomew could move if he so wished. Dathan kept an eye on the old sod just in case he tried to do a runner, but now it seemed the scientist had got the unspoken message that intimated the threat of some unexplained horror should he try to escape, and so Bartholomew remained seated in a self-inflicted paralysis.

That delighted Dathan Greenwood, because he didn't have to actually *hurt* anyone to frighten them. There was enough of the independent Dathan left that knew that inflicting actual injury on a person was quite wrong, and he was relieved that all that had been required of him was menace. He wasn't sure he could perform any act of violence, not only because he knew it was wrong but also because he feared recriminations from the police and such authoritative bodies; he didn't want to lose his freedom but he didn't want to lose this status either. But, luckily, he'd only been required to scare, and he was very good at that, which was why he never failed.

"Why are you doing this?" Bartholomew asked at length, daring to speak – *able* to speak – but not daring to move even though he could if he so wished.

Dathan thought about that question and realised that, in truth, he couldn't answer; or if he were to answer, he would have to say that he did it because of the wonderful feeling it gave him, even if he had no idea why he felt that way. He was pretty sure that his fetishes didn't extend as far as erotophonophilia, so it had to be coming from somewhere else, though God knew where.

Suddenly his head started throbbing and he felt himself cross the room to Tim Taylor's desk where he opened a drawer and took out a letter opener. This doesn't look good, he thought; what the hell am I supposed to do with this?

Insert it in the human's body at any point that guarantees death, said a voice in his head. *You will be rewarded greatly for this!*

"But you said I wouldn't need to hurt anyone," protested Dathan. "At least, not much anyway!"

The first time is the hardest. Once you have done it, it gets easier.

"And you'd know, right?"

Absolutely right. Now go and do as we ask.

"No," Dathan said to the ceiling, not sure how the voices were going to take the refusal. "I don't want to kill. I *won't* kill. You said I wouldn't have to!"

So, you fail us for the first time. The voice in his head was more taken aback than angry.

"I can – I will – do anything you say, but – please – not murder."

The laughter rang out in his brain then, echoing around his skull and his vision began to blur. He felt as if he were going to made to do it, and the tiny bit of Dathan Greenwood's will that still belonged exclusively to him, made the effort to fight the impulse to stab the old man where he sat.

But instead, Dathan was allowed to stagger away from Martin Bartholomew, trembling outside and in as if he, Dathan, were the one being threatened, and as he backed up towards the door, he pointed a shaking letter opener at the old man.

"You *dare* solve those equations," Dathan snarled, stabbing the air with the letter opener's blade to reinforce the point, "And you won't live to regret it!"

Bartholomew had watched the scene with dread; the man was obviously psychopathically crazy, which had petrified him more because there was no way to reason with people like that, and, terrified as he was, in spite of Dathan's refusal to kill him, Martin Bartholomew totally believed that at some other time, Dathan could and would do it...

*

Larry sat in the aisle seat so that Marcia could have the window to look out of. He'd bought her some sweets and a couple of small bottles of lemonade – there was a toilet on the coach and while it wasn't very pleasant, he'd noted, it was at least usable – but he had no doubt that she'd get bored before she fell asleep. He'd offered to get her a comic, but she didn't want one. Nor a magazine, nor a book. She did ask him for a postcard, however, and now she was examining the three-for-a-pound trio that she'd chosen: one of Big Ben and the Houses of Parliament, one of the River Thames and the London Eye, and one an aerial view of a good portion of London, which she 'd decided was probably her favourite.

Larry smiled as he watched Marcia still enjoying what was to her a great adventure, until gradually his eyes closed and he began to snore gently. Marcia was glued to the scenery outside – lots of red buses, lots of black taxicabs, peculiar-looking statues in the ……… centre of the road? And so many people! Marcia wasn't sure if she would ever come here again, but she sure hoped she did!

And she was so intent on making the most of being here right now that she didn't notice the light that crept up Larry's leg like a .gunsight light … seeking its target and eventually disappearing into Larry's open mouth, where it suddenly blinked out as if Larry had swallowed it.

*

Martin Bartholomew gave himself a good brush off mentally and tried to pretend that what had just happened had been nothing more than – what? A daydream? Might as well have been, because saying that a man really came in here and threatened his life made even less sense. On reflection, it seemed almost ridiculous; surely his imagination was running away with him? He must have fallen asleep, that was it, and this business, coupled with the image of that chap on Tim's computer monitor, triggered off a series of illusions which his mind released as a safety-valve and, naturally, being intelligent, the dream was so lifelike, he'd thought it'd actually happened! Yes, that was the explanation; much more commonsensical than the idea that his life had just been threatened, silly old bugger that he was!

Silly old dead bugger if you touch those figures...

The voice penetrated Bartholomew's thoughts like a knife, and although it wasn't the voice of the young man he'd just dreamed about, it was just as menacing, if not more so.

"Okay, okay," he muttered to no-one. "I'll leave them be."

And with that, he gathered the papers together untidily, stuffed them in a large envelope, and sealed the flap. It wasn't much of a safeguard but it was indicative of his willingness to comply. Chances were they wouldn't be able to pull it off anyway, he tried to convince himself – although he wasn't buying that excuse at all.

*

Addilyn and Kaden arrived back at the RAS library an hour later, Kaden swearing about the London traffic under his breath, Addilyn clearly desperate to get on the road – though whether to be getting on with saving the world or to be getting out of London, Leslie Billinghurst wasn't sure. She was marginally more cheerful than was Kaden, but both were clearly drained, both physically and mentally. He suggested they stay overnight somewhere and get an early start after something to eat and some sleep, but they both insisted that they needed to get going.

"*Tempus fugit*," said Addilyn. "And we don't have time for *tempus* to be *fugitting*!"

She smiled lamely at Leslie, and he smiled back, appreciating her attempt at joviality which, whilst being most admirable, was being most equally as unsuccessful.

He led them both down the short corridor where Tim's room lay to the right, and then turned left down another, slightly longer one, to where a door on the left some halfway down announced Dr Martin Bartholomew 's abode. He knocked, opened the door when invited to, and left them to it.

"Just keep in touch," he whispered as Addilyn walked in and he had Kaden to himself for a moment.

"I will," Kaden promised, then he too walked into the room, glancing back as the door behind him clicked shut.

"Right!" said Bartholomew without preamble. "I've put some recommendations in this here package with the figures, and the amendments and additions I've made." Martin Bartholomew handed Kaden a large sealed envelope which was bulky and rather heavy.

"A lot of recommendations from the weight of it," Kaden smiled.

"It's an important matter," snapped Bartholomew.

"Okay, okay, I was only trying to relieve some of the tension!" Kaden passed the envelope to Addilyn. "I know it's an important matter and I'm grateful for your help, because God knows, those numbers made no sense whatsoever to me."

"It's sealed," remarked Addilyn. "Any reason?"

"Your young man just said you didn't understand any of it," pointed out Bartholomew. "Were you going to take it out and read it on the way up even though you know you'll never make head nor tail of it?"

"Professor Bartholomew, if I wanted to read it I would simply break the seal," pointed out Addilyn. "I was just making an observation, not accusing you."

"I'm sorry." Martin Bartholomew came around his desk and offered his hand to Kaden, who shook it warmly. "I suppose it was a futile attempt at hiding it from you, as if that would do any good. All this is really getting to me. It's hard to accept that you could be dead within the month if things don't work out, but it's a distinct possibility. It's also hard to accept that you could be dead within the hours if you try and do something about it. I suppose that's the trouble with us scientific gurus – we don't believe in anything supernatural, no life in the hereafter, and dead is dead and no question for us. It's just not something I enjoy contemplating."

"It's not enjoyable for any of us," replied Kaden. "But the quicker we get these data to Jodrell, the quicker they can start working on a solution. Stay close to the phone tomorrow, Professor; if they don't phone you first thing, I most certainly will."

"Thank you." Martin Bartholomew managed a weak smile but the moment Addilyn and Kaden had left the room, the smile vanished and an angry scowl replaced it. If looks could kill, the glance he'd just thrown at the two young people would definitely have proved fatal.

Just outside the door, Leslie Billinghurst, who was waiting to bid Addilyn and Kaden farewell and safe journey, noticed the change in his boss's expression and alarm bells immediately sounded in his head. It would have been understandable had the old man regarded them sadly, hopefully, gratefully, even pityingly; but the look of sheer hatred on Martin Bartholomew's face did not bode well with Leslie Billinghurst at all.

SEVENTEEN

Kaden had suggested to Addilyn that they return to the hotel and have a meal before they set out back up north, but Addilyn had looked at him incredulously and asked: "Do you seriously have an appetite?"

"No, not really," he'd replied. "But bodies need sustenance or else they don't function properly."

"And the chaps at Jodrell need these figures." Addilyn lifted the padded envelope and waved it. "Otherwise none of us will be functioning at all!"

And so they'd compromised by skipping the meal but stocking up on bottled water, fruit and a couple of packs of sandwiches each, and vowing to stop later on at a service station for something a bit more substantial. Addilyn was so keen to get going that she didn't even ask the owner for a refund from the full week accommodation she'd paid for her room at the inn.

Kaden volunteered to drive first and Addilyn was more than pleased to comply. She was tired as well as restless and she didn't deem herself psychologically competent enough to drive in London; already she had sworn at a cyclist and shouted unmentionable descriptions at a black taxi cab driver who had cut out in front of them, only to turn off the road again some twenty yards later. Kaden had chuckled both times and when Addilyn shot him the most annoyed glances ever, he chuckled even more. She'd be sure that, had she not loved him so much, she'd have seriously fallen out with him.

"So are you tempted to open that?" Kaden asked now.

"Not much point," shrugged Addilyn, knowing that the 'that' being referred to was the bulk of papers that Martin Bartholomew had given them. "As Dr Bartholomew correctly pointed out, I wouldn't have a clue what they meant."

"I thought you might memorise them," Kaden commented.

"I don't memorise anything," replied Addilyn. "Some part of my brain somehow works out a relationship between them that constitutes a sequence, but if I can't remember what triggered the reason my brain needed to work out the relationship in the first place, I don't recall the numbers. It's sort of like setting the mental ball rolling, but whilst other people can stop thinking things whenever they want to, sometimes I can't and they continue uncontrolled. Stupid, eh?"

"No, it's not stupid at all."

"Well, *I* think it is. I mean, the whole OCD thing is stupid."

"You have OCD?"

"I thought you realised that."

"I knew you had a – problem – but I wasn't sure quite exactly what it was."

"Well, it's OCD and sometimes when it gets bad, it can be debilitating. So, you gone off me now?"

"Not a chance. Tell me more about the numbers."

"Well, the forming of a sequence is a very complex way of coping with the stupid OCD. I had to devise an equation to use when the compulsion threatened to become too much. I used to call it a compulsion equation but now I just call it an equasion with an 's'."

"It's just as well you're intelligent then," observed Kaden. "Someone else with the same type of OCD – "

"Would come up with some way to cope with it that suited the particular individual," finished Addilyn. "There's a little fraction of the brain hell bent on survival and maintaining sanity, and even if it can't completely override the illogic of the disease, it can offer an escape clause, a sort of exhaust valve to cope when things get too frustrating, when there's an overload of compulsory flotsam."

"Gee, ain't brains great?" Kaden winked at her to show he meant no offence; it was a habit of his to make light of things he didn't really comprehend.

"Mine ain't!" Addilyn replied in an equally light-hearted tone that suggested that she wasn't quite as annoyed with hers as she sometimes claimed. "But seriously, Kaden, if you find it too much to deal with, I'll understand."

Kaden remained silent, but indicated left and pulled the car up at the earliest opportunity, switching off the car engine before he turned to face her and looked her directly in the eyes.

"Addilyn, I'll say this once and once only, and my words will remain the case for the rest of our lives together: one, I will never find your OCD and any related problems too much to deal with; two, if I don't understand quite what you're going through then I will expect you to tell me so that I *can* understand what you're going through; and three, your OCD is part of someone I happen to love with all my heart and therefore, as a part of that someone I love with all my heart, I love your OCD with all my heart too. I won't run at the first little obstacle, at the first silly argument, even at the first *serious* argument, so forget whoever hurt you in the past because I'm not them. When you're ready you'll tell me, but until you're ready, just rest assured that you're stuck with me for a very, very long time."

Tears welled up in Addilyn's eyes, and she smiled and nodded before leaning over to kiss

Kaden's lips very gently.

"Thank you," she whispered, and she didn't add that they might not *have* a very, very long time together. She thought it, though, and she guessed that Kaden did too, but neither of them was prepared to spoil the beautiful moment, especially when further beautiful moments were not at all guaranteed.

*

Marcia wondered how she coped on the way down being cooped up for so many hours because the journey, if she were honest with herself, was just plain *boring.* There was nothing to see out of the window except lots of cars on a motorway that was the same mile after mile after mile, and although she was tired she couldn't settle enough to sleep because her seat wasn't that comfortable and anyway the coach was jiggling about and it was too bumpy for her to relax.

Not like Larrilee, who was fast asleep and gently snoring; not loud enough to annoy other passengers but loud enough so that Marcia knew she wasn't alone, and that was rather comforting. She would have appreciated someone to talk to though, and she regarded her Larrilee and tried to formulate a way of waking him that wouldn't seem like her fault, but then she dismissed the idea as being totally selfish. Larrilee was older, a *lot* older than she was and he needed his rest. She was quite capable of keeping herself amused and if she were bored, well, live with it, she told herself. It wasn't the end of the world.

Just as she was about to turn back to the window, Larry snorted and as Marcia turned to smile at him, even though he wouldn't know she was smiling at him, she noticed two little lights escaping his open mouth, and her heart raced excitedly.

"Daji?" she cried, quietly but forcefully.

No, NOT your Daji!

The voice – voices, there were two of them in perfect synchronisation, she realised – sounded sharp, strict, angry, and as Marcia watched the little spots of gold flicker up to the top of the coach and out of it completely, she began to cry as if thoroughly scolded.

*

"I wish you would stop *bothering* me!"

Leslie Billinghurst shrugged the outburst off as he'd shrugged off a dozen such outbursts this morning since Addilyn Mackenzie and Kaden Taylor had left the observatory. For some reason, Martin Bartholomew was in a foul mood and he could only put it down to the stress the old man felt at the prospect of the world ending, which was of course an excellent reason to be angry and worried, but not for him.

Leslie Billinghurst no longer feared death. Oh, he had done, as most people do, when he reached an age when he realised that he wasn't immortal after all, which was around fourteen after his beloved grandmother had died and he realised that human beings were finite, but since then he had received confirmation that death was not the end.

It had been on his twentieth birthday. He'd been celebrating end-of-year exam success, and coupled with the big two-oh festivities, he had drunk far too much and should never have tried to cross the road when he couldn't focus on anything and so wasn't sure whether any traffic were coming or not. He stupidly decided to take a risk and dashed out of the shelter afforded by the canopy outside the wine bar into the dark, rainy night and had almost got halfway across the seemingly deserted road when he felt an agonising pain in his left side and was vaguely aware of someone screaming, before he blacked out completely for – apparently – several days.

There was no tunnel. It was dark, but he felt aware and the darkness was comforting, relaxing, rather than frightening or disorientating. Then, when the eyes that he didn't have adjusted to the lack of illumination, he began to see small lights, little golden orbs that sparkled against the background blackness like a myriad of little stars or Christmas fairy lights. They bobbed too, the little lights, as if they were on springs, dancing in a kind of synchronised routine that made him smile with lips that he didn't have.

Then he heard a voice, or rather his brain identified a voice within itself: "Hello," it said. Nothing else, nothing grand, nothing revelationary, just "hello" and if he had been able to, he would have laughed. Instead, however, he wondered how to reply with no vocal chords and no throat when suddenly he heard the sound, or rather his brain identified a voice within itself that sounded very much like his, which said "hello" back.

The simplicity of it was charming, and the fact that he found himself wondering why he had expected anything else was silly. Suddenly it was clear to him that nothing was complicated, that humans just made things complicated by trying to find too much hidden meaning in everything. He wondered why he hadn't realised it before: all that love of money, love of power, love of authority, it was so finite, so inappurtenant, so inconsequential...

Enough. The voice sounded in his head, loud, strong, authoritative. *Think no more, realise no more. Or else you cannot go back.*

Go back? The question was aimed more at his own self than anyone else's, and his first reaction was astonishment at the thought that he *could* go back.

Sometimes it is necessary. Sometimes it is not necessary but it happens anyway.

But he didn't *want* to go back! He realised now what it was all about back there and he didn't want a part of it! He wanted to stay here where it was cosy, straightforward.

"I don't want to go back!" he moaned. "Please, I don't *want* to go back!"

"Shh, now," said a soft, female voice that belonged to an A&E nurse attending him. "You're in hospital, Mr Billinghurst and you're going to be fine."

*

They found the little caf□ which was off the beaten track near the opening of a bottleneck formed by the curvature of the River Severn totally by accident, but it was one of those accidents that was propitious and lucky because they also allowed dogs, something Addilyn had not found so commonplace outside of Cumbria. Furthermore, although they had missed breakfast time at the small restaurant, the proprietors were happy to accommodate their request for two full Englishes because, they explained, they cooked everything from fresh as ordered anyway. So the wait might be a little longer than in some other establishments, but it would be worth it.

And it was. The plate in front of each of them was as much a delight from a visionary aspect as it would prove to be from a culinary aspect; the food was hot, the eggs runny where they should be and solid where they shouldn't, the aroma was appetising and the plates were full. What was more, Shadow had his own paper plate of three sausages, a spoonful of beans and another spoonful of scrambled eggs.

"Well, our canine companions need a good start to the day just as much as we humans do," remarked the owner's wife, and the way Shadow tucked into his breakfast, the dog obviously agreed.

Kaden, meanwhile, smiled at Addilyn who smiled back, both silently acknowledging that they were absolutely ready for this food.

"Well, we're halfway," commented Kaden, pausing for a sip of freshly-ground coffee and a rest to allow what he had consumed to go down. "Another hour, hour and half should do it."

"We could have done it in one go," pointed out Addilyn. "Only two and a half hours."

"What, and miss *this?*" Kaden pointed at his half-empty plate with his fork.

"It is rather delicious," admitted Addilyn. "I was hungrier than I thought."

Kaden nodded and began eating again.

"Maybe," said Addilyn a few minutes and two sausages later, "I should open the envelope Bartholomew gave us, primarily because we don't know who to contact when we get to Jodrell."

"I see no harm in it," shrugged Kaden. "We've already seen what Tim wrote, and if there's anything secret about what Bartholomew's added, well, I think we've earned the right to be privy to it."

"Not to mention that it might not even matter in the long run."

"Don't go there. We'll find a way – all of us, I mean, not just you and me. Bartholomew, Billinghurst, the Jodrell chaps, anyone else they think should get involved. We're not totally without our resources."

"Forever the optimist," chuckled Addilyn, smiling.

"And not a cocked eye in sight!" retorted Kaden, and he was smiling too.

*

Not only was Leslie Billinghurst fine, he was considered a miracle by the hospital staff whose experience in such cases as his had suggested that he wouldn't last the night. And he *had* died, the machine print-outs attested to that, as would have Leslie Billinghurst himself if he weren't suppressing the reality of the experience and attributing it all to an elaborate dream. Yet here he was, left leg in plaster, right arm in plaster, a black eye, a thick lip and he feeling sorry for himself because of the rotten hangover he had (as if the former problems were not enough) but definitely and very much alive.

"You must feel so blessed!" enthused another nurse, this one employed on the ward that he now inhabited. "You're obviously a tough 'un, either that or God hasn't finished with you just yet!"

"Gaaagh," replied Leslie. "With a head like I've got, oblivion might well be preferable..."

"*Leslie Billinghurst, don't you DARE!*"

The voice was harsh, cross, admonishing, and his grandmother's; it was this latter realisation that bothered him more than anything else. His eyes snapped wide open and he stared ahead, blinking several times because his grandmother just could *not* be standing at the bottom of his bed, her arms crossed over her ample bosom, a scowl on her face, and a foot tapping on the ward linoleum that he couldn't see but he just knew her right leg would be patting the ground, the same as it always had done. Around her head, however, tiny golden dust motes caught the light and sparkled while they moved, and Leslie had a vague recollection of having seen them in his dream, although already the details were fading into obscurity.

"You won't remember them, but you'll remember me!" his grandmother said, stiffly.

"Grandma?" His voice was small, and he felt small too. She had always been an intimidating woman, his grandmother, one of the old school who did not suffer fools or silly grandchildren gladly; indeed she thought the latter part of the former and had treated them as such. This resulted in very well-behaved children around her who asked 'how high' when she said 'jump' and who for some reason loved her more than any other children could possibly love *their* grandmothers.

"Never wish you were dead, Leslie Billinghurst!" Her voice had softened now but he could tell that she was still angry with him. He rationalised her anger as a part of his own guilt at not being thankful that he did indeed survive a bad accident, and he wondered if there would be any permanent damage to a brain that could conjure up such imaginative reveries.

"I'll 'dream' you, my young man – "

Yes, he remembered those words; with other verbs of course, according to the situation, but her tellings-off nearly always started with –

"Leslie, if you want to think of me as a dream, feel free to do so."

Now her voice was so calm and caring that he *knew* he was dreaming.

"There's no pleasing you, is there?" She chuckled, then: "Remember me however you wish, remember me not at all even, but remember well these words of advice: get yourself well, get yourself a degree, get yourself a good job and do your best to make a difference. You have a brain, so use it rather than killing it off with booze."

"Yes, grandma."

"Now go to sleep and let your body recover."

"Yes, grandma."

"And – Leslie?"

"Yes, grandma?"

"I always loved you best."

And those were the last words Leslie Billinghurst remembered hearing his grandmother say to him as he dozed off into a sound and deep slumber, and if, in years to come, he sometimes pretended that they weren't part of a very authentic-seeming dream – well, it was understandable because everyone wants to be approved of and loved

*

If Addilyn and Kaden left the caf□ smiling, they weren't smiling now, a quarter-hour down the road.

"Where's my phone?" Addilyn growled as Kaden kept driving because he intended to continue to Jodrell Bank in spite of the revelation because he'd decided that that was the best thing to do, even now. "I'm going to give that bastard a piece of my mind!"

When they had finished their breakfast and paid for it, washed up a bit, given Shadow a run and then returned to the car, Kaden had offered to drive again while Addilyn got to work on the envelope's contents, looking for named contacts or memorising the figures, whatever she wanted to do that might give them the upper hand in this ridiculous but real situation. It made sense and Addilyn concurred, and once she was settled and ensured that Shadow had water from the little bottle-and-tray combination she'd bought back in Keswick, she tore open the envelope and took out the wad of papers. It had taken her about ten minutes before she'd erupted and began calling Dr Martin Bartholomew all the names under the sun, then furiously patted her jacket pockets to find her mobile.

"What's up?" Kaden had enquired.

"There's nothing new with these figures," fumed Addilyn. "Bartholomew hasn't done anything with them!"

"Are you sure?"

"Of course I'm bloody sure! He's written this bloody note to me –

" '*Addilyn,*

" '*I know you'll open this before you get to Jodrell so I just want you to know, I can't help because I don't want to die. And before you scream that we might all die anyway, I know that already, but at least I'll have time to prepare. I'm a coward, I know it, but in my opinion you are sentencing all those to whom you show these figures to a sudden and not-so-quick death. Forgive me, but I cannot bring myself to do the same.*

" '*Martin Bartholomew PhD (amongst others)*'

"And what gets me is, he's practically accused me of being hard-hearted enough not to care if I cause people's deaths! Where's my mobile? I'm going to give that bastard a piece of my mind!"

Finally Kaden pulled up on the hard shoulder of the motorway they had just recently joined. Addilyn had found her mobile phone, but realised she didn't know Bartholomew's number, which made her swear more and begin to cry in anger and frustration. Kaden took the phone from her, meeting with little resistance, and took her in his arms and let her cry for a moment. When she had stopped, and she pulled away from him to apologise for being so stupid, he smiled and stroked her cheek very gently.

"I won't say 'love is never having to say you're sorry' because it's corny," he said. "But there really is no need to say sorry for being human. After all, there's not much you can do about that! "

Addilyn tried to laugh but barely succeeded; her anger was dissipating, but at a slow enough rate for some to remain to frustrate her.

"And I don't think taking it out on Bartholomew will do much good," continued Kaden, "Because I'm guessing he feels crap for saying that. He's really frightened, Addie, and true fear makes cowards of almost all of us."

"We're not running away," pointed out Addilyn.

"Maybe because we believe it's not the end; I mean, I used to think it was, I used to – I used to not know what the hell would happen when I died and I think I wanted to believe so I started to because the alternative was unthinkable. In itself, that made me soppy and weak in my own eyes and so I tried to act tough and not believe even though I still hoped. What I'm trying to say is, we don't all manage as well as –

"Me?" interrupted Addilyn. "The cold-hearted Addilyn Mackenzie whom nothing ever bothers?"

"The emotional and totally human Addilyn whom everything bothers, but she can live through it because she's strong-willed and determined."

"Don't judge others by my own standards, eh?"

"More like, do unto others as you would have them do unto you; I assume it can't have been easy admitting to your – problem – and reactions can't have been favourable all the time."

"They were favourable none of the time. Even my parents decided they couldn't hack it."

"Well, that's unfortunate, it's sad, and it says more about them than it does you. But in the here and now you are coping with it, you are loved by someone who is happy to cope with it with you, and you are strong-minded enough not to let an old man, whose scientific knowledge has led him to believe there is nothing magical about the world any more, upset you so much."

Addilyn stared at him for a moment, then: "Where have you been all my life?" she asked.

Kaden chuckled a little embarrassedly.

"No, I mean it. Why couldn't I have met you a decade ago?"

"Oh, stop it, I'm not that special."

"Says you. I can't believe a hundred women haven't tried to snap you up by now."

"Who says they haven't?" Kaden chuckled, still uncomfortable.

"No, I'm serious." Addilyn paused because she suddenly realised she really was. "Why haven't you married? It doesn't make sense. You're too lovely not to have been loved before."

"Addilyn, please..."

"No, Kaden, I want to know. You and I are a two-way deal. You support me, I support you."

"It's nothing much, honestly..."

"Spill."

Kaden spilled.

*

I am tired of their killing. I am particularly tired of their killing my offspring. How many times does he have to die before he gives up on them?

He will never give up on them.

Maybe it is time for us to give up on him.

I will never give up on him.

Then they will continue to kill him.

And I will continue to weep and to hurt and to hate them for what they do.

Until your hate is all used up could be a long, long time.

A long, long time indeed, for it is infinite. As is my love.

*

Addilyn didn't know whether to laugh or cry. She had been imagining all sorts of things: was he actually gay but denying it, even to himself? Was he a criminal, on the run, the guise of a police officer the most efficient way to hide? A wife-beater? Maybe he already married and just stringing her along. Her heart beat in her throat while he told his story but now she felt so relieved that she felt she could fly; over-sensitivity was something she, at least, could live with forever.

Kaden's fault was taking things too personally and it apparently drove would-be life partners up the wall. At school, being shouted out would result in tears because he thought criticism, even directed at his misbehaviour and no doubt deserved, was aimed at him as a person and that his whole being, his very existence, was a mistake. If someone glanced at him in the street, it was because something was wrong with him, and he became self-conscious and worried and that in turn resulted in a kind of clumsiness that ended in Kaden becoming embarrassingly flustered and girlfriends frustratedly leaving him for someone more secure.

There was more, of course, but Addilyn got the picture; Kaden didn't say anything about his early childhood but she was pretty sure something had happened. Yet he'd worked through it, and after much time and even more determination, he'd arrived at himself today – calm, confident, contented. Addilyn wished she could do that too – God knew she'd tried – and rather than frustrate her, the whole episode made her admire him even more. No crying to the authorities for Kaden, blaming childhood treatment for all kinds of behaviour that other irresponsible people claimed; it was his problem to work out and work it out he did, yet without a hint of righteousness afterwards. He hadn't forgotten the struggle and that's why he understood so well what Addilyn was experiencing and she suddenly felt a surge of, not so much love as, a *bonding* with him..

She was just about to tell him so when her

phoned rang in her hands; she didn't recognise the number but she answered it anyway.

Hello, Addilyn? It's Leslie, Leslie Billinghurst. I'm just on my way up to you now. I know what Bartholomew's done, or rather hasn't *done, but I've managed to work some of it out myself, and the rest I'll do when I'm up there or maybe the chaps can do it themselves. Anyway, I'll meet you at the Discovery Centre this afternoon, yes?"*

"We'll find each other somehow," replied Addilyn, and she turned to Kaden to explain the call.

EIGHTEEN

Leslie Billinghurst threw his calculations into the small storage compartment underneath the seat, closed the seat down, leapt on his Honda Fireblade and revved the motorcycle before speeding away from his place of work far more dramatically than was necessary. But he wasn't showing off – there was no-one to show off to even if he'd been the type to do so, which he wasn't – nor was he being flamboyant for the hell of it; rather he was taking out his anger and frustration on a machine that wouldn't be aware of it because he'd been morally obliged not to take it out on his employed who did.

Leslie didn't understand while the stupid old goat refused to help Addilyn and Kaden. Okay, so it was high;y likely that their suspicions regarding the scientists' deaths were valid, and maybe Bartholomew would have met with a violent end, but how long did his refusal to help buy him? Maybe a few years, that's all, whilst he robbed the population of earth a combined four hundred aeons or more and how that was logical, Leslie didn't have a clue. Because that's what scientists were supposed to be – logical, yet the old duffer had shunned logic and even consideration, and allowed his emotions to get the better of him.

Okay, so the old bugger might have been afraid, but Leslie was sure that Addilyn and Kaden were afraid too, and he knew damned well that he himself was! But Bartholomew was old (comparatively, anyway – had to be late sixties, surely) so shouldn't he have been sensible and more mature about it? Didn't he have children and grandchildren to try to save? (did he? Leslie realised that he had never socialised with his work colleagues and they had never shown any desire to socialise with him; consequently he knew very littler about any of them.)

Leslie shrugged mentally; he supposed her was better off than most in this situation because death held no fear for him now that he knew there was something afterwards. So was it belief – or rather *non*-belief – that influenced Bartholomew? Again, Leslie realised that he didn't know the old scientist well enough to be aware of his opinion one way or another; he just knew that, personally, he wouldn't live with himself if he'd done (or not done) what Bartholomew had, knowledge of an afterlife or no.

He was just turning right out of the side road that led from – or up to, depending on which direction you were travelling – the observatory and he had to admit his mind was still on the illogical behaviour of some human beings when he pulled out without really checking if anything was coming. It was such a quiet road, and no-one usually came up here on foot, so when he suddenly had to swerve to miss hitting the young woman, he was as much wondering what she was doing up here as whether or not he had injured her in any way.

He handled his motorcycle with practised ease, then brought it to a halt only a few a yards away; he dismounted, took off his helmet, walked towards the woman who seemed to be all right and asked somewhat ambiguously: "Hi, can I help you at all?"

"I was looking for my brother-in-law and his girlfriend. Well, he's not exactly my brother-in-law, but he would have been... Kaden Taylor and Addilyn Mackenzie, have you seen them?"

"Oh, are you Darcy Allen, Tim's intended? I've heard about you, but I'm new, so we probably haven't met."

"Well I was, but not any more obviously."

"Yes, well, I'm sorry I didn't come to the funeral, but – well – you know, as I said, I didn't know you so I thought I might be intruding..."

"Have you seen those two or haven't you?" Darcy interrupted him rather brashly.

"Oh, I'm sorry. Yes, yes, I've seen them."

"Up there, are they? Good! Because I have a few things I want to say to them."

"Oh, they're not here."

"You said you'd seen them."

"I have – I did – but they left for the north this morning. I'm on my way there now myself, as a matter of fact. And I really must get going, they'll be waiting for me..."

"A scientific pow-wow?" asked Darcy, a little sarcastically.

"Well, actually, that might well be a apt description," shrugged Leslie, then: "Can I give them a message? Ask them to ring you?"

"No, but you can give me a lift. My car's packed in, which is why I'm on foot in these infernal shoes." Darcy lifted one foot so that Leslie could see the high heel.

"Is it far?"

"I have no idea; I thought you'd know that!"

"Miss Allen, I have no idea where your car is, so I can't tell you how far away it is. And I can't give you a lift to it either unless you tell me where it is!"

"A lift to my car? I don't want a lift to my car, I could walk to it if I wanted to. No, I want a lift up north to wherever Kaden and Addilyn are and you're going."

"Oh, no, no... oh, I don't know about that..."

"Do you really want me to go to the newspapers?" asked Darcy sweetly. "Because I will. I'll tell them that Spaceguard and Jodrell Bank are in collusion and I might throw in Manchester University just for the hell of it. You willing to have maybe their lives on your conscience?"

"How did you know I was going to Jodrell bank?" asked Leslie, half-annoyed, half-curious.

"It houses the biggest power in the Merlin array," replied Darcy. "There's nowhere else like it in the UK and Tim often talked about how they assist you sometimes."

Leslie hesitated for a moment, then: "Okay, but I'll have to go back and pick up my spare helmet," he said."And I want you to know that I don't appreciate being coerced by blackmail!"

"Noted," smiled Darcy, hopping on the back of the motorbike and holding tight onto Leslie's waist. "Now, let's get going, because I'd hate to be the reason for your being late for your pow-wow..."

*

When they eventually met up with Leslie Billinghurst in the public cafeteria that served the Jodrell Bank Visitors' Centre, neither Addilyn nor Kaden could believe that he had Darcy in tow, that the two of them were chatting amiably and that Darcy was actually not only smiling, but seemingly smiling genuinely. They had many questions to ask him but tact and diplomacy, along with old-fashioned good manners, prevented them from airing their curiosity as to what the hell the young astronomer had done to bring about the transformation in Kaden's almost-sister-in-law.

For her part, when Darcy saw the looks of bewilderment on their faces which they had tried hard, but failed miserably, to conceal, she laughed lightly. "Bet I'm the last person you expected to see!" she commented, and whilst Kaden just nodded, Addilyn wholeheartedly agreed, and out loud too.

"Well, I do read," Darcy continued, "And I was aware that Tim was worried about something, although he didn't discuss his work with me other than sometimes telling me about an exciting find in simple term that even I could understand."

"Oh, but I'm sure Tim didn't mean to – " began Kaden, but Darcy intercepted his defence of his brother.

"Yes, he did," she said, "And it's my fault he did." She paused, then: "It's a long story," she smiled – a little sadly, Addilyn fancied – and chuckled humourlessly as if at some distant memory which she suddenly didn't find as funny as she once had. "Maybe one day, if we have the time – if anyone has any time at all – I'll tell you about it. I think it might amuse you."

"It doesn't amuse you," Addilyn observed, not unkindly.

"You reap what you sow," replied Darcy, and it turned out that as far as she was concerned, the matter was closed, for rather than elaborate, she changed the subject by recalling aloud how, earlier, Leslie Billinghurst had done his best to run her over.

*

Marcia was worried about Larrilee because he had slept the whole way from London, not even arousing when the coach stopped halfway through its journey at Birmingham and people got off nosily enough to wake the dead; indeed, she would have been afraid her Larrilee was one of these had he not been still snoring gently, reassuring her that there was breath in his body yet even if there was no awareness in his mind.

Even when they got to Keswick and Larry reluctantly moved himself out of the coach, they caught a taxi back to their house because he felt too tired to wait for a bus, he said. Marcia had never known Larrilee get a taxi before – both he and Josie considered them a waste of money and vastly overpriced – and when they got in, he didn't even answer Josie's questions, just kissed her cheek and told her "later, love" before he went upstairs to bed without anything to eat.

Marcia ate with Josie and told her as much as she could, but she knew that Larrilee would know more about the strange day out than ever she herself would. Besides, she knew that Josie had never been very happy with Daji so she pretended ignorance much of the time; Larrilee would have to fill her in tomorrow once he'd had a good sleep. Marcia finished her egg and chips and then she too felt sleepy, and at Josie's insistence she lay on the settee to watch the television with a mug of hot milk and a chocolate biscuit.

*

The first meeting wasn't so much a coming together of minds with a mutual intent on saving whatever they could each according to his or her particular ability,as an almost clandestine herding of non-staff by staff in authority which made Addilyn angry even though she understood the motives behind the actions.

Leslie Billinghurst for his part also saw the entire affair as the big boys putting the infants in their place; Jodrell Bank, as Manchester University's department of Physics and Astronomy as well as its Centre of Astrophysics, was a far bigger outfit than any of those so far involved in the UK, and Leslie was sure that the representatives of these departments were just making sure their visitors didn't forget that fact. Okay, so he himself had been afforded a certain degree of courtesy as his knowledge in the field commanded, but he was aware that Addilyn, Kaden and Darcy had been treated almost as interlopers whose presence was more to be grudgingly tolerated than justifiably accommodated.

Presently, a middle-aged, tall, fairly handsome, well-dressed gentleman walked into the room, closed the door behind him and smiled at the small assemblage with the most genuine smile any of them had seen so far today. None of them expected he was pleased they were there, but at least he was making the effort to look as if he were, and doing an admirable job of it too.

"I'm Dr Nigel Cavendish," he said as he seated himself, not at the head of the boardroom table at which the others were seated and waiting, but at the side so that he looked like one of them. "But don't let the name fool you. I'm not posh, I'm a Northerner, and as I understand you are too – at least most of you – I think we'll get on just fine." They all chuckled on cue, then Dr Cavendish continued: "I will try and explain what we're doing in lay terms, and then if you have any questions, I'll do my best to answer them as far as I can or am allowed. Is that okay?"

They all nodded, knowing that even if it weren't, that's all they were going to get; as far as Addilyn was concerned, all she needed to know was that everything would be A-okay and that they all had a future, and in fact that was roughly the wish of Kaden, Darcy and Leslie Billinghurst too.

"Right," said Cavendish, clutching his hands on the top of the table and leaning slightly forward as if he were about to impart something exclusively for their little group and no-one else, "Well, basically, what the Lowell telescope does, for those of you not so familiar with our branch of study and research, is receive messages from space in the radio-wave portion of the electromagnetic spectrum. As you may – or may not – know, everything with a changing magnetic field produces radio waves so the first thing to do is see if there's anything there or if its just a – er – a misunderstanding."

"You mean 'joke'," commented Darcy. "As if my Tim would play a prank of this magnitude. Did he also corroborate on the murder of all those scientists?"

"Miss. Allen, it's very likely that Professor Taylor's observations will prove genuine," smiled Cavendish. "He is not unknown to us here. But any preventative measures we take will cost the government a lot of money and I cannot put it to them without facts laid out in black and white, indisputable facts that they cannot argue with."

"But what about the tendency for whoever assists – " began Addilyn.

"We are professionals, Miss Mackenzie, and as you represent someone who has helped continuously and is still here to tell the tale – along with Mr Taylor – I don't foresee a problem. If it transpires that you are somehow being 'protected' as your story suggests..."

"You don't believe us," Kaden said sadly.

"Of course he doesn't believe you," snorted Darcy. "His kind can't see beyond mathematics and science. But when Les – Professor Billinghurst – explained on the way up about what happened at his observatory, I certainly believe it. And my Tim will not have died for nothing, because I for one am willing to help regardless, if I can." She paused for breath then: "Run your tests, Dr Cavendish, and you'll find the asteroid there just as my Tim said it was."

Addilyn and Kaden exchanged glances; this was a Darcy Allen that they had never met before, and they found that despite their previous opinions, they were rather warming to her.

"Yes, well, as I said, Miss Allen, we held Dr Taylor in very high esteem," said

Cavendish, wanting to get the meeting back on a course that he felt more comfortable with. "And what we'll do is, point the Lovell antenna at the co-ordinates he gave us, and if we get a reply, so to speak,. We'll be able to verify that something is there. Then we can ascertain its size, speed, distance from us..."

"I find it curious that you haven't picked up on it before," remarked Addilyn.

"We may well have," replied Cavendish. "There are a lot of things out there that the Lovell converses with, but recently much of our time has been taken up with e-MERLIN, the old Multi-Element Radio-Linked Interferometer Network with an upgrade of optical fibre intercommunication which greatly improves the quality of results and merits the 'e' prefix. But we have a schedule, Miss Mackenzie, drawn up years in advance because a lot of people want to use our facilities and so we are always extremely busy. If the Lovell is pointing somewhere else when something appears, it's easy for us to miss it."

"So those outfits that *did* detect it, like Leslie's, just happened to be looking in the right place at the right time?"

"Well, that's a very simplified way of putting it, but apart from the fact that their sweep of the sky is a lot wider than ours, that's about the gist of it."

“Well, we won’t be the only ones looking now,” commented Kaden.

“Probably not,” agreed Cavendish. “But there haven’t been reports of any more associated deaths...”

“Are you saying we *are* the only ones looking?” asked Kaden, incredulously.

“I’m not saying anything, Mr Taylor, because I don’t know. But logic dictates that unless those deaths were completely independent of what seems to be going on, either people have stopped looking or those responsible for the deaths aren’t so bother about secrecy any longer.”

“So you give credence to the possibility that something is manipulating us?” asked Addilyn.

“I have studied your report, Miss Mackenzie, but I find the idea of some fort of alien intelligence very hard to swallow indeed. I’m a scientists, and things are supposed to make physical sense, but while there have been so many factions on this planet seeking even a mere *hint* of extraterrestrial life without so much as a beep, you’re basically saying that one seems to have slipped through everybody’s fingers!”

“That’s maybe because you regard them from the point of view that they’re out there, up there and - as you yourself admit – as physical as we are,” said Darcy. “That was one thing that Tim always complained about: humans who refused to accept the possibility that existence could come about under circumstances so alien – excuse the pun – to us that ET could come up and bop us on the nose and we would be too metaphorically short-sighted to even see him."

Cavendish regarded her for a moment, was about to say something in reply to that, then changed his mind. "Well, no doubt we'll get to the bottom of it eventually," he smiled instead, and the way in which he unclasped his hands and placed them palms flat on the table indicated the imminent conclusion to this little gathering. He stood. "I'll contact Dr Billinghurst when he have something to report," he continued. "And I will send one of our assistants to see you out of the building momentarily, if you would be so kind as to wait."

And with that. Cavendish strode out of the room so quickly that it was obvious he was keen to get away.

*

They are determined.

He always said they were, but their determination is misplaced.

He says that too?

He does.

Then why does he not concede defeat? It is a pointless exercise which results only in his own pain and disappointment.

And mine.

Then for you he should cease his efforts.

He will not.

He is cruel to make his mother suffer so.

He says I knew how it would be, and I do.

So the hurt and the frustration continues.

Maybe it is time we helped them. Those to whom I allowed free reign should be pulled up and checked. They go too far now, for it does naught but reinforce our son's determination.

You admit you were wrong?

I admit I acted out of a selfish regard.

Very well, if you deem it judicious, I shall assist you.

*

As they'd left the site of Jodrell Bank, Addilyn had the distinct feeling that they and what the experts considered were their silly, preposterous little ideas were not at all welcome here in spite of how much they had done to ensure that the right data was in the hands of the right people, and her opinion had not changed since. Now, as she sipped her wine and watched with kind amusement at the way Darcy and Leslie were getting on so splendidly, she tried to forget that she should feel indignant at the way they'd had to fight to remain even a small part of the operation, being also quite aware that the Jodrell Bank senior personnel were all for sending her, Darcy and Kaden home, whilst Leslie was to remain as special dispensation for his minimal usefulness but even then Addilyn doubted that he would be consulted much.

It was Darcy who had twisted their arms, not with her favourite threat of going to the newspapers, but by remembering something that Tim had told her about a senior astrophysicist at the University of Manchester and a certain pupil and threatening to go visit *Mrs* senior astrophysicist, as she put it. Whether or not Darcy knew the identity of said scientist, Addilyn wasn't sure, but no-one was going to risk it just in case she did. They were accommodated in a small B&B a mile away, basic expenses only paid for, and as she watched Darcy slap Leslie playfully then kiss his arm better through his coat she wondered if Darcy might suddenly and inexplicably disappear...

"Is that okay with you, then, Addie?"

Kaden was saying.

Addilyn snapped out of her reverie. "Sorry," she grinned gingerly. "I'm away with the fairies. Is what okay with me?"

"If you and I call it a might," answered Kaden.

"Oh, yes please," smiled Addilyn, finishing her wine in a couple of noisy gulps and standing up. "I'm plum tuckered out!"

"See you at breakfast, then," said Leslie, and he nodded his appreciation at Kaden as if he didn't think Addilyn would know why they were tactfully withdrawing.

"Night," added Darcy, but when Addilyn turned to wish her good night in return, she and Leslie were heads-to-dead giggling like a pair of lovesick teenagers at some private joke.

"Jealous?" Kaden ribbed her as they left the bar and walked into the cold night air.

"Not a bit," replied Addilyn, linking her arm in his for the walk back to the B&B. "Who wants lemonade when they've got champagne?"

And who wants to die before they have a chance to properly appreciate it, she thought, though she wouldn't have dreamed of saying so out loud.

NINETEEN

The following morning, Josie Hodgson called in their GP even though Larry told her not to bother him for something as unimportant as sleepiness, something which, he insisted, would quite simply be cured by sleeping more! But Josie suspected that there was something more wrong with her husband; he had never before slept so much, eaten so very little (or, as was the case now, nothing at all); besides, he was very cold to the touch and he looked a bit pasty. Josie didn't like that and she phoned the doctor even as her husband fell back asleep and snored gently for the two hours it took for the doctor to arrive on Larry's home visit.

Marcia kept looking in on her Larrilee but he didn't hear her, didn't awake and hold out his arms for her to run into for a cuddle, and she kept asking Daji to come and help, but Daji was ignoring her and Marcia was very cross with him; she sat on the settee between visits to her adopted parents' bedroom and formulated just what she was going to say to him when he did eventually return to her – so far, it wasn't very nice at all but Marcia didn't care.

Presently the doctor arrived, went in to see Larry Hodgson and returned to the sitting room less than a half hour later. Josie was waiting with Marcia, both seated on the settee looking at the adjoining wall as if they had x-ray vision and could see what was going on through it, and when the doctor opened the sitting room door that linked the two rooms, Josie knew immediately that it was serious just by the sour look on a face that was usually comfortably cheerful.

"I'll arrange an ambulance," he said to her.

"What's wrong with him, Dr Preston?" asked Josie.

"They'll run tests," the doctor prevaricated.

"What's wrong with him?" Josie asked again.

"I'm can't be sure until we get the test results." Preston was evading the question for sure.

"Okay, what do you *think* is wrong with him?" Josie was beginning to lose patience, but she didn't press the matter because just then Marcia hurried up to her, threw her little arms around her waist, buried her face in her abdomen and started sobbing uncontrollably.

*

Dathan Greenwood didn't know where he was, what he was doing, or even if he were the same person he'd been a month ago. He felt as if he'd been taken over by – *something*, he knew not what, possessed by a strong will that was not his own, forcing him to act in ways that he would have refused had he had any say in his own actions...

He was headed north but he didn't know why. He had to get to it before the others had a chance to program it, yet he knew not what 'it' was. But no way could it be allowed to achieve its destination, whatever that destination was. Of course, it wasn't being dispatched from here, it was going to be built he knew not where. But here, up north, thy had the data which would steer it and he had to get to that data data and destroy it completely this time.

He knew there were others worldwide being controlled, like puppets in their total uselessness to act independently, but the strings seemed to be on the inside, not on the outside.

He wondered if these others felt as angry and frustrated as he did, as he broke the side window of the dull green Audi, reached in, opened the driver's door, clambered in and drove off as the ignition somehow fired up without his having to do anything.

*

They'd taken a trip to the fairly-nearby Teggs Nose Country Park in order to give the long-suffering Shadow a good run and a few hours of fresh air. They also did it to pass the time while they waited for a telephone call that was as elusive as their comprehension of this entire matter. But it was a dry day – chilly, cloudy, but not raining – and it was better listening out for their mobiles' ringtones out here than it would be in their hotel room. At least it was for Shadow, and Addilyn had decided that that was a good (and deserved) thing. He had waited in the room, quiet and uncomplaining, leaving no reminders whatsoever that he had not been out for a walk for some hours, and Addilyn was proud of him; she promised herself that if they ever got out of this situation alive, she was going to spoil the darling dog rotten – God knew he deserved it!

The park was a half-hour drive from their B&B and the other side of Macclesfield, on the edge of the Peak District which parts of the park overlooked. Dogs were allowed to run free so long as they were controlled, and Addilyn knew there would be no problem with Shadow because he was so well-behaved that she didn't actually have a lead for him, that and the fact that she didn't expect to be staying away from home quite so long. The walk they took was around two and half miles, of which they had done well over half. They had passed the quarry and the reservoirs and were now climbing up the hill which was purported to give pretty spectacular views. It wasn't hard-going, but it was frosty and some of the pathways took pedestrians close to sheer drops which they kept well away from.

Once at the top, Addilyn admired the view for a moment or two, trying not to compare it with the ones at home – she had a habit of doing that and almost always arriving at the (biased) conclusion that nothing quite measured up to the beauty of the Lake District scenery. Then suddenly, as the realisation that this beauty might not last much longer sank in, her thoughts turned again to her own mortality and, try as she might to prevent it, she burst into hopeless and angry tears.

"Hey, hey!" Kaden was at her side in an instant and, as he held her close, her head resting on his chest, her body wracking with each stifled sob. "Let it all out. You deserve to."

"I – I'm sorry," Addilyn sniffed at length, "I'm acting like a stupid little girl."

"You're not stupid," Kaden smiled, "And you're not all *that* little..."

Addilyn chuckled in spite of herself. "Good quality things come in little packages," she observed.

"Small but expensive," countered Kaden.

"I won't strain your purse strings, she said, sobbing spasms still punctuating her words. "I want time, not money."

"And we'll have it." Kaden tightened his grip on her and he felt like crying himself.

"You think so? You think they'll be able to pull this off?"

"I don't see why not."

"And what of Daji and whoever – whatever – wants us destroyed?"

Kaden said nothing.

"You know it's no random coincidence that the asteroid is going to collide with us, right?" Addilyn pushed gently away from Kaden just far enough so that she could see his eyes when he replied.

"I suspected as much," he admitted.

"So even if they manage to divert the asteroid, who's to say that it won't 'mysteriously' regain its collision course?"

"You can't think like that, Addilyn..."

"I *am* thinking like that. I'm thinking that maybe there's an enemy out there we don't stand a snowball in hell's chance of defeating. And can you honestly say you disagree?"

"I don't disagree, Addie." Kaden took her hands in his. "But I hope."

"Now who's cock-eyed?"

"If there's someone – something – trying to destroy us, there's someone – Daji – trying to help us. He wouldn't have tried to warn us if he wasn't on our side."

"But is he enough?"

"I don't know. I don't know who or what

he is, as I also don't know who or what our adversary is. But what I *do* know is, we're not going to give up, we're not going to quit fighting."

"We're not going to quit hoping, eh?"

Kaden smiled. "That is one thing we will *never* give up." he paused to pull her back to him and kissed her on the forehead. Then: "Come on," he said. "Shadow's been sitting there patiently waiting for us to carry on walking for the past ten minutes. I think it's time we obliged!"

Addilyn concurred and allowed Kaden to lead her along the path back to the car, listening to his idle chatter and loving him for trying to lighten the situation even as she knew it wasn't really working for her. He continued on the drive back, and Addilyn hoped and prayed with all her heart that she would have more time to appreciate this man.

When they arrived back at the B&B, Leslie Billinghurst was waiting outside, squatting and fussing a tame sheep which belonged to the owners – they worked a farm in addition to running their B&B business – and Addilyn knew straight away that he had some news for them from the look on his face and the fact that he'd been waiting for them.

"What's new?" she asked anxiously, getting out of the car whilst Kaden stayed to ensure her door was locked after Shadow got out from the back seat.

"There's a meeting in the morning," replied Leslie, waiting until Kaden had joined them and then walking with them to the front door of the B&B. "I don't know any more than that, but from the tone of voice, I'd say Cavendish has something quite good to tell us..."

*

Josh Greenwood had walked past the shop window three times now, and Don Gittins just knew that there was something wrong, but he wasn't sure whether he should go out and ask the boy or wait for Josh to come in and talk in his own time. He had hardly seen anything of the boy since Addilyn had gone on leave, as he liked to call her absence, but Don was aware that Josh's dad's birthday was close and he still had the beer mat out the back all ready and waiting for Josh to collect – after he'd paid the balance of fifteen pounds.

Maybe that was what the problem was, Don mused; Josh might well be trying to summon up the courage to come in and tell him he couldn't afford it this week, or this month, or at all, even – and Don wished the boy would just get on and do it because he, Don, wasn't a bad man and he would come to some arrangement whereby Josh could maybe work off the balance by helping him clear the back out. Or something like that.

Don sighed; that attitude, he told himself, is the reason you will never be a rich man. But Don didn't care. There were more things to life than money – and with that thought, he crossed over to his shop's door, opened it, stepped out and interceded Josh's pacing on the boy's next pass.

*

At ten o'clock the following morning, they were waiting in a small, almost empty office for the arrival of Dr Nigel Cavendish, who seemed to have deemed the room quite sizeable enough to host such an informal talk as this was intended to be. As they had been reminded when they were showed to this office, they were lucky that the scientists bothered keeping them up-to-date at all; generally speaking something like this was on a need-to-know basis and civilians – Addilyn thought they more likely meant '*plebs* – were not usually informed of what was going on.

Kaden and Leslie pretended to be adequately impressed, but the girls were less grateful; Darcy because she hated being considered the stereotypical dumb blonde, and Addilyn because she suspected that, as long as the hierarchy were unsure about their peers' deaths and the idea of 'extraterrestrials' appearing to Marcia and Addilyn (as Larry had innocently informed Erik Croptom back in London what seemed like a lifetime ago) could not be totally suppressed, they wouldn't let Addilyn go just in case she received a further visit, and not letting her go meant keeping all the others.

Addilyn wondered where Daji had gone, what he was doing, why he ignored them when they needed him the most. She wondered if Marcia had been contacted by him and vowed to make a point of asking her when next she saw the girl, if she ever did...

Nigel Cavendish entered the room rather noisily and Addilyn was grateful for the distraction; her thoughts were getting far too maudlin.

"Right," he said when he had seated himself at the head of the table at which they all sat. "Well, it seems there *is* something there after all."

"You sound surprised," commented Darcy.

"Not 'surprised', Miss Allen," replied Cavendish with a sigh, "More 'disappointed'. It would have been so much better *not* to have had an asteroid on a collision course with Earth."

"An asteroid?" Leslie Billinghurst sounded perplexed. "How far away is it?"

"About six months," replied Cavendish,

knowing the unit of measurement the young man wanted,

"How?" Leslie was indignant. "Spaceguard would have picked it up – if not us here in the UK, then one of our member locations..."

"It is rather odd..."

"Odd? It's far more than odd! Either we would get zero impact notice or several years' worth! How the hell does an asteroid large enough to detect now suddenly materialise 250-odd million miles away?"

"Your guess is as good as mine, Dr Billinghurst. However, we can investigate the whys and wherefores later. Right now we need to find a way to divert it. We can't explode it because the danger to Earth would merely be supplanted by the resultant shower of smaller but just as deadly meteors..."

"So how do you propose to divert it?" asked Addilyn. "I mean, I'm not that well-versed in the intricacies of space science, but even I know that you have a choice of blowing it off course either from Earth or from space."

"NASA has mitigation plans with deflective techniques," answered Cavendish, "Although for obvious reasons I cannot go into them. And the global nuclear arsenal stands at around 23 thousand warheads. That's more than enough power for a stand-off explosion."

"Or we could use a robotic lander." Leslie took up the thread almost excitedly. "With mounted thrusters, it could conceivable push the thing off course."

"Into Mars might be an idea," commented Darcy.

"Mars?" asked Addilyn.

"There's a theory that asteroids harbour ice underneath their rocky exteriors," shrugged Darcy. "A collision with Mars could in theory supply the planet with enough water to encourage life evolution."

"Oh," said Addilyn, not knowing what else to say.

"I think the life on *this* planet is enough to be concerned with for now, don't you?" Dr Nigel Cavendish wasn't annoyed but there was more than a mere hint of anxiety in his voice. "But before we approach anyone, we need to consider who, and how many, we will be putting in jeopardy."

"I hardly think it matters at this point," opined Kaden. "We'll all be dead within the year if someone doesn't do something."

"As it stands, I agree," said Cavendish. "But we need to confirm impact status before we think about starting a global panic."

"That would involve the e-MERLIN array, right?"

"Yes, Dr Billinghurst. I don't see the need

to involve anyone other than our own immediate contacts until we're positive we have our facts right."

"I suspect they're sitting having very similar considerations on the other side of the Atlantic and Pacific too," observed Darcy. "But the question no-one wants to ask, so I will: why do you trust us to keep quiet?"

"Because you could have said something long before now," replied Cavendish. "And of course we have had your backgrounds checked. Certain people have had to be informed of the situation, although we have kept them to a minimum. But..." – Cavendish got up from the table and regarded them all one by one – "I personally don't think you want to endanger anyone you don't have to."

And with that, he left the room and Addilyn suspected that he was accusing them of, to all intents and purposes, killing him.

*

They will not desist.

They MUST desist!

I commanded them but they refused.

Then we must destroy them. That is the only way we will stop them.

That will not be easy. They are powerful.

So are we. We just need to be MORE powerful.

For my son I will do my best.

I know you will. Now let us rid the world of these vermin while your son tries again – futilely, I might add – to finish what he started.

*

They were driving back from the meeting, Addilyn and Kaden in their car, Darcy and Leslie Billinghurst on his motorcycle. They had not spoken since they'd left the meeting and although they had made no such plans, Kaden knew to drive to the little pub just down the road from their B&B because he knew that was where Leslie Billinghurst would assume Kaden was going. There would be a discussion about what had been said, but it would be a futile one; the matter had been taken out of their hands now, and all they could do was wait.

"Sucks, doesn't it," commented Addilyn, as if she could read Kaden's mind. "After all we've done, all we can do is sit and wait while someone else takes over. I kind of feel pushed out."

Kaden shrugged. "Maybe they're more qualified than we are to take care of it," he replied.

"Bollocks they are," humphed Addilyn crossly. "They have the instruments, but that's about it. They are no more qualified to deal with this than we are. Unless it was hushed up pretty damn well, I don't recall there being a possible end to the world before."

"Sounds almost too ridiculous to be true," mused Kaden.

"Like a plot of a science fiction story? Well, isn't that why they wrote those stories, because it was the sort of thing that was believable and therefore frightening?"

"And the sort of thing that, while it would give you nightmares, you never in your wildest dreams thought would actually happen."

"It was always on the cards."

"Did you ever expect it to in your lifetime?"

"Well, no, but – " Addilyn stopped speaking as her mobile phone rang. She pulled it quickly from her jacket pocket to see who was calling her, then took the call. "Can I phone you back, Josie?" she said, trying to sound as normal as she could. "I'm – well, I'm a bit tied up just now."

"*It won't take a moment,*" Josie was saying.

"I'll ring you when I get back to the B&B," Addilyn assured her. She really didn't feel like chatting just now. "Give my love to Marcia, won't you. And Larry. I hope he got back okay."

"*He got back okay but he's dying.*" Josie's voice was so flat that Addilyn knew she wasn't kidding.

Addilyn froze. "What?" she whispered, forgetting that she didn't feel like talking.

"*Cancer,*" said Josie quietly. "*A sudden onset, apparently.*"

"Very sudden," mused Addilyn aloud, and suddenly she heard a scuffle at the other end of the phone line and Larry Hodgson's voice saying '*oh, give over, woman* in as loving a tone as she had ever heard.

He took the phone from his wife.

"*Lass, don't you worry about me,*" Larry was saying to her now. "*We both know that this isn't just pure bad luck, and we also know that nothing can be done about it. Just get on with what you're doing and pray that they don't start taking things out on Marcia.*"

"Who's 'they', Larry?" She wanted to know if Larry knew any more than she did.

"*Marcia thinks they're more of Daji's kind, but older. Personally, I have no idea.*"

"Well, that makes two of us. But, anyway, we have other things to worry about, so you take care of yourself, Larry, and take care of Marcia too. We'll be back up there as soon as this thing is sorted."

"*I'm not so sure it will be, Addilyn, but I wish you all luck anyway.*" He paused for a moment, then: "*And if it turns out they can't do anything,*" he continued, "*Come back anyway, lass.*"

"Die at home in the comfort of my own home, eh?" Addilyn chuckled humourlessly.

"*Die here with us where you're loved, both you and Kaden,*" Larry corrected her, and suddenly Addilyn realised that a tear was trickling shamelessly down her cheek.

"I'll keep you informed," she said chokingly and, without a word of farewell, she terminated the call.

"You okay?" Kaden asked her.

"I'll be better when I've had a word with... *DAJI!*"

For a moment she felt nothing, then the deep, sonorous voice boomed around the car as if it were coming out of large speakers turned up full blast:

He whom you call 'Daji' is preoccupied, but please rest assured he, and we, are doing what we can.

And with that, the voice fell silent and somehow Addilyn knew that its owner, whoever or whatever that might be, was no longer present.

TWENTY

Nigel Cavendish was trying to concentrate on the figures displayed on the computer screen in front of him, but the dancing light that he could see from the corner of his eye kept distracting him. He couldn't even see where it might be coming from; it wasn't sunny, no lamp light could have been reflected from whatever was lodged behind the small grille in the skirting board, located in the near corner of the room by the door. A couple of times he got up and bent down to try to see inside the grille, and once he even poked a pencil through to try and dislodge whatever it was, but as soon as he returned to his desk, the light reappeared and started jigging around again, more frenzied, he fancied, as time passed. Eventually he tired of the mystery and called for security to come take a look.

*

"I have to admit, I didn't think they could do it so quickly!"

Kaden stared into his empty glass as if the ice cube at the bottom were the most fascinating object in the bar, then looked up to see Addilyn nodding her agreement at his observation.

“Makes you wonder, doesn’t it,” she said.

“Well, that’s the government for you,” remarked Leslie Billinghurst. “That and the fact that the probe can be launched from anywhere outside of Earth’s orbit and thereafter the robotic lander diffused and steered by remote control. So they didn’t really have to calculate for a pinpoint landing or rendezvous anywhere specific for the task. It was just a matter of getting it up there. Not that that’s any insignificant feat, mind you, especially in view of the security involved...”

They had been informed earlier that day, three days after the latest meeting, that a probe had been launched; that, and the fact that it had apparently all gone off as expected, was the extent of detail they were prepared to go into. Leslie Billinghurst had theorised the probability of using RAF Kinloss or Lossiemouth in Scotland as a space port, but hypothesis was all they had because Jodrell Bank weren’t talking. Furthermore, after again phoning Martin Bartholomew on his mobile but failing to contact him, Leslie had instead approached Spaceguard officially, only to be told that he had been dismissed *in absentia* and therefore no longer had security clearance for any such information. That, it seemed, included the name of the brash young lady to whom he had spoken; under normal circumstances, Leslie would have taken himself up there and demanded to know what the hell was going on, but these circumstances were anything but normal and he would find out what was happening after this present predicament was sorted, if it mattered at all by then.

"So when will they start the diversion process?" asked Darcy.

"As soon as the computers sort out the range and direction," replied Leslie. Then they can start feeding the numerical data to the robotic lander; I assume they'll try from space before they attempt a landing."

"If it's cheaper, they probably will," observed Addilyn drily.

"Well, wherever or whenever," said Kaden, "Do you think they'll bother informing us of the outcome?"

"I'll be banging on their front door asking if they don't," replied Darcy. "After all you've been through, you two at least deserve to be treated better!"

Addilyn threw Kaden a glance and although he was certain he didn't visibly acknowledge it, Darcy sighed, sat back, crossed her arms and said:

"You want to know, don't you."

"Know what?" asked Kaden innocently.

"Yes," put in Addilyn. "We do."

"Well, it's not a Jeckyll and Hyde complex,

so you're completely safe," Darcy commented with a smile.

"In your own time," said Addilyn. "I know how hard it is to share confidences."

"Oh, it's simple really," shrugged Darcy. "I once overheard Tim telling a friend that an intelligent woman was the last thing he wanted in a girlfriend. That was the evening we first got together; I spotted him across a crowded room, though 'wow' and was closing in on the kill when I heard him say it. I spent almost an hour eavesdropping on and off to make sue I knew exactly what he preferred, and then I became it."

"So you changed just for Tim?" Kaden seemed troubled.

"No, I didn't change," replied Darcy. "I acted."

"Which would be one hell of a lot harder," observed Addilyn.

"Yes indeed," agreed Darcy. "For one thing, my aloofness was constantly being mistaken for haughtiness, when in fact I didn't want people to see through the fa□ade. I could only relax with my close friends who knew the score."

"I'm wondering if my brother would appreciate being deceived," mused Kaden.

"Would he appreciate being loved so much?" retorted Darcy. "It may have been the wrong thing to do, but it was done for the best of reasons."

"Well, we'll never know," interjected Leslie. "I just hope you'll be yourself with me."

"I'll never live a lie again," Darcy assured him. "It's far too much hassle."

And that was when the explosion sounded, with Addilyn and Kaden both doubting it was a kitchen accident this time.

*

"Dear Lord above!" effused Nigel Cavendish.

The security officer had removed the grille's cover and was now shining his flashlight into the gap revealed, picking out a dark, cubic object with a small timer on top but with no lights; indeed, the dancing light had now vanished so Cavendish could only conclude that it had somehow come from the reflection of an unknown light source in his office as it bounced off the object's black shiny surface.

The timer was set for ten minutes from now; that, Cavendish calculated, was long enough for the bomb to be removed and taken somewhere remote nearby. There wasn't time to contact specific bomb disposal experts, but some of his security staff had the relevant render safe procedures training and so they were quickly summoned and they set to work while Cavendish took his mobile phone from his jacket pocket, opened it and proceeded to tap out a text message.

The other security staff soon arrived and the officer in charge removed the cap carefully and then lifted it onto a wheelbarrow-shaped transporter. They were going to take it to pieces later, but suddenly Cavendish ordered that it be taken away and remotely detonated. The officer in charge regarded Cavendish as if he were crazy and tried to argue that the thing had been rendered quite harmless, but in lieu of explaining that he was afraid that it might have been designed by extra-terrestrials who didn't necessarily follow earthly blueprints and therefore it could possibly go off whether or not the cap or anything else had been removed, he merely barked the order again ion a severe enough tone of voice to be obeyed.

As it happened, his extreme caution was justified; just after the bomb had been transported to the outer limits of the resident arboretum and placed in a large clearing which usually housed a garden set out in the style of the Solar System, it blew thirty seconds before the timer was due to reach zero and it was never publicised that the officer in charge was killed instantly.

*

As the other three dashed outside, Leslie Billinghurst fell back as he felt his mobile shudder in his pocket and stopped to take it out and read the message that had just been sent to him. His sigh of relief would have been audible to his friends had they not already exited the inn, but behind him an overhearer commented.

"Sounds like it's good news," said a somewhat hysterical male voice.

Leslie turned to see a man who must have been in his late thirties, maybe early forties, and who, by the looks of him, needed a day or two – or maybe a *week* or two – off the booze.

"Yes." Leslie didn't want a conversation with this undesirable, so he just nodded a vague acknowledgement to what he assumed was a friendly gesture and then hurried out to where Addilyn, Kaden and Darcy were standing looking in the direction of a large cloud of dirty grey smoke. Other people too were watching, presumably waiting for the sound of sirens belonging to the emergency services that must surely arrive soon, but Leslie knew that they would not be coming.

"It's okay," he whispered to the group of his three friends. "It was a contained explosion."

"Who told you that?" Kaden asked.

"Because it sure as hell didn't sound contained to me. The blast wasn't muffled at all and there's too much smoke."

"Nevertheless, Cavendish says it's all under control," insisted Leslie.

"It *is* coming from the direction of Jodrell," pointed out Addilyn.

"And there are no emergency services," added Darcy. "Which means they didn't see a need to call them."

"Well, I don't trust that man much," Kaden admitted. "Half the time he doesn't seem to know what he's doing, and the other half he seems to know too much!"

"Oh, well," shrugged Darcy, "So long as no-one's hurt. We might as well go back in and finish our drinks, then."

The others concurred, and as they made their way back to the front entrance of the inn, they didn't see the dishevelled man whom Leslie had met earlier leave by a side door.

Which of course was exactly as Dathan Greenwood had planned it.

*

They are strong, my husband. Very strong.

But we are stronger.

We may be stronger but we are not more.

Then ask your son to assist us.

I think I must. We have much to undo.

Too much to undo all at once.

I concur.

So we shall start by visiting the old man.

After which we need communication with the others.

If they will listen.

They never have before.

Then we shall tell them only what they need to know.

The rest can be saved for a later time?

Indeed; but give them that later time and maybe they will eventually listen.

We can but try....

*

Don Gittins had ended up raking young Josh Greenwood – without the drinks mat – home with him that evening. After what the boy had told him, he could hardly have done anything else.

Don hadn't known Lena Greenwood excellently well, but from what he did know of her, he wouldn't have put her down as a prude. She seemed always cheerful, a smile on her face, a friendly greeting for acquaintances and stranger alike, a general disposition that suggested nothing of malcontent with her husbands – requests.

But Josh Greenwood had poured out the whole story, as if he were confessing to church minister, as if, once the flood gates opened, he could not stem the flow of his words until they were all spent. And for his part, Don had listened silently; first incredulous, then horrified, and lastly with tears filling his eyes. When Josh had finished his narrative, Don had merely looked him in the eyes, no words sufficient to describe what he was feeling for the lad, and opened his arms to the boy who welcomed the offer of comfort with as much need to accept as the giver had to invite.

*

That night, Leslie Billinghurst was not in an amorous mood, and the way that Darcy accepted this without question or complaint momentarily moved him to rueful guilt on behalf of male-kind, who generally didn't take to that kind of snub so readily or so compliantly.

He didn't dwell on it for long, however; he was tired, he had the warm feeling of good wine in his stomach and a beautiful woman lying beside him, and for once he had more than a little faith that Cavendish and his team could actually pull off this entire annihilation prevention attempt. He was therefore so relaxed – in comparison to how he'd been feeling for the past week, anyway – that he dropped off to sleep within a couple of minutes.

And awoke to the sound of his grandmother singing as she always did when she was in the kitchen and baking cakes and jam tarts on a Sunday morning. Obviously the vestiges of an otherwise unremembered dream, he reasoned, and he turned over in what he thought was his bed, promptly falling off the old wooden kitchen table that used to grace the centre of the large farmhouse room in which he had, as a boy, spent so many hours helping his grandmother on baking day in return for licking clean the bowls of delicious, raw cake mix.

As Leslie picked himself up off the floor, he tried to work out how he could know he was dreaming yet not wake himself up, and a dismal thought passed through his mind...

"No, you're not dead," said his grandmother, turning to face him, wiping her hands on her apron as she often did when baking.

"But *you* are..." whispered Leslie.

"There's no such thing," huffed his grandmother. "All that happens is, the body stops functioning due to wear and tear, but your essence – your thoughts, your feelings, your imagination – all that goes on and on. Think of your essence as electrical energy and your body as a light bulb; when the light bulb breaks, you just replace it."

"So am I in the afterlife at the moment?"

"No, we're sort of meeting half way. Daji needed you to know things but he also needed something – some *one* – you were comfortable with. Speaking human to human is better for you, isn't it?"

"So are you Daji or are you my grandmother?"

"I'm neither. I'm a psychic projection of a material body that you once knew, which Daji plucked from your memory. I could have been anyone but Daji determined that you would take your grandmother more seriously than anyone else."

"And what about the dream I had when I was younger? The one of my grandmother?"

"After the accident when you drank too much and almost killed yourself? That was the same sort of image as this, but it was your grandmother's own thoughts and feelings in those words."

"You sounded quite like her then," Leslie chuckled humourlessly.

"I know."

"How do you know?"

"I just do."

"That's not enough,"

"Nothing is enough, but I can tell you only what you need to hear..."

"Who is Daji?" interrupted Leslie.

"Daji is – he is young again."

"Again? Has he been young before?"

"You would call it, I think, reincarnation although that is not strictly what it is. Maybe 'rebirth' would be a better word."

"He's lived before?"

"Not 'before'; that implies that he has died, but he has not."

"Time travel?" Leslie was aware that the idea was absurd but he couldn't think of anything else. "I mean, has he gone back in his own timeline or something?"

"Interesting interpretation, but again not quite right, although very close. If you can imagine timelines emanating from your essence in every direction, an infinite number in case they are needed, Daji is a little along one of them. Does that make sense?"

"Not a bit."

"I cannot think of another way to explain. But suffice it to say that Daji has been here before and will be here again in the future."

"'Here' as on Earth?"

"Indeed."

"Is there a record if him being here before?"

"There are many, but Earth does not seem

to want to know. That is why his mother freed the evil ones to destroy it."

"Daji's *mother*?"

"It is complicated and I have little time in which to try and do a great many things. But I have to let you know that we will assist you as much as we can in your attempt to avoid destruction, but there are many more evils than there are virtuous. Therefore I cannot guarantee success."

"You think we might fail?" Leslie suddenly wanted this dream to end so that he could wake up and pretend it was nothing more than too much wine and not enough nourishment.

"You have the right idea. If you can carry it through, you will succeed. But there are many who wish to stop you and we who are against them are but few."

"So what do you suggest I do?" snapped Leslie, exasperated. "*Pray*?"

"Who to?"

"I don't know!!!"

"Then there us little point in praying." Leslie's grandmother regarded him for a moment with the saddest eyes that he had ever seen. Then she turned her back on him. "Go," she said adroitly. "They begin their attempt the day after tomorrow at ten fifteen in the morning."

"How do you know that?"

"You never, ever learn, do you?" sighed Leslie's grandmother and Leslie fancied he heard tears in her voice. He wanted to apologise to her, to hug her, to speak some more which whoever she represented...

He awoke with a start, feeling as if he'd been falling and had just landed back on the bed. Beside him, Darcy stirred.

"You okay?" her voice said sleepily from under the duvet.

"Just a dream," he replied. *But NOT just a dream,* he thought, *because dreams are memories animated by the imagination to make them recognisable and comprehensible and how the hell did I know that?*

"Because you're learning," said Darcy in her sleep.

*

Larry Hodgson awoke at the sound of a buzzing close to his ear. Too early for flies, he told himself irritably; bloody things had no right to come in here and interrupt the sleep he so desperately needed.

"Go away!" he snapped irascibly, flailing at the air with the hand which was free of the duvet. His eyes tightly shut against the growing alertness that threatened unwanted wakefulness.

Cannot do that.

The voice was in his head but it also came from close to his ear. He opened his eyes to see a small golden orb hovering a few inches from his face.

"Daji?" he asked, incredulous.

Not Daji, but of him.

Larry snapped awake then and began to sit up, but suddenly an invisible weight pressed him back down again, a force too strong for him to resist.

No, do not rise, Stay still.

Larry's eyes widened as he watched the little light close in on him slowly, but instead of touching his face as he expected, his mouth opened as wide as a short-sighted dentist might wish it to – but of its own accord – and then he saw the little glowing orb vanish from his line of sight, only for it to appear again a few moments later.

You may close mouth now.

Larry did, then: "What are you *doing*???" he asked, panic-stricken.

Made better.

"'Made better'?" reiterated Larry.

Made better, confirmed the intracranial voice before its owner flew upwards and vanished through the bedroom ceiling.

TWENTY-ONE

The following day and a half seemed like a month and a half, and although it would have made more sense, in view of the present circumstances, for them to want the time to go as slowly as possible – *seem* to, this is – all that they wanted was for the launch time to arrive so that they would know once and for all whether or not they were going to die.

Opinion was split; Leslie Billinghurst was still quite confident that it would all work out, in spite of the knowledge that there were more against success than failure, while Addilyn looked on the dark side, as was her wont, seeing nothing but blackness ahead because that was what life had taught her to expect. Kaden, for his part, was just waiting to see what happened, maybe cautiously optimistic but not wanting to tempt fate by being to vociferous about it, whilst Darcy honestly couldn't have cared less.

It suddenly occurred to Addilyn that Darcy might well be depressed, missing her fiancé more than any of them had realised, though for Leslie's sake she was trying to keep her feelings under wraps. Maybe if they all came through this unscathed, she would have time to mourn for Tim and come to terms with what had happened; maybe Leslie Billinghurst was a pleasant distraction during this difficult time which was compounded, for Darcy, by the loss of the man she was going to marry.

Addilyn for one refused to judge her – grab happiness with both hands while it's there, was Addilyn's credo – and Kaden seemed quietly accepting of the situation too. Maybe that was because they had more pressing things to worry about for the time being, but maybe that in turn had emphasised to them just what was and was not important in life. After all, Darcy could cry a million tears, remain a spinster for a decade, and it still wouldn't bring Tim back; it was no insult to Tim that Darcy chose to carry on living in his absence, just a mature decision on Darcy's part to make the most of a bad job. In fact, Addilyn envied the younger woman that ability; it would have seen her, Addilyn, through so much of what she had had to go through over the past three decades and maybe she wouldn't have become quite so bitter. As it was, just as she was beginning to find some happiness in her life, Addilyn was more than aware that she might have to kiss it all a very premature goodbye.

On the day itself, it had been decided that Leslie Billinghurst alone should go to Jodrell, as he knew a lot more about the calculations that Tim Taylor had bequeathed them, why and how they mattered, and what Jodrell

Bank would be doing with them at the appointed time. The other three, it had been agreed, would wait back at the B&B, where Kaden now stooped to fuss the friendly sheep and Addilyn knelt to fuss Shadow, neither animals displaying any signs of hostility or jealousy whatsoever.

"Not long now till we know," commented Kaden.

"It still feels totally like a dream," sighed Addilyn. "I still think I'm going to wake up at any moment with my head resting on my desk and a note from Don Gittins saying he'd locked up and gone home but had secreted the shop key wherever."

Kaden chuckled. "Wouldn't he have more likely woken you up?" he asked.

"I don't know," shrugged Addilyn. "I've never fallen asleep at work before."

"You haven't fallen asleep at work now."

"More's the pity. I'd much rather all this was a dream."

"Even the bit about meeting me?"

"You'd still exist, and now I know your intentions towards me, I could confidently look you up and instigate proceedings."

"That's comforting to know." Kaden paused, then: "Shall we go and see if Darcy's okay?" he asked. "I don't think she should be alone at a time like this."

"Good idea."

They both stood up and, with Shadow, made their way back to their room where they left Shadow with a bowl of water and some dog treats.. Then they went up the stairs just outside, and to the right of, their bedroom door to where Darcy and Leslie's room was located.

*

It had taken a lot of emergency planning and not just a small dose of bootlicking to get what they wanted – no, *needed* – and it was that very point that had angered Dr Nigel Cavendish almost to the point of telling his counterpart at NASA to forget the whole damn thing, then praying fervently for a miracle. Because that, even now, was what it was going to take, even with the loan of the Harrier AV8BII (which was British anyway so why they made such a fuss, he didn't understand) and a thermonuclear physics package (which was admittedly American) which was now in orbit around Earth.

Cavendish glanced at his watch – he really had to stop checking it every two minutes – but it still wasn't time. In fact, there was time for coffee before they began transmitting the data calculations to the prone in the hope that the explosion it would orchestrate would act as a radiated vaporiser and subsequently as a thruster. Then the asteroid could go on its merry way and Joe Public need never know they'd been in danger.

Which idea didn't sit squarely with Cavendish either; all this secrecy was, in his opinion, an indirect insult to the general public's intelligence, never mind the amount of mistrust that a subsequent discovery of the potential danger would engender. Okay, so maybe the public would react by panicking, by looting, with misplaced violence because there was no-one really to blame yet they had to take it out on someone – but surely not all of them? Was it really all right to risk their wrath when their reactions were really up to them and not to the bearer of the news? Was it really all right to hide the truth because, when it came down to it, the authorities deemed to public too damned ignorant to react with propriety? There was a big enough 'us-and-them' divide in society as it was – and Cavendish refused to believe that it wasn't as bad as before because it *was* as bad, just a lot more tactful – without handing the people (whose taxes paid for the majority of what they worked with) more ammunition with which to shoot the governing bodies down. And even though they'd chosen remote Stornoway Airport as the launching port of the jump-jet which was carrying the probe, there was always the possibility that someone unauthorised had seen the silver-grey dip-winged jet take off and wondered what he hell an aircraft like *that* was up to...

He was about to go for a coffee, having decided that the caffeine boost would likely be advantageous once everything started happening, when his office door burst open and Leslie Billinghurst marched in, followed closely by two security guards who were looking sheepish, guilty, worried and angry all in one go. For his part, Dr Nigel Cavendish merely laughed.

*

It was easier the second time round because this time he knew were he was going. He got in through the small vent at the back of the building, seeming to bed impossibly to squeeze through the duct pipes as if he could melt and will and then re-solidify. Accompanying him were a host of gold orbs, fluttering around him like a myriad of infatuated fireflies.

Once through the labyrinth of pipes, standing now in a room empty of people and absent of any light other than that coming from a flickering computer screen, he stopped as if gathering his thoughts. Then he strode towards Nigel Cavendish's desk while the fireflies disappeared through the closed door.

He seated himself at the computer and prepared to hack into it to destroy all the data that Tim Taylor and others had died to cach□.

There was nothing left now of the man he had once been; for one thing, Dathan Greenwood had always been totally computer illiterate.

*

She′d made a quick and clandestine exit via the fire escape because she knew Addilyn and Kaden would want to come too, and although she couldn′t blame them for that, she also needed to go alone. She somehow knew there was going to be trouble, although whether it was merely her own intuition or whether some kind of subliminal awareness had been afforded her by someone, she didn′t know and she didn′t care about. She felt as if she owed Tim something – she′d lied to him by not being herself, she′d found happiness too soon after his demise – and she was going to make sure she repaid him, because quite frankly she was beginning to wonder if she actually wanted to face life without him after all.

*

Josie Hodgson just couldn′t believe it; she

knew her husband had spirit, but this had to be more than just a refusal to let things get him down.

This morning, Larry Hodgson had been up at the crack of dawn, acting as if he had won the lottery, singing in that totally out-of-tune baritone voice that she'd always loved to hear.

"What's got into you?" she shouted through the open bedroom door as she got out of bed – the first time she'd got up after him since they'd learned of his illness – and came through the hall into the sitting room, still dressed in her nightie with a cardigan throw over her shoulders.

"Eh?" Larry came in from the kitchen with a mug of coffee for himself and glass of milk for Marcia, who was lying on the settee grinning. "Aw, lass, I thought you might want to have a lie-in! Let me make you a cuppa."

"No, no, I'll do it." Josie motioned for him to sit down next to Marcia. "In a minute. First of all, I want to know what all this singing and jollity is about."

"I disturbed you. No wonder you couldn't have a lie-in..."

"Never mind the lie-in! What's making you so flamin' *happy*?"

"Larilee's all better!" explained Marcia excitedly, sitting up now whilst drinking the milk Larry just handed her, upper lip coated with cream. "The bad stuff has all gone!"

Josie looked at Marcia, then at Larry, a puzzled expression clouding her features.

"It's true," Larry said. "I phoned Dr Preston first thing, and he's arranged for tests this morning. But I already know I'm cured."

"But how?" Josie didn't understand; cancer didn't just disappear, that much she was sure of.

"You remember Marcia's little friend?" Larry put his coffee down, stood up and took Josie's hands gently in his. "You used to call him 'DJ'?"

"You're not going to tell me an imaginary friend cured you, Larry – ?"

"Oh, Josie, Daji was never imaginary, and I think deep down you know that."

"It's a far-fetched, totally ridiculous claim, Larry Hodgson! Whether or not this Dodgy thing is real, I'm sure you don't expect me to believe it can cure cancer just by – what is it supposed to have done anyway?"

"Now, don't you worry about what he did, pet," soothed Larry as he turned them around and gently pushed Josie to sit where he had been sitting on the settee. "I'll get you a cuppa and then we can all go to the hospital and you'll see that my cancer is completely gone. You'll believe the hospital, won't you?"

Josie believed. When the tests came back negative, when at Larry's insistence she was shown the X-rays so that she could see with her own eyes that the growth had disappeared, Josie had no choice but to believe. But she couldn't help feeling comfortable too; when things – *miracles* – like this happened, there was usually a price to pay....

Suddenly a clattering came from behind her seat and she turned to see a nurse staring crossly at three bed pans (luckily empty) that were now strewn across the linoleum floor. Slowly, her gaze turned on Josie.

"You just *won't* accept it, will you?" she yelled at Josie, her young eyes drilling into the older woman's, her expression one of exasperation as well as annoyance. "Whatever is done for you, you just keep on denying it!!!!"

Josie felt suddenly afraid. She got up and hurried out of the corridor into the public area of the hospital, followed by a dozen or more pair of eyes whose owners wondered what she had done to merit that rebuke.

Marcia followed quickly behind her, but Larry hesitated, lingering as he wondered whether he should ask the nurse to elaborate, making up his mind not when he heard the poor girl denying that she'd said anything. The nurse in charge of course begged rather indignantly to differ, but Larry Hodgson believed her; her vocal chords might have produced the words, but he doubted that her brain had composed them.

*

"Well, that's charming!" effused Addilyn. "She sneaked off and didn't even think to notify us!"

Kaden shrugged. "It wouldn't have been 'sneaking' if she'd told us," he observed.

Addilyn shot him a glance.

Kaden grimaced. "Looks, kill, mince-meat," he said lightly, then: "Maybe she just wanted some time to herself," he suggested.

"She was having time to herself! Leslie's not here, she was on her own, in my book that's being by yourself!"

"Until we interrupted her solitariness. Maybe she wants rime to herself somewhere where she *won't* be interrupted." He paused. "And the bedroom door was open. She see,s to have left in a hurry," he added. "Can we be sure she's okay?"

"We can," Addilyn assured him. "She'll have wanted to leg it in a hurry just in case we caught her. She'll be there by now."

"'There'?"

"Jodrell."

"You think she's gone to Jodrell?"

"No, I think she's gone into Macclesfield to do some shopping." Addilyn paused, then: "Of *course* she's gone to Jodrell!" she sighed.

"Where else would she go? She's gone where we all want to be. God knows why we agreed that Leslie should go alone; we *all* want to be there!"

"I'm not sure I do." Kaden sounded pensive. "I mean, of course I'd like to know how they're getting on, but I'd only be in the way. They know their job, Addie; let them do it."

"You think Darcy won't be in the way?" countered Addilyn. "You think Darcy should go but not us?"

"I'm not responsible for Darcy, Addilyn," said Kaden calmly,"And I don't care about her a fraction as much as I care about you. So let Darcy do whatever she wants, and if she gets in the way, that's her problem. Me, I think we should stay here and wait till Leslie gives us the all-clear."

"or not."

"I prefer optimism," shrugged Kaden.

"I prefer it too," said Addilyn. "It just seems to have slipped by me somehow."

Kaden chuckled quietly. "Well, let me text Leslie, then," he said. "We'll give him half an hour to reply and then, if we haven't heard anything, we'll make our way. Agreed?"

"I suppose," said Addilyn, as she began to count down, in her head, the seconds from one thousand, seven hundred and ninety-nine, ninety-eight, ninety-seven....

*

He crept from location to location. There were a half dozen rooms from which the great telescope could e operated, but at the moment they were using only the main control room, and he very much wanted to keep it that way. He could have merely closed the programs down and switched the machines off, but smashing them up was much more fun, much more satisfactory, a physical manifestation of the antipathy he felt towards the pathetic little humans with their big ideas and tiny brains....

It was only at the fifth console that he paused in his destructive course to sit down at the desk and, when a handful of little golden sparks appeared around him, to rapidly type in a program that would override the control room's instructions and render the radio dish useless.

When he'd executed the program, he smashed the monitor screen and exited the room, intending to make for the control room. He thought he heard something, and decided to take a detour before continuing to ensure that all record of the data needed for input in order to deflect the asteroid was totally eradicated.

*

When she got to the visitors' centre's gates, Darcy anticipated problems getting past security, but there were none. The entrance was not manned, and if the security cameras picked her up and transmitted her image to some security monitor, either no-one was there to see it or no-one cared. Darcy supposed that she should have felt grateful, but in fact the quiet made her feel very uneasy; okay. So the visitors' centre had been closed for the time being and therefore there was no attendant general public from which a busy noise would emanate, but she really thought there'd be *some* sign of life.

She realised then that even nature had fallen silent – there were no birds chirping, no sheep bleating, no cows lowing, nothing to suggest that the surrounding farmland was populated, and there wasn't so much as a slight breeze either. If the great dish of the Lovell telescope hadn't been soundlessly turning ever so slowly – and she marvelled at the absence of noise from both the horizontal and vertical drive motors which had to be sizeable to move a dish almost a quarter of a kilometre in circumference – she would have believed to whole place to be deserted.

She knew from her associations with Tim Taylor and Leslie Billinghurst the location of the control room, and she entered a single-story white building to her left, via a pathway, through a grey iron door that clicked open at her approach. She might have wondered at that, but she'd spotted the sparks at about the level of the combination lock and so assumed that some electrical circuit had shorted and caused the lock to release.

Once inside the building, she padded quietly across the stark, cream-coloured polished floor to another door which was open and which gave out to a dark, internal corridor.

She had advanced only a couple of steps when she heard a crashing sound like the shattering of glass, and she dodged back into the room she had just exited, heart pounding, temples throbbing, breathing heavy. To try and decide what she was going to do next.

She was of course ignorant of the fact that in a few minutes, as Dathan Greenwood slinked noiselessly along the corridor towards her, the choice of action would not be hers to make.

*

"That's another one!"

Leslie Billinghurst heard the frustration in the control room assistant's voice and totally understood it because he felt frustrated himself. This was the fourth program that had irretrievably stopped working, and he didn't need any of his degree qualifications to work out that it was subversion. He contemplated going to see if he could find the guilty party, maybe even try to power up the programs again; anything was better than just standing here watching everything go wrong.

"Number five just went down," the assistant continued.

Dr Nigel Cavendish swore under his breath, but loudly enough for Leslie to hear. "So control is limited to us," he mused, not really speaking to anyone in particular so much as voicing her own thoughts out loud.

"That's confirmed," reported the assistant.

"And there's every reason to assume that whoever – whatever – powered down those five other control programs is going to be headed here to power down *this* one..."

"Dr Cavendish, are you implying sabotage?" The assistant turned away from his monitor by swivelling around in his chair and, instead of facing the window through which there was an unobstructed view of the impression dish, he faced his superior, questioningly but calmly.

"Yes," replied Cavendish, "I am."

"Then I would suggest we begin data transmission now, while we still can."

"Do it!" urged Cavendish, half-whispering, half-commanding.

The assistant sprung into action, reading and touch-typing the data into the computer faster than Leslie had ever seen anyone type before.

Just then, his mobile phone vibrated in his jacket's inner pocket. He knew that it was officially prohibited to keep mobiles switched on when this close to the telescope, but also knew that this rule was more for the general public than for the staff, who were less in number and more likely to use their mobiles responsibly.

He took the phone out and accessed the message; Kaden was asking what was happening, and Leslie was unsure as to how to reply. Would it do any good to tell Kaden about the problems, thus possibly garnering panic for him, Addilyn and Darcy, but definitely having no effect, positive or otherwise, on the situation? If he said all was fine and they later learned differently, would that affect their friendship or, in the case of Darcy, something more?

Leslie was still debating the alternatives when the door burst open, knocking him back towards the corner of the room, and in strode Dathan Greenwood, pushing a bruised and befuddles Darcy Allen before him.

The surprise kick-started Leslie's brain and made up his mind for him; he quickly answered Kaden's enquiry:

IT'S A SHAMBLES, NEED HELP FAST.

TWENTY-TWO

It was a miracle that they didn't crash; taking the narrow country lane bends at almost a ton wasn't the best of ideas, but if Kaden had read the implied tone of Leslie's message correctly, speed was of the essence.

Addilyn hadn't said a word since he'd told her the message, and Kaden wasn't sure how to read that at all. Was she angry? Was she panicking inside and trying to hide it from him? Was she numb? Was she determined? Was she all those things and more as well? Kaden realised her really didn't know her very well at all, and even though he wanted so badly to remedy that, he now began to seriously question whether or not he'd have the chance. Things were going badly, Daji seemed to have disappeared from their lives just when they needed him most, and all in all he was far from optimist about the future.

It was easy for the to gain access; no-one on the gate at the entrance, doors ajar or wide open, the place seemingly deserted. Addilyn and Kaden exchanged glances and there was no need for words; the question – *what the hell is going on here?* – was written all over their features. They negotiated desolate corridors, peered into empty rooms, and eventually came across one which housed a shattered computer monitor.

"Wow," was all Kaden could think of saying about that.

"Oh, dear Lord!" was all Addilyn could think of saying about the various sounds of utter pandemonium that was coming from a little way along the corridor from where they now stood, paralysed with uncertainty.

Then she sprinted towards the noise and Kaden just had time to think that at least he knew her well enough to know that she wasn't going to make anything like a subtle entrance, before she'd barged into the room in question and he had to run to catch her up.

*

The room was in an uproar. Although no windows were open, a gale-force wind seemed to be blasting through the air, shuffling papers ad sending them flying through the air like squadrons of flimsy vellum aeroplanes. Mugs of tea and coffee were upturned, their contents spilled onto surfaces and dripping therefrom like a loose-washered tap, while orbs of light jetted around like loose sparks on twinkling collision courses. There wasn't so much panic from the humans present as a kind of numb (and dumb) silence; they simply could not believe what they were seeing because their brains possessed no precedents by which to understand it.

The telescope dish, for its part, was now dipping towards the ground as if hanging its head in shame at a job badly done. Nigel Cavendish was typing frenetically on a keyboard but it was if its parent computer were ignoring its signals because the input was just not valid. The assistant was poring through a variety of paperwork that he was copying from not long ago but which was now strewn over desk and floor, but no sooner had he picked a sheet up than he threw it back down again with a desperation that was bordering on hysteria; whatever he was looking for very clearly eluded him. Both he and Cavendish kept throwing pernicious glances at Dathan Greenwood as if the man standing at the back of the room, stationary apart from the occasional tightening of his grip on Darcy Allen each time she was stupid enough to try and break free of him, were responsible for the commotion – an idea as ludicrous and impossible as was what was actually happening.

Then suddenly, for the second time in a half-hour, the door crashed open and admitted yet more unauthorised personnel.

*

Darcy Allen had stopped struggling at long

last, and Dathan Greenwood was thankful for it because the thing that controlled him was also privy to his nervous system and those long nails of hers damn well hurt.

As Dathan's eyes scanned the beautiful chaos that his sparkling little comrades had caused, Darcy was wondering about her next move. They were at the back of the room, a little to the right of the door, on the opposite side of which Leslie Billinghurst stood, looking as unsure about what to do as Darcy herself was. Indeed, everyone in the room appeared unsure about what to do, and that wasn't good – or, from Dathan's point of view, excellently good.

Darcy looked around her for something to use as a weapon; she had raked at her captor several times but he seemed to have a very high tolerance threshold for pain. To her right, on a table that stood against the back wall, was a plastic tray holding cutlery – four metals spoons to be precise – which hadn't yet been toppled by the unnatural maelstrom that had swept the the control room. If she could just reach over and snatch up one of them, she was sure she could think up some way to use it to inflict more pain than even Dathan Greenwood could endure.

The opportunity presented itself a few seconds later as the door blasted inwards and Dathan was pushed off-balance. As he fell, he let Darcy go in an automatic reaction in which his hands splayed outwards to take his weight as he hit the floor. Darcy used the opportunity to grab a metal teaspoon, stabbing it into Dathan's face as he recovered his stance and turned to grab her again, embedding it squarely in Dathan's eye socket. The action sickened her but she refused to look away as she rammed it even further into the softness until the spoon handle met bone and Leslie Billinghurst came up from behind, taking Dathan's head in an arm-lock and twisting savagely until he heard the dull cracking of a broken neck.

Darcy threw herself into his arms, and they both looked down at Dathan Greenwood, and then at Addilyn and Kaden, who were regarding the corpse with such indifference that it frightened Leslie that everyday humans could be capable of such violence without conscience, even in the name of survival.

*

Josh Greenwood suddenly let out a loud sob.

"What's up, lad?" enquired Don Gittins, who was making coffee for them both at his shop before he showed the boy the basics of checking the direction of the wood grain prior to carving by removing a piece out of a corner, curving out to finish the cut so the wood didn't splinter, then checking the run of the darker streaks of material; he intended to take Josh on as an apprentice once he had finished school.

"Dad's dead," whispered Josh, tears rolling down his cheeks.

Don crossed over to the boy and gave him a comforting hug; for a reason he couldn't altogether fathom, he didn't doubt the accuracy of Josh's statement.

*

As they all watched, a thousand or more little golden orbs exited Dathan Greenwood's dead body and instead began searching out Tim Taylor's papers and other data records, dropping onto them and igniting them in tiny but nonetheless destructive flames. Others flew around the room, tormenting its occupiers or maybe distracting them, until all paperwork had been incinerated and there was no record of the co-ordinates needed by the space-born probe.

Dr Nigel Cavendish leaned his head in his hands and groaned loudly, elbows on the keyboard because it didn't matter now if he inadvertently typed anything in. He might have had better odds than an infinite number of monkeys on an infinite number of typewriters eventually producing an infinite number of copies of the complete works of Shakespeare, but the co-ordinates they had yet to program in comprised a hundred-plus sequence, so to Cavendish it was equally as unlikely as to be virtually impossible.

Kaden, for his part, was still looking at Dathan's corpse, maybe his policeman's training kicking in because he found he was mentally examining the reason Darcy did what she did, while Addilyn was just staring out of the window, her gaze on the magnificent radio dish which seemed now to be sharing their desolation, bowing its antenna towards the ground. Tears formed in her eyes, but she tried to blink them away, especially when the telescope slowly came to life and began to lift its concave head.

The numbers, Addilyn! A voice echoed through her head and she recognised it as Daji's. *Remember the numbers!*

"Oh, thank God you're back," she breathed.

"Sorry?" Kaden overheard and mistook the comment as being aimed at him, and he hadn't been anywhere.

I and mine will keep the others occupied while the co-ordinates are entered, but they're many and they're strong, Addilyn. Urgency is of the essence, we can't hold them forever!

"But..." stammered Addilyn. "I don't

understand..."

You don't need to understand! Daji's voice was yelling at her. *Just remember and shout out the numbers!!!*

The numbers...

... began to appear in Addilyn's mind as she recalled the many occasions on which portentous clues were presented to her: on her hallway wall during a dream, on the neighbouring headstone at Timothy Taylor's funeral, in the car when she'd read Tim's papers not understanding anything about them – premonitions, in fact, that had haunted her all her life in the guise of a mental illness just so that she would assign meaning to a long string of figures that would eventually save the world. Mysterious ways indeed, she reflected...

"Dr Cavendish, input coming your way!" she shouted, and after a double-take, Cavendish somehow knew he had to stop looking at her as if she were crazy and turn back towards the console, and momentarily his fingers were poised ready to type and Addilyn began.

"Fifteen." *One is white, five is blue, the Scottish flag, her best friend was Scottish...*

"Forty." *Four is yellow, zero is infinite, the endless sunshine on a day abroad with her Scottish friend so many years ago...*

"Seventy-five." *Seven is lilac, five is blue,*

ultraviolet rays, sunbathing on that holiday...

"Sixty-eight." *Six is green, eight is red, green grass and that ridiculous red hat her friend wore to hide her shaved head.*

"Nineteen." *One is white, nine is dark, the darkness that claimed the bright white light that was her friend in spite of all the chemotherapy...*

Tears began to form in Addilyn's eyes as she continued to tell herself the story, the memory encoded in the figures that she now recalled as they sequenced themselves before her mind's eye, the plot twisting and turning, incorporating more components, each represented in a numerical pattern that made sense to only her, people, events and experiences both good and bad that had affected her sufficiently to merit a permanent, if arcane, place in her memory; a classified method that was far from what the so-called experts defined as a way of coping, because it was in fact an obscure but personal way of remembering, of ensuring that things important enough for whatever reason took on a memorable and recallable aspect so that their significance would never be lost, occurring and reoccurring on a daily basis in mundane, repetitive ways...

Nigel Cavendish, when Addilyn had finished, when he also had finished, sat back in his seat and waited. For a few seconds, nothing happened, then suddenly he noticed that around him there was total silence.

The wind had died down and flaming shreds of paper fluttered to the floor, going out as they flew downward, and then lay in crematorial stillness.

Cavendish's assistant looked at the blank computer screen in front of him as if he dare not move lest the ruckus start up again.

Darcy was still in Leslie's arms but she looked uncomfortable; this may have been her discomfort at what she had done to Dathan Greenwood, or maybe it was something else that she needed to address at another time.

Addilyn was still staring out of the window, now for the first time in many minutes seeing the radio dish smiling broadly at the sky, its antenna high and proud, like a tongue poking out in cheeky but harmless silliness. For the past one hundred and thirty-six numbers she had seen nothing except the digits in front of her eyes, coming and going, nearing her mind's eye's field of vision, then receding in order than others might take their turn for her attention.

Kaden padded over to her, the quietness of his footsteps unnecessary but nonetheless seemingly called for in this moment, and as he stood behind her to look at the telescope too, his hands on her shoulders, his mouth brushing against her dishevelled hair, a loud, persistent beep emanated from Cavendish's computer.

"Oh, my God in heaven above," he breathed, his voice barely above a whisper, "It worked..."

*

Larry Hodgson looked up from the newspaper crossword her was doing and looked through the sitting room window towards the cloudless, blue sky. A strange feeling had just come over him; strange but not at all unpleasant.

"We're going to be all right, aren't we." Marcia's comment was more an enquiry for verification than a direct question.

"Yes," said Larry, and somehow he knew he was speaking the truth. "Yes, thank God, we're going to be absolutely fine..."

*

It becomes more of a struggle every time.

That is because evil is finding a foothold, which is why it is even more essential that I keep trying.

Your mother deplores it.

You imagine I enjoy *it? No, I do not, but*

it has to be done. In every way possible it has to done until one day they finally learn!

And the evil ones? The ones who refuse to acknowledge and live for the truth?

I will metastasize them. Deliverance will be subject to passing by me first.

So what now?

We continue the fight. This is but one disaster averted. Evil has nothing if not a bottomless pit of deleterious ideas. They will not give up.

So neither will you.

Never.

*

They were standing outside the buildings on the grass, looking up at Jodrell Bank's expansive radio dish, smiling smugly.

"That was close," commented Nigel Cavendish, wiping his brow with a crumpled handkerchief he'd retrieved from his pocket. "We'll have to up our NEO programme after this!"

"I don't think a warning would've made any difference," Leslie said. "Although Dr Taylor and his peers were aware that something was coming, it couldn't have been predicted, not without assistance in keeping it predictable."

"Well, it makes no sense to me," sighed Cavendish, "But I'm relieved that it all worked out in the end, and I thank you all for your help." He paused, then: "Of course they are a few formalities to be observed before you can go home," he added, suitably sheepishly.

"No-one would believe us anyway," chuckled Kaden, humourlessly.

"I think he's more concerned about the corpses," commented Addilyn drily.

"There'll be one almighty cover-up, that's for sure," agreed Darcy. "I'm surprised we're even being allowed to live..."

"Really, Miss Allen..." began Cavendish, and then he saw the big grin come over her face, and he matched it with one of his own,. "There will be measures to ensure secrecy" he admitted after a moment, "But I think I have enough clout with the authorities to convince them that a signing of the Official Secrets Act will suffice."

"And who wants to remember it all anyway?" added Addilyn.

"Well, I do, for one," said Darcy. "Just recently, I've been doing and thinking, feeling and experiencing, things that I never thought I was capable of. I believe I need to rethink my whole being."

"Does that mean – " began Leslie.

"We don't live far apart, and I'll keep in

touch," Darcy smiled. "But I need time. And space."

Leslie nodded, then: "And you two?" he asked Addilyn and Kaden, as if to detract his attention from the disappointment and hurt he was feeling.

"I don't know," said Kaden. "Do you need time and space, Addie?"

"Yes," replied Addilyn, "I do. I need six months to plan the wedding and I shall require a yard at least around me for all the flashy lace and tulle I'm going to have on my wedding dress!" She grinned mischievously at Kaden, then: "I don't need to think," she said seriously. "I already know..."

★

Lightning Source UK Ltd.
Milton Keynes UK
UKHW021320090223
416761UK00014B/180

9 781326 526610